QUEEN OF THE FLAT-TOPS

Queen of the Flat-Tops is the breathtaking saga of the U.S.S. *Lexington* and the Battle of the Coral Sea.

Queen of the Flat-Tops is the incredible story of a stunning victory, something to make every patriot's heart leap.

Queen of the Flat-Tops is the soul-stirring tale of a gallant defeat. Just to read of a great ship's last hours packs pride, awe and a minute-to-minute thrill. It renews your faith in your country.

Queen of the Flat-Tops is "absolutely the best war epic ever written."

—*Cleveland Plain Dealer*

THE BANTAM WAR BOOK SERIES

This is a series of books about a world on fire.

These carefully chosen volumes cover the full dramatic sweep of World War II. Many are eyewitness accounts by the men who fought in this global conflict in which the future of the civilized world hung in balance. Fighter pilots, tank commanders and infantry commanders, among others, recount exploits of individual courage in the midst of the large-scale terrors of war. They present portraits of brave men and true stories of gallantry and cowardice in action, moving sagas of survival and tragedies of untimely death. Some of the stories are told from the enemy viewpoint to give the reader an immediate sense of the incredible life and death struggle of both sides of the battle.

Through these books we begin to discover what it was like to be there, a participant in an epic war for freedom.

Each of the books in the Bantam War Book series contains illustrations specifically commissioned for each title to give the reader a deeper understanding of the roles played by the men and machines of World War II.

QUEEN OF THE FLAT-TOPS

THE U.S.S. LEXINGTON
AND THE CORAL SEA BATTLE

STANLEY JOHNSTON

BANTAM BOOKS
TORONTO • NEW YORK • LONDON • SYDNEY • AUCKLAND

QUEEN OF THE FLAT-TOPS
*A Bantam Book / published by arrangement with
E. P. Dutton Inc.*

PRINTING HISTORY
*Dutton edition published September 1942
11 printings through October 1957*

*Bantam edition / March 1979
2nd printing ..... May 1979
3rd printing .... August 1984*

*Cover painting by William F. Draper
courtesy of the Navy Combat Art Center,
Washington Navy Yard, Washington, D.C.*

*Drawings by Greg Beecham.
Maps by Alan McKnight.*

*Bantam Books are published by Bantam Books, Inc. Its trade-
mark, consisting of the words "Bantam Books" and the por-
trayal of a rooster, is Registered in U.S. Patent and Trademark
Office and in other countries. Marca Registrada. Bantam
Books, Inc., 666 Fifth Avenue, New York, New York 10103.*

PRINTED IN THE UNITED STATES OF AMERICA

H   12 11 10 9 8 7 6 5 4 3

Dedicated to

THE U.S.S. *LEXINGTON*

to the men who fought on her
and to the country that bred them . . .

The author gratefully acknowledges permission of *The Chicago Tribune* to reprint the substance of the chapter called SMASHING THE JAPS AT LAE AND SALAMAUA, copyright by *The Chicago Tribune*.

PREFACE

The *Lexington* was something more than a ship in the years before the war. When she was lost hundreds of men throughout the services mourned her passing as they would a dear friend. Many of our Navy fliers, and many of our admirals and senior officers received their initial training in sea-air operations aboard her.

After this generation passes on the memory of the *Lexington* will continue to live just as we still remember the *Monitor* and *Merrimac*. Those two, the world's first two iron-clads, ushered in a new era of naval warfare when they fought their battle. In the same way, the *Lexington,* in the battle of May 7th to 8th, ushered in a new chapter of naval fighting, for hers was the first engagement fought between aircraft carriers. Of all the assembled ships (the enemy's and ours) involved in the action, sea battle though it was, not one single ship fired a gun at another. The sinking and shatterings were accomplished by airplane-carried bombs and torpedoes. The ships' guns were used solely as anti-aircraft weapons.

The *Lex*—as she was affectionately known throughout the Navy—was the realization of the dreams of that small group of Navy men who fostered the development of flying throughout the days when to many senior officers the airplane was known as "the flying machine," or "that new fangled contraption."

In those early days only the British and Japanese navies possessed aircraft carriers.

The British developed theirs in 1917–18 to provide floating flying mats which could accompany the fleet and from which fighting planes could be launched, to provide protection against possible attacks from German shore-based torpedo planes and to act as scouts.

The Japanese built their first carriers in order to evade the terms of the Washington Limitation of Armaments Treaty. Limited to 3 in the 5-5-3 ratio of that treaty, Japan built battle-cruiser hulls on which quickly removable flight decks were placed. They intended, in the event of war, to tear away the flight decks and put heavy guns on the mounts already installed. Photographs of early Japanese carriers bear this out.

As soon as the Japanese saw the *Lexington* and *Saratoga* and learned through espionage our own Navy airmen's plans for using them, they themselves commenced building ships designed throughout as carriers. Finally, in the last two years before the present war, the Japs went to the other extreme by converting hulls, originally laid as heavy cruisers, into carriers, which they knew by this time from their own experiments in China were the most powerful fighting vessels that could be devised.

A carrier's main defense is her aircraft. The result is that as long as she can keep her fighting squadrons in the air she is the most nearly invulnerable of fighting ships.

The war of today must be won or lost with the weapons now available. This is not to say that better weapons should not be forged whenever progress makes it possible. But today and now the carrier is a prime weapon. Some day aircraft of sufficient range and power to conduct midocean war may be developed and produced in sufficient quantity to replace aircraft-carriers —but I have not as yet heard that either we, or the enemy, have devised such a super-machine. Therefore in the absence of a better method of conducting sea-air war it is foolish to say we should discontinue constructing carriers because one day a plane with such capabilities *might* come into being.

There have been charges that the carrier is an "egg-shell," easy to destroy, that a battleship can withstand more punishment.

This arises from a general misconception of what armor *is*. The Nazi super-battleship *Bismarck,* the British battleships *Barham, Prince of Wales* and *Repulse,* and our battleships lost at Pearl Harbor, fell quickly to airplane-fired missiles. The *Lexington* also was the target of a ferocious air attack, but unlike the supposedly thick-skinned and impregnable battle wagons which all sank quickly, the *Lex* steamed at 25 knots and was in fighting trim for hours after the enemy aircraft passed over. Internal fires which only started later —admittedly as a result of previous damage sustained —finally resulted in her loss. She stayed afloat until all of the surviving members of her crew were taken off, then her blazing hull was sent to the bottom by torpedoes fired from one of our own destroyers.

The people of the United States can take comfort from the victories won by the Navy in the Battle of the Coral Sea, and a month later at Midway. Our sea-air battle forces met and defeated superior numbers of the enemy. We won because the tactics for battle evolved by the services during years of peace were superior to those of the foe, when carried out by our fighting men.

The equipment used by the two contestants in the air was practically equal. But the controlling factor was that little extra initiative and pugnacity on the part of the American commanders and men.

Who are these men? We see them proudly wearing

their uniforms when they are on leave from training establishments or from the battle fronts. They are incredibly brave in battle and the stories of their great courage and ability are not exaggerated. I have seen men fight and die in two wars, men from many nations, and under many circumstances, and I am proud to say that I have never seen men combat and die more gallantly than did these, the boys who grew up in our villages, towns and cities, the fathers, brothers, cousins, uncles and friends of every one of us, who have proven themselves as valiant and daring and audacious as men only can when fighting for their country.

S. J.

September, 1942

CONTENTS

QUEEN OF THE FLAT-TOPS

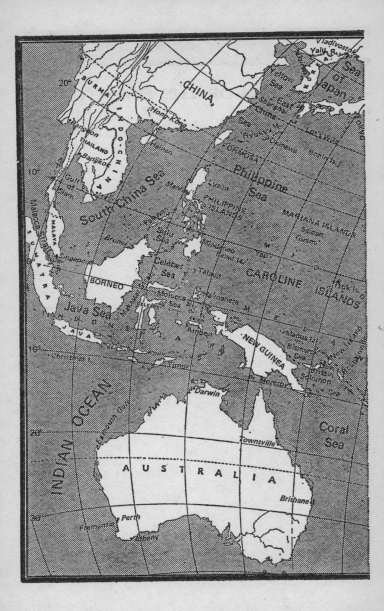

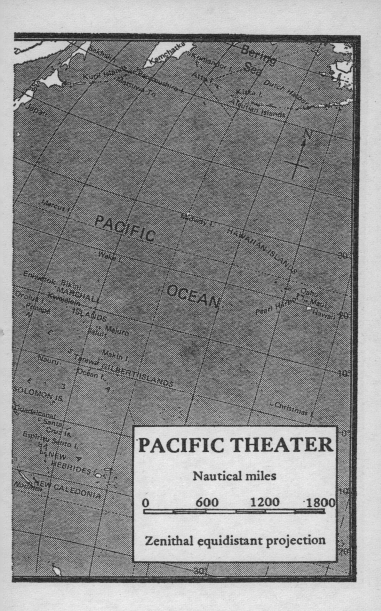

1

THE LEX CROSSES THE LINE

The mid-Pacific is a sapphire ocean: hot, humid, arched over by a blinding sky. From this void the sun bends low, exerting its power so that sailormen broil in their own essential juices. Even 30 feet below the surface—depths where water is drawn for big ships' condensers—the ocean has a temperature of 85 degrees Fahrenheit. It is an almost opaque, an intense Gulf Stream blue. The blue of vast deeps. And propellers whipping this dark water at racing speeds churn out wakes that float away to the horizon like dual ridges of snow.

As was the case with other vessels braving the heat and deadly stifling moisture of the equatorial ocean's springtime last April the *Lexington*'s innards were almost as wet as was her outer hull. Droplets of saline crystal clinging to the steel plates outside the anti-torpedo bulges were matched by purer drops of nature's distillate that formed everywhere within her. The great man o' war—888 feet long—sweated like a man in a Turkish bath. Beads of moisture combined to form rivulets which forever coursed down floors, walls and roofs, the bulkheads, decks and side plates—of this great floating city.

Aboard the *Lex* there was no relief from the heat and sweat. The *Lexington*, you must remember, was started as a battle cruiser and launched in 1925. As fighting ships go she was old. She had none of the comforts of later carriers, cruisers and battleships. Air conditioning was not known when she was designed. And it never had been added because a fighting ship—especially in a war—is stripped down to her bare essentials. As a result, even the breath of the mechanical hurricane forever blowing through her bowels was hot and humid. While it changed the air within her, it did nothing to cool the interior or the crew.

The scorching tropic sun sizzled on the flight decks, the Island, and the ship's anti-aircraft guns, bared so that they could search the skies in all directions around her. The deck plates, stanchions, gun barrels and breeches, railings and all the Island's structure became so hot that flesh touching them was blistered. On deck the normal forward progress of the big carrier—20 knots or about 22.5 miles an hour—was enough to keep a strong breeze forever blowing. Even so the temperatures on deck often reached 90 to 95 degrees Fahrenheit.

Below, under the flight deck where the crew's living quarters were situated, temperatures were over 100 degrees Fahrenheit from a few minutes after dawn until late at night. The coolest it ever got there was about 95 degrees. This of course was the result of the burning of thousands of gallons of fuel oil in the 16 huge boilers that supplied superheated steam for the *Lexington*'s turbines. These turbines, moving electric motors, generated 209,000 horsepower—the most power ever put into any vessel, either of peace or war.

The heat from these boilers, of course, was terrific. It started in the engine-room plates and through the conductivity of the enormous steel hull, riveted and welded into one homogeneous mass, spread throughout the ship. The hot seawater did little or nothing to reduce the temperatures. The result was that the *Lex*'s crew continually lived in sweat-soaked clothing and breathed and moved through a mist only slightly less moist than the element in which the mighty ship itself floated.

In the engine rooms the heat approached at all times the utmost limits of human endurance. With the blowers operating at their best the temperatures ranged up toward 120 degrees Fahrenheit by day. At night they dropped for a few hours to 112 degrees. Through even these temperatures the engine-room crews operated like the rest of the ship in shifts of four hours on and four off. Four and four . . . four and four. White-faced engineers—and they throve on it. No sun tan on their skins yet they carried on with courage and quiet endurance.

Perhaps I lay too much emphasis on the heat. Men of the *Lexington,* however, will not soon forget their campaigns in the tropic seas, nor the constant, forever-irritating heat and sweat they endured.

Soon after I went aboard the *Lexington* I began to wonder what effect the heat had upon the personalities of the crew. At first I thought it strange that no effects were visible. No one was cantankerous, no one gave way to petty fault-finding, the military version of these minor hysterics in which some women indulge. Instead the men were quiet, relaxed, easy. There seemed no rough spots in the ship's routines, even though fully one fifth of the men aboard were on their first cruise.

After a time I realized that in the Navy where the numbers of men in the crew of even a big ship like the *Lex* are relatively few compared to Army corps or divisions, there is no place for prigs or pigs. Men must be good to hold their own. Anyone who lasts *is* good because the poorer material is weeded out. A ship's code of behavior is so enforced by custom, good sportsmanship, and the example of the ship's leaders —be they the immediate commanding officers or younger men whom the crew sees at closer range—that newcomers unconsciously fall into line. War is a serious business. It needs to be seriously studied and conducted. But it need not take all the fun out of life.

I think I began to understand the *Lex* and her crew best when we were five days out of Pearl Harbor last April 20th. Five days and nights of steady steaming in the midst of our escort at a 20-knot pace had brought us close to the Line. And it is here that we take up our story directly for the first time.

The Line is the equator and in war or peace the American Navy makes its crossing an occasion for celebration whenever there are Lowly Pollywogs aboard its ships. And when is there a ship without them? A Lowly Pollywog is any person who (1) has never crossed the Line; (2) has never genuflected to

Neptunus Rex; or (3) is in the unfortunate position of being unable to prove he has done either or both the above.

Aboard the *Lex* on this voyage, as mentioned already, were more than 500 raw recruits—all Lowly Pollywogs. They ranged in age and rank from boys 17 and 18 years old, to ensigns and young lieutenants who never had crossed into the realms of King Neptune. All, regardless of age and rank, were ripe material for the mild hazing which the initiations and "homage" to the sovereign and ubiquitous ruler of the Raging Main are wont to take.

This time the initiations were to be unusually complete, all aboard were darkly told by the Ancient Shellbacks—those who could prove they had been initiated and *had* crossed the Line. There was a special reason. It happened that on the voyage preceding this trip the *Lexington*'s crew had consisted of about 60 per cent Lowly Pollywogs. They had included not only enlisted men but also officers up to the rank of commander. And the Lowly Pollywogs had taken over the ship, contrary to all tradition and propriety, and soundly walloped the Ancient Shellbacks on the "crossing" day.

Now the Shellbacks, with appetites whetted, were to remove their dishonor by thoroughly initiating a new and well-outnumbered group of Pollywogs.

The five days at sea had shaken the crew into ship routine. The new men had found their places as signalmen, anti-aircraft gunners, pilots, air gunners, as officers directing small gangs of men, air crewmen, as engineers, firemen, butchers, bakers, messmen, medical assistants or as clerks. They had become part of the ship's community. But any unity, any friendship that had developed was temporarily shattered when the Ancient Shellbacks began to ferret out the Pollywogs.

Even in matters of pure fun, Naval tradition calls for an orderly process. So it is with the Ancient Rites. Each mess, or each department on the ship handles its own Pollywogs in preliminary ceremonies that take place on the two evenings just prior to Crossing Day. At these hearings the Pollywogs—regardless of rank or station—are put through early tortures, are indoctrinated with respect for the Court (invariably a group of, for the occasion, sadistic "old timers"), and are generally browbeaten and robbed of small sums of money to provide cigarettes, Coca-Cola, candy bars, or ice cream which is avidly devoured by the waiting Shellback pack.

Every preliminary Court is headed by a Grand Inquisitor—a direct representative of Neptune. He is flanked by a scribe—Davy Jones' helper, for Davy is King Neptune's personal scribe. Around the Court gather self-appointed fellow inquisitors, tormentors, kibitzers, and those whom the Navy knows as "nibitzers." A kibitzer, of course, is one who peers over the shoulder of an active player in any game and contributes unhelpful suggestions—a low fellow! A nibitzer is the lowest form of kibitzer—so low, in fact, that three nibitzers, each standing on the others' shoulders, can pass beneath a snake without knocking off the highest man's tall hat.

Collection of the Pollywogs' names began early all over the ship. The first ceremonies were held on the second evening before the ship was due to reach the crossing point. I watched the gathering in the mess headed by the Executive Officer, Commander Mort Seligman, an old Navy test pilot who began his Navy career by commanding a trawler that helped in the great sweeping up of mines from the North Sea after World War I.

The mess was two decks below the flight deck, about amidships. In it were six long tables with seats for 22 men each. The room was almost square. Walls, ceiling and floor were painted white. Tables and chairs were of dark wood. For dinner—the evening meal—the officers wore white ducks, and the high-collared Navy jacket, which, if cut loosely and worn without shirt or singlet beneath, is as comfortable a garment—if the stiff high collar is left open—as one can wear under these conditions. We were of all ages, from the early twenties to the late fifties—some deeply tanned, some with the pallor of 'tween-deck workers. We were lean, fat, stocky, and slender.

It was a meal in which there was much good-natured

repartee. After the messboys had served the confection
and coffee the tables were cleared quickly and the
Senior table, in the center of the starboard end of the
wardroom, transformed into the bar of Neptune's
Court.

I remember the scene well. All of us looked on with
expectant amusement as the Court formed. We pulled
back our chairs—all 130 odd of us—and settled over
cigarettes or pipes. Commander Walter Gilmore, big,
heavy, jovial with graying hair and an office paleness
to his cheeks, assumed the exaggerated character of
Grand Inquisitor. His jury—as prejudiced a group of
Shellbacks as ever convicted a Pollywog—surrounded
him.

Commander Arthur J. White, senior surgeon aboard
the *Lex,* was assistant kibitzer. Quiet, slender, easy-
going, with a humor that hid behind a poker face and
his ever-glowing pipe, the doctor was a dangerous
man to have interjecting rapier questions—which is the
duty of a good kibitzer.

At his right was Group Commander William Ault,
senior aviation officer aboard ship. He was six feet two
of whipcord; more than fifty years rested lightly on his
shoulders. His thin long face was deeply tanned. A pair
of sharp eyes drilled you when he peered your way,
yet he was easy, friendly. Now his lips twisted in an
anticipatory smile that bode ill for the accused who
must come before him. Bill Ault had been a Navy
pilot for twenty years and still was active leader of the
ship's air squadrons. In attacks he led a command
group of four planes and used to dive-bomb, himself.
His leadership was of the highest sort—leadership
which led. The Navy had recognized it by ordering him
to report as commander of one of the new converted
aircraft carriers when next the *Lexington* made port.

Alas, the *Lex* didn't make it. And Bill Ault too is
among the missing. When last we heard from him, by
radio about noon on May 8th, he told us that he and his
gunner had been hit by Japanese bullets, and their
plane was shot to pieces around them. Bill said they
were going down in the sea—somewhere along that 200
miles of ocean between us and the enemy. When he

radioed us he was returning after having led the *Lex* squadrons in the ship's last great fight. But that was weeks ahead and none of us were thinking of the future that night.

The rest of the jury consisted of Lieutenant Commander Weldon Hamilton, skipper of the *Lex*'s 18 dive bombers; Lieutenant Commander Bob Dixon, skipper of the scout-bomber squadron; Commander Heine Junkers, the squat, powerful chief engineer, as purposeful in his quiet way as his four huge engines. All were seasoned men, sure of their own abilities, accustomed to command. Hamilton with his wavy black hair was perhaps the handsomest of the trio. Dixon, quiet, precise with a body trained down fine like a prize-winning athlete and with an air of do-or-die determination about him was the personification of a Navy airman.

Because this was the senior officers' mess with virtually no victims from its own tables, the young pilots and a dozen or more young ensigns and junior-grade lieutenants from the junior officers' mess were called before this court. These young pilots, only a couple of months out of the Navy Air School at Pensacola, Fla., and the other young officers were a keen, trim lot. Disciplined, yet headstrong and likely to take a tack of their own, they made wonderful "victims."

One of the first was Ensign Lee, tall, poised, good looking, and one of the better jitterbugs, as my vision of him dancing at various Honolulu night spots before the voyage started, bore out. Mr. Lee made a bold decision when his name was called, and he positively swaggered as he strode before the bar.

"Have you ever crossed the Line?" came the question of the Grand Inquisitor.

Brazenly the young man asked: "What Line?"

Snarls of rage rose from the assembled Shellbacks. Groans, hoots and denunciations. Here was an impudent young Pollywog poking fun at the Royal presence. Even Lee's stout heart must have had misgivings as he saw the results of his defiance.

Covering their delight with melodramatic frowns of evil intent, the jury demanded: "What Line do you think?"

"Oh," was Lee's reply, "if you are referring to that highly imaginary line, that line that no one has ever been able to see, that line that holds in the earth's waistband, that is supposed to be somewhere around here—then I've never crossed it."

More snarls, groans, moans of anguish rose. Mutterings of "mutiny," "He takes liberties with the Royal Domain, then sneers at the old salts"—and similar remarks in undertones were heard.

With merely a glance at his exercised jury—each man was gesticulating, shouting, asking some question that was lost in the general turmoil and confusion—Inquisitor Gilmore instantly found Lee guilty of being the Lowliest Pollywog. He was dismissed as the Court's decision was acclaimed. The dismissal, however, was granted with instructions to appear before the Court on the morrow, prepared to pay penalties and forfeits for his conduct.

The Court went on for hours. Some Pollywogs adopted the most abject attitudes. They were promptly stepped upon hard, told off for lack of backbone, denounced as spineless and worthless 'wogs. Others followed Lee's example. They were browbeaten into a state of dejection, declared to be mutinous, denounced as lacking in respect and reverence for the Supreme and Omnipotent Ruler of the Sea, and condemned. It was soon apparent that the court and jury were sitting with one purpose in view, to convict and condemn any and all. It was an inquisition in which justice and right were totally absent, in which the prisoner had no rights, hopes or chances of escape. But it was all in fun.

You may be very sure my own case was soon called. I had heard something of what was coming and had made certain preparations. There had been outspoken glee over the opportunity of initiating a newspaper correspondent. I'd been warned that I was to "get the works," in fact, and I had helped things along by appearing very ignorant of what was coming.

When I was called that first night I had my documents ready. And I startled the court by promptly claiming my rights and putting my foot on the Court's table. By this I indicated I had crossed the Line in the

Pacific, the Atlantic, and Indian Oceans. In fact Line-crossing has been something I've been doing frequently ever since I was born. The Court was most reluctant to accept my proof and my papers were scrutinized for flaws. Eventually, however, I was recognized as a Shell-back—to the disappointment of all in the room. My rating was such that I took my place at the judgment table as assistant scribe.

"Lieutenant Commander Paul Ramsey face the Court," intoned the scribe. Ramsey, skipper of the *Lex*'s fighter squadron, had been sitting in the crowd enjoying the spectacle. Confident in his own knowl-edge that he had long ago qualified as a Shellback, he kibitzed, shooting in cunning questions from time to time to nonplus hapless defendants.

The call surprised him, startled him out of his usual debonair poise. Rising quickly, he glanced up and down the forbidding line of faces glaring now at him, raised his expressive eyebrows and with exaggerated innocence demanded: "Who? Me? Not me," all the while tapping his chest with his index finger.

"Yes, you. You heard. Take the stand," came the Grand Inquisitor's stern voice.

Quickly appraising the situation and deciding that he was in for trouble, Ramsey stepped forward to meet it, gave his long handlebar mustache a cavalier twirl, and awaited the inevitable questions.

That mustache was the result of a vow taken weeks earlier that he would not shave his upper lip until his guns had shot at least two Japs from the sky. Later af-ter a wet dinner just before the cruise started Paul raised his sights rashly to 10—five for a side. Tonight this fungus had reached gigantic proportions and from constant twirling stuck out on both sides of his face in a fashion reminiscent of the horns of a Texas steer.

Ramsey was a serious and efficient fighting man who exercised his squadron constantly and prepared every man for the air battles that fighter units seek. His presence and that of his squadron aboard the *Lex* indicated that he was highly rated by his superiors. But when he was off duty, as now, he was a delightful shipmate. His penchant for jest and his ability to turn the sharpest thrusts against their originators made him a constant target in the mess.

Consequently the packed wardroom waited with amused expectancy for the bout of wits they expected forthwith. Paul, standing without a trace of egotism but with a twinkle of expectancy in his eye, was at his best. The Court, realizing that here they had a prisoner who would hand back as much as he received, consulted momentarily in a huddle of heads before commencing the inquisition.

"Before charging you with being a low, despised Pollywog we ask if you would like the Court's defense counsel to act as 'prisoner's friend.' We feel you are entitled to this protection," Commander Gilmore began smoothly.

"But I do not," Ramsey replied. "If I am going to hang I will say the things that hang me myself. I don't want any assistance from this Court's prejudiced, iniquitous, perfidious, back-stabbing counsel."

To this the Court reacted like a group of politicians caught with their collective fists in the pork barrel. Eventually, however, they quieted, ceased defending themselves by casting reflections on Ramsey's ancestors, and proceeded to give the victim "the business."

"We understand you claim to have crossed the Line and further that you have been telling unsuspecting ensigns that you are a fully rated Shellback," Gilmore made it sound like a charge.

"Yes, of course. It's perfectly true I am," Ramsey replied.

"Have you any written document to prove that you crossed the Line and were duly initiated into the mysteries of the raging main?"

Ramsey's face reflected his anguish. He suddenly remembered he had no such document aboard. Knowing and rightfully fearing the penalties that would be assessed him he began casting about for a way out.

"Why, ah, no, I haven't documentary proof," he mumbled, "but I did cross the Line aboard the *Wyoming* in such-and-such a year, as everyone knows."

"We aren't interested in what everyone knows. But perhaps there is someone here—some *friend* for example—who will stand out and vouch for you. Remember, this *friend,* assuming you have even one, must be a proven Shellback."

This is an ancient snare, as Ramsey well knew, but he was desperate. Turning and surveying the wardroom, he sought some shipmate from the *Wyoming*'s cruise. His eye settled on Commander Duckworth, air officer on the staff of the *Lexington*'s skipper, Captain Fred Sherman.

"Ducky, you can vouch for me. We were together on that cruise. Remember?"

"I never saw the prisoner before this moment," Duckworth, with straight face, informed the Grand Inquisitor as the crowd jeered Ramsey.

Ramsey's case seemed to parallel the rest—once called, no quarter was given. Paul saw he was beaten, temporarily at least, and he threw himself on the dubious mercy of the Court. Of course the jury took the position that he had attempted to foist himself off as a Shellback under false pretenses, a serious matter, they assured him. He was dismissed with orders to present himself the next evening for sentence.

During the next few hours Ramsey spent most of his time in the *Lexington*'s library where he went hunting for ships' lists and rosters of crews on various vessels. After a three-hour research he dug up a Navy list that proved beyond doubt he was aboard the *Wyoming* when she crossed the Equator. Next evening he presented this incontrovertible document and thus evaded the difficulties he was certain would overwhelm him on crossing day.

When the Shellbacks had finished that night they were assured of a goodly number of choice 'Wogs for the coming Roman holiday. Those of us who had been given "charges" to prepare—long indictments of specific 'Wogs—burnt midnight kilowatts in our cabins concocting dire, involved, and tongue-twisting calumnies. All were designed to show what a base and worthless individual a Lowly Pollywog is on the night before his initiation.

The second night's fun consisted of repeating the wardroom Court scene. This time no proof was being requested. Every victim was called before the Court to receive penalties. These were of the wildest and most bizarre sort. The pockets of the victims were hit slightly—all the old Shellbacks sweltering down there having developed enormous thirsts for soft drinks and ice cream.

Everyone was watching the words and demeanor of the victims to discover a case of "contempt of court." Practically anything was contempt of court. Commander Gilmore would say:

"Look at him! Standing there with collar unbuttoned! Shoes not polished! No crease in the pants! Tie not straight! Lounging, eh? Has table No. 2 got plenty of coke over there. No?—supply a round of coke for table No. 2!—there are only two dozen there!"

The next victim might be one of the young pilots.

"Oh, ho! A pilot." The Commander's words dripped scorn. "Why aren't you wearing your fur-lined flying jacket? In fact it might be a good idea to put your entire winter suit on—pants, boots, jacket, helmet, gloves. Then come back and report to us."

The poor victim would disappear and then come back dressed and with the perspiration already coursing down his face. He would then take his place in the line waiting for the Court's disposition, but strangely enough he would be entirely invisible to the Grand Inquisitor for perhaps an hour. It would be a period of very real torment but of course did no harm except to the victim's self-esteem—if any.

During the first night of interrogation one young ensign made the serious tactical error of admitting before the bar that he was attached to the ship's Naval Intelligence. That was greeted with hoots, jeers and howls, for every Shellback knows there is no such thing.

When he reappeared that second night he was greeted thus: "Oh, here's the young 'intelligence' officer." There was a hurried, whispered conversation at the Court table. Then:

"Young man, what do you do with the color-headed pins you use on the charts?" (A question revealing that the questioner knew his job well.)

"That's a naval secret." (The young man was doing pretty well.)

"Right. Then go and get a large box of them and bring them here."

This young man was called to the front of the line as soon as he reappeared, and the questioning was instantly resumed.

"So! You are in Naval Intelligence! Then you would know of all the countries in the world?"

"Well, ah, yes."

"Then make a large map of Australia on the left side of your coat using those pins for the outline. No —don't take the jacket off. Leave it on. We don't mind if you prick yourself occasionally."

Halfway through someone said: "What *are* you doing?"

"Making an outline of Australia," was the surprised rejoinder.

There was a babble from the table. "It's upside down." "It's wrong way round." "It's not straight." "You've got north pointing downward."

Finally it was agreed to let him proceed according to his own pattern. As one of the jury sadly remarked: "What more could be expected from a Naval Intelligencer."

When he stopped pinning himself and looked up there was a lot of criticism as to the outline, and he was rigorously cross-examined on the location of harbors, rivers, the Great Barrier Reef, and other points. Finally a very confused, embarrassed, heated, and futile young man was "allowed" to buy a gallon of ice cream for one of the tables before being turned over to two Shellbacks who would prepare him for and see him through his initiation.

The Court closed that night with appetites whetted anew for the initiation proper of the morrow. It began for some of the poor Pollies before dawn. Coming in for breakfast I ran into the first of them. Two ensigns clothed and blacked as Minstrel Singers were presenting themselves as I entered. Each had a special little chore of his own which had to be repeated in every department of the ship. One had to enter, bow, and

then sing "I Love You." The other was required to
declaim an involved and highly suitable poem. It was
a poem about a man with a wheelbarrow, a hoe and
a plough, but we never did get the sense of it because
of the singing that drowned out part of the performance. The two acts, it seemed, had to be done together.

Ensign H. B. Shonk followed them at close range.
He wore short whites, a singlet with shoulder boards
indicating he carried the rank of commander, and a
paper Napoleon hat. Round his neck was a rope carrying two Coca-Cola bottles lashed together for an
imaginary set of binoculars. His act was to peer around
all points of the compass and into every corner of the
ship and then report: "No enemy aircraft in there."
Poor Shonk, he was busy doing this all morning long.
He was a good victim, however. Shonk, it turned out,
was an "off-the-arm poet." He evened his scores with
the various Shellbacks, long before the voyage was
over, by his poetical castigations.

You must not forget that despite all the surface
horseplay the *Lexington* was a ship of war coursing
toward enemy waters. Half of her company was constantly on duty as usual. Not a whit of vigilance was
ever relaxed. The air patrols went off regularly, the
radio department was as diligent as ever, the engineers
and gunners were at their posts. But it was amazing
how it "happened" that not one of the Pollywogs
found himself doing watch that morning. Somehow this
was the case no matter where they were assigned on
the ship.

What came next convinced me that no one should
ever cross the Line for the first time aboard an aircraft
carrier. The flight deck is far too long, and the deck
personnel, not to mention the rest of the ship's company, by far too numerous. I say this because the final
act of the initiation cermonies was to run the gauntlet
—from one end of the ship to the other—between two
lines of husky, healthy young Americans each of whom
took a lusty whack at your posterior with a canvas tube
stuffed with wet paper. This I assure you makes quite
an effective flail, especially when multiplied by 500

The Royal Court

over the period of time it takes you to run 800 feet. Every Pollywog's initiation wound up that way.

But before this grand finale, each man is called before the Royal Court. Up forward King Neptune, the Queen, and the Royal Baby (invariably the fattest man on the ship) are ensconced on their thrones. They come aboard with all the ceremonies granted a reigning monarch, early in the day, and throughout the forenoon "welcome" the newcomers.

Each victim is led before the King, stripped more or less. Then come forward vassals of the Court who wield brushes dipped into strange pigments—egg yolk, shellack, iodine, banana oil, lemon extract, and other even stranger and more mysterious concoctions. These pigments are used to "anoint" the bodies of the now nearly shellbacked Pollywogs. Strange devices, heraldry, and mystic symbols are embossed on their torsos. They make their final genuflections, go down on their knees and then commence their run. Usually they start with their belts unbuckled by the foresight of the "high priests." The result is that they stagger and stumble down the lines of men.

For much of this I stood on the signal bridge, 25 feet above the deck. From there I could see each Shellback rear back, swing and hear the "plock" as the various blows got home. One short stocky Marine about halfway down the line had a beautiful backhand stroke that seemed to snap with unusual vigor. The runners would hold a steady pace until even with him. Then his arm would sweep around, his wrist would flick, and with a yell of momentary agony the unhappy runner gave a great leap, thereafter to increase his speed.

"On carriers in non-war time," Ensign Hansen, the ship's signal officer who stood beside me, said, "we had a fine old practice. It used to frighten the wits out of even the boldest. It involved using the main airplane elevators that bring the planes from deep inside the ship up to the flight deck.

"The Shellbacks would rig a huge canvas tank of water on the elevator and then lower the lift at its deepest—about 70 feet below the flight deck. The Pollywogs would be led to the edge of this chasm and ordered to peer well into the water tank below them. They would be led away, more ceremony would follow, whereupon they were blindfolded and immediately led back to the edge of the elevator. There they were told that the tank was below them and ordered to jump in.

"Still blindfolded as they were, there was almost none who went voluntarily. Usually they had to be pushed. Of course while they had been away from the elevator, it had been brought up until it was only five or six feet below the flight deck—but the victims, didn't know that. There'd be great shrieks as each fell, and they almost always got great gulps of water, because they hit with a splash after falling only a fraction of a second."

This gentle practice was suspended for the duration aboard the *Lex* because her planes and elevators were kept ready for instant action.

From the *Lex*'s bridge I looked out over our task force and could see that aboard every other vessel homage was being paid the Ruler of the Raging Main. Aboard the cruisers and destroyers with us at this time, scenes quite similar to those aboard the *Lex* were being enacted.

When I went below for lunch I ran into my cabin boy, Duke, a slender happy-go-lucky Negro youth from Harlem. He had joined on in New York, where he had worked with a band. He was a most intelligent and enthusiastic youngster who spent his spare time playing his accordion. It was his "hot" musical style that had won him the name Duke, after "the" Duke Ellington.

"How's it feel to be a Shellback, Duke?" I asked him.

"Well, sir, they certainly poured it into me," he replied, massaging his bruises. "Several of those boys in that line-up there certainly is hot with them flagellators. I won't be able to sit down for some days."

"Never mind. Think of it. Next time you cross the Line you'll be with the Shellbacks passing it on to the Pollywogs."

"Ah can't hardly wait for that time." He flashed his teeth at me. "I'll be right there handin' it out."

Neither of us could know that the Duke had just crossed the Line for the first and last time.

2

SHIPS WITH WINGS

As the U.S.S. *Lexington* ploughed across the line that white-hot morning she was carrying the hopes, dreams, achievements and contributions of a whole generation of Navy airmen. The *Lex* and her sistership, the *Saratoga*, were the floating laboratories through which our own Navy, and the Japanese, had learned how to equip and then how to operate sea-borne aviation. Exercises with these two great ships first taught our Navy leaders the potentialities of the Air Striking Force and exerted tremendous influence upon the design of all other fleet vessels.

In other words, it was the *Lexington* and *Saratoga* that transformed the whole concept of naval warfare. The flight decks of these vessels brought about the greatest advance in the art of sea fighting since the addition of armor and steam to warships. But on that morning, just about a week out of Pearl Harbor, I didn't know the *Lexington*'s history. That was to come later after hours spent in the ship's library, and after I had attended dozens of lectures at which the strategy of carrier fighting and Navy sea and air tactics were unfolded for her young pilots.

I discovered after some research, with the assistance of the ship's executive officer, Commander Mort Seligman, that our *Lexington* was the fourth ship of the United States Navy to bear this name. There was little enough available concerning her predecessors, but we found that the first *Lexington* was a brig of 16 guns, the second a sloop of war with 18 guns, and the third was a sidewheel ironclad steamer of Civil

War vintage—she was a shallow-draft vessel for navigating inland rivers, I believe—with seven guns.

The present *Lexington* was our first really big aircraft carrier. She was a floating aviation field. Her 900 feet of flight deck, extending from her bow to her stern, formed a runway that could be turned into wind from any direction. And her great motors could be used to create a mechanical wind over her deck by driving her at any desired speed up to 33.9 knots (38 miles an hour roughly). Even on a calm day the air flow along the *Lexington*'s deck, when she was merely cruising, was equal to that of a brisk wind on a flying field ashore.

Best of all she was a mobile field. Under her own power the *Lexington* could cover more than 700 miles in a single day and night. In her first long sea run, from San Pedro, Calif., to Honolulu (June 9 to 12, 1928), she covered 2,228 nautical miles in 74 hours and 34 minutes. On that voyage she averaged 30.7 nautical miles (34 land miles) an hour including the first hours during which she was gradually accelerating to full speed.

Below the flight deck was the hangar deck where her planes could be stored. Then there were the engine and plane overhaul shops, store rooms, motor-test rooms, fabric departments, parachute rooms, and all the other shops and stores necessary to the equipment of a complete military air base. Giant elevators, fore and aft, could raise or lower complete planes from these inner storage or shop spaces to the flight deck. When raised until flush with the rest of the flight deck the elevator platform formed part of a complete and unbroken surface from bow to stern.

The *Lexington* originally was one of six battle cruisers included in the three-year building program authorized August 29, 1916. The original contract for her hull and machinery was signed on April 20, 1917, but work on her was not started until 1920, due to the entry of the United States into World War I. As one of these cruisers the *Lexington* was being designed for both great speed and heavy guns—a sort of American counterpart of the British battle cruiser *Hood*. Her planned tonnage was 43,500—the approximate weight she displaced at the time she finally was sunk in the Coral Sea.

The *Lex* was about one third finished and the *Saratoga* a little further along, when the Washington Limitation of Armament Conference was called late in 1921. By treaty during this conference the United States called off its tremendous Navy building program and at first all six of the battle cruisers were ordered abandoned or scrapped.

The late William A. Moffett, one of the Navy's first leaders to believe in the future importance of aircraft, had just been made an admiral, and had succeeded a few months before the Armament Conference opened in organizing the Navy Bureau of Aeronautics which even today handles all Navy aviation affairs. Through Admiral Moffett's personal influence the first two of the battle cruisers were saved for what generally was understood to be experimental service after conversion to carriers. A supplementary contract for the conversion was signed in the case of the *Lexington* on Nov. 2, 1922, and the work was recommenced.

The long delay between authorization of the conversion and the contract signing was caused by the redesigning of the entire interior of the *Lex* and *Sara* as the Navy soon came to know them. All the superstructure planned earlier for the battle cruiser had to be eliminated and the smokestack, bridge and navigating offices of the vessel were concentrated in an "island" raised above the flight deck and placed on the starboard side. Tankage for aviation gasoline, for oil, and for water was placed on the port side to offset the weight of the "island," and the four pairs of 8-inch guns which were mounted off center to starboard.

In order to make the *Lexington* virtually unsinkable the interior was elaborately compartmented. In all there were more than 600 separate compartments —each of which could be locked from the others by watertight bulkheads, steel scuttle hatches and heavy doors. Of these compartments, 117 were assigned to the Supply Department of the vessel. Thirty-one were set aside for storage of technical aviation material, 70 for general ship's stores, equipage and provisions. Sixteen compartments were utilized for galleys, bakery, butcher shop, general mess, issue room, clothing-issue room and the ship's store or canteen.

Part of Admiral Moffett's conception was that all aircraft carriers should be fast long-range vessels. Therefore the *Lexington*'s original battle-cruiser propulsion machinery was retained. This consisted of 16 big oil-fired steam boilers supplying power for four electric-turbine generator sets, each designed to produce 33,200 kilowatts per hour. These four generating sets were linked to eight big motors which in turn were paired on the four propeller shafts. The designers intended that a total of 45,000 horsepower should be delivered to each shaft—enough to turn the huge water screws 317 r.p.m.

Subsidiary power plants consisted of six 750-kilowatt direct-current turbine generator sets. This equipment operated the steering gear, anchor windlass, ventilation fans, lighting systems, radio, telephone, telegraph and electric pumps distributed throughout the ship. The elevators, searchlights, fire-alarm systems, cooking apparatus, refrigeration, ammunition hoists, and other special and secret apparatus were electrically operated. I am including these details here because they contribute directly to a bettter understanding of the events immediately preceding the great old ship's end—an end that came less than three weeks after we passed the equator.

The *Lex*'s earliest trials disclosed that her propulsion equipment, produced by the General Electric Company, exceeded design specifications materially—by 29,000 horsepower, in fact. Instead of 180,000 horsepower her turbines and motors delivered 209,000 horsepower—more, as I said before, than that of any other vessel except the *Saratoga*.

With all this power the *Lexington*'s great bulk and breadth, 888 feet long by 106 feet wide, could be maneuvered almost as readily as a destroyer one twentieth of her weight.

Armament of the *Lexington* originally included eight 8-inch rifles. These were in heavy turrets fore and aft of the island which was a combined bridge, funnel enclosure, masts, range-finding and radio tower, and ventilation outlet. By 1941, however, these turrets, with their heavy guns which were only approximations of a cruiser's arms, were removed.

The Navy had officially decided that the *Lex*'s airplanes alone were sufficiently powerful offensive weapons. This was, of course, before we were in the war and before the correctness of the Navy's theories were proved in battle.

I was particularly interested in the removal of the turrets later on because a 1,000-pound Japanese bomb skimmed the flight deck a few feet ahead of the bridge, barely cleared the starboard rail and exploded in the sea alongside us. Its explosion shook the *Lexington* and drenched all of us on the bridge with an enormous column of seawater. That bomb, had the turrets been retained, would have struck flush on the top of the forward barbette and probably would have destroyed the island, the entire operating center of the ship and, incidentally, me.

For defensive arms the *Lexington*'s commanders had adopted the British and German systems. They literally made her a pincushion of small rapid-fire anti-aircraft guns. These were of two calibers, 20mm and 1.1 inches. In all, more than 100 of these were spotted around the ship in batteries of four. Each unit was commanded by a young gunnery officer whose sole duty in battle was to keep his own particular segment of the sky clear of enemy planes.

In addition to the light quick-firing "machine guns" as the 20mm and 37mm guns are called by the Navy, the *Lexington* retained her batteries of 5-inch dual-purpose anti-torpedo plane, anti-high altitude aircraft guns. These were disposed at bow and stern on each side in units of three. The small gun batteries were all manned by sailors and sailor crews operated half the 5-inch batteries. Marine crews had charge of the other six 5-inchers and the healthy rivalry between the two units in practice shoots sure was something to behold.

But I'm getting a little ahead of myself. I want to return to that period in the Navy just prior to the commissioning of the *Lexington*. While yet a captain, William Moffett became interested in Naval aviation and gathered around him a group of younger officers whose technical knowledge assisted him in evaluating air possibilities. When he became an admiral he assigned some of these younger officers to develop special types of places and engines for carrier work, special catapult mechanisms for ships, and commenced work on the Navy's still secret arresting gear to assist planes in alighting on carrier decks.

One of these younger officers was E. E. Wilson, then Aviation Aide to the C-in-C of the Battle Fleet. Mr. Wilson (who had reached rank of commander when he resigned in 1930) now is president of United Aircraft Corporation. He "grew up" in Naval Aviation according to his own words. Recently he wrote me a long and informative letter showing in brief, but most illuminatingly, his personal recollections of those important years in which this new arm was coming of age. I am going to quote extensively from this letter which paints the men and the times:

"In World War I," Mr. Wilson wrote, "I was chief engineer of the battleship *Arkansas* in the North Sea. My ship was based in the Firth of Forth, and near us were anchored the great British carriers. The one thing the British Grand Fleet feared at that time was that the Germans would discover the possibilities of the torpedo plane (which the British had pioneered during the early years of the war). Beatty (Lord Beatty who then was commander of the battle-cruiser squadron) took every precaution against possible German use of this weapon. He had several large carriers in active commission."

These carriers with their airplanes, and the land planes that were carried above the battleship and battle cruiser turrets were simply a counter against the possibility that the Germans might have land-based torpedo planes, Mr. Wilson writes. He says that had the Germans had shore-based torpedo-carrying aircraft at the time of the Battle of Jutland, they could easily

have taken part in the action. It was fought near
enough to German territory.

Sopwith Camels, very light land-fighter planes were
used for take-offs from the battleship turrets. These
practiced at fields ashore and were ferried alongside
the vessels and hoisted to the turret tops before the
fleet went to sea, Mr. Wilson adds. They retained the
wheels for alighting on land, and it was these planes
and practices together with the British carrier program
that were the inspiration for our carrier force, he
claims.

"American Naval aviation centered in some anti-
submarine patrol work on what was called the Northern Bombing Force. This was commanded by Kenneth
Whiting, now Captain, U.S.N., Inspector of the
Eastern District, New York City. Whiting was one of
the earliest Navy pilots and was fully alive to the
British carrier development. To a great extent he is the
father of the American carrier program. He sent Lieut.
Godfrey de Chevalier to Rosyth, Scotland, to observe
British carrier tactics, and de Chevalier was berthed
on my ship.

"This aroused my interest in the new activity, so
when the war was over and I came home I got an as-
signment at the Naval Training Station at Great Lakes
as officer in charge of the Naval Aviation Mechanics
School. Such schools had been established all over
the United States by the Bureau of Navigation under
the direction of Dr. Charles E. Lucke, of Columbia
University, one of the engineering consultants for my
company today.

"The Navy Department decided to concentrate these
schools at Great Lakes in order to train several thousand men required to replace the wartime force dis-
charged to their homes. I commanded this school for
two years and then went to sea on the U.S.S. *Wright*,
the first Navy seaplane tender.

"Capt. William A. Moffett had been Commandant
of the Great Lakes Station as everyone in the Middle
West knows. He had become much interested in Naval
Aviation. After the war he went on duty as captain of
the *Mississippi*, but went back to Washington in 1921

for the avowed purpose of establishing a Naval Bureau of Aeronautics. On his way he stopped in to see me at Great Lakes and asked me to join him in the Bureau, but I had to go to sea to qualify. So, after the Great Lakes tour, I put the *Wright* in commission as a kite balloon ship and plane tender at New York.

"I served on her a year, mostly in the Caribbean, and this was the beginning of our patrol schedule based on seaplane tenders.

"Meanwhile Admiral Moffett had succeeded in getting the Bureau of Aeronautics organized. I went to sea on the *Bridgeport* as executive officer to qualify for executive duty, and in March, 1924, was ordered to the bureau in charge of the engine section. Lieut. Commander B. G. Leighton, since retired and now managing the Intercontinental Aircraft Corporation at Miami, had the engine section and was busily engaged in developing the air-cooled radial engine. I took over this duty and pushed the development to the point where we had two competent companies, Wright Aeronautical and Pratt & Whitney Aircraft, in production on such engines.

"The fundamental problem in the carrier development was to get the maximum number of aircraft in the relatively small space offered by carrier accommodations. The cooling system of the liquid-cooled engine meant additional weight, which, in turn, increased the size of the airplane and reduced carrier capacity. That story alone is an interesting one.

"In the Bureau at the time was Kenneth Whiting, now a captain and in charge of the carrier program. The Washington Arms Conference had scrapped most of the new vessels but Admiral Moffett had managed to save the *Lexington* and *Saratoga* . . . for conversion to carriers. Meanwhile Ken Whiting had succeeded in converting the *Langley* for experimental purposes. The Bureau was very busy developing the special type of airplanes needed for the carriers, including fighter, torpedo and bomber planes.

"After the engine development had progressed considerably I went to Pensacola, received my wings, and returned in charge to the Design Section of the Bureau.

There I had the opportunity of supervising the completion of the new aircraft around the air-cooled engines intended for the carriers. In October, 1927, I was assigned to the Aircraft Squadron, Battle Fleet, at San Diego, as senior aide or chief of staff to Rear Admiral Joseph M. Reeves, now retired but in Washington as liaison between the Navy and the Maritime Commission.

"Serving with me on the staff was Capt. Frank D. Wagner, now in the Bureau of Aeronautics of the Navy Department as operations officer. Wagner was a combat pilot and I know of no one more competent than he in the field of aircraft operations and air tactics.

"When I arrived in San Diego, Capt. J. H. Towers, now Chief of the Bureau of Aeronautics, was Captain of the *Langley* and this was our only carrier and on which Admiral Reeves had been training the air squadrons scheduled to go aboard the *Saratoga* and *Lexington* when they ultimately joined the fleet.

"In 1928 we made a cruise to Hawaii on a Fleet problem. At that time, the *Langley* actually carried 42 of the new Boeing fighters and Vought observation airplanes, and we carried out an attack against Hawaii that in many ways resembled the Japanese action at Pearl Harbor. The *Lexington* joined us and became our flagship for the return to San Diego, and later the *Saratoga* joined us. We spent a year in the development of our carrier tactics, training of the crews and in tactical exercises with the fleet.

"In the autumn of 1928, Admiral William Veazie Pratt, then Commander in Chief but now writing for a news magazine, sent out the usual fleet problem as the basis of operations for the next year, 1929. This included an attack on the Panama Canal. Admiral Reeves, in his estimate of the situation, proposed that we abandon the usual stereotyped battleship operation and detach the *Saratoga* on a wide, southerly detour, with instructions to run the gauntlet of the defending forces and attack the Canal, launching aircraft at a distance of 200 miles.

"When the Commander in Chief's new orders came

out there was no mention of this new idea. Therefore the Admiral and his staff flew in three airplanes to San Pedro to call on the Commander in Chief. I had Admiral Reeves as my passenger.

"We went aboard the *California* to see Admiral Pratt, and Admiral Reeves outlined his plan. He pointed out to Admiral Pratt that we had succeeded in developing an entirely new task force. He coined the phrase at that time, 'The Carrier Striking Force,' and gave Admiral Pratt a detailed plan for the approach. Most of these details had been worked out by Capt. Wagner.

"Admiral Pratt was much impressed. He said that he would adopt the suggestion, but instead of changing the orders which were already out, he would put to sea and make the change en route to Panama. This would give us the benefit of an exercise in complete change in orders.

"Before doing so, however, he pointed out to Admiral Reeves that if we were to lose any pilots in this long-range operation, it would go hard with the command. Admiral Reeves replied: 'Our record for the past year discloses no mechanical failures in many hours of over-water operations. Our experience indicates that we need expect no such thing (as mechanical failures and pilot losses) against Panama, and the risk is therefore warranted.'

"Under the general plan of the problem, the *Langley*, *Lexington* and *Wright* were assigned to defending forces. There were also shore-based aircraft and the military in the Panama Canal Zone. The *Saratoga* was the only carrier in the attacking force, supposed to represent a Japanese fleet.

"We put to sea, according to schedule, and down the Mexican coast, stopping in the middle of the day. Our vessel sent boats to the flagship for guard mail and the guard mail contained the new orders.

"One of the problems was that there was no destroyer at that time able to keep pace with the *Saratoga* on this long, high-speed run. The *Omaha*, flagship of the commander of the destroyer division, Admiral Senn, was therefore detached to act as a plane guard for the *Saratoga.* Admiral Senn flew his flag on the *Omaha,* and Capt. Stark, until recently Chief of Naval Operations, was his chief of staff. We had the extraordinary situation of a senior admiral plane-guarding the flagship of a junior admiral.

"The *Saratoga* went far to the south and west, in the direction of the Galapagos Islands, and began the approach to the Canal at 30 knots. Twenty-four hours before the attack we were nearly a thousand miles from the canal and even though there is a cul-de-sac on the Pacific side, this spread the defending vessels very thin. The weather was squally during daylight so there was no need to send aircraft in the air. However, at the end of the day the weather cleared and we launched some of the fighters. Almost immediately they reported the destroyer *Breck* as in contact.

"Meanwhile the *Saratoga* had run the *Omaha* out of fuel and that vessel had slowed down. My chief worry was what to do about a plane-guard vessel for the attack in the morning. Just at this moment occurred one of those extraordinary incidents that disclose the fortunes of war. We were all standing on the bridge, watching the *Breck* approach, when the chief signal quartermaster said to the Admiral: 'I think the *Breck* thinks we are the *Lexington.*'

"The Admiral said: 'Well, what will we do with her?' And I said: 'Let's tell him to plane-guard us.'

"Instantly the Admiral gave the signal. As the flags reached the yardarm the *Breck* swung into position and took her plane-guard station directly astern where we promptly 'disabled' her. Later she reported having rigged a jury radio and notified the enemy of our approach.

"Just at dark the cruiser *Detroit,* with Capt. R. Drace White, now with the Budd Manufacturing Company, suspected what we were doing and deviated from its scouting station and picked us up. He trailed us all night long, waving his searchlights in the air and urging the enemy to concentrate on us.

"During the night our squadron commander was concerned lest we be caught on the deck (i.e., hostile planes surprise attack while our squadrons on deck instead of in the air) and suggested to Admiral Reeves that he launch ahead of time. We had planned to launch two hours before daylight. I felt, however, we should not change the plan, and we stood on. We launched aircraft on schedule, 200 miles at sea.

"The details of this are most interesting, but I won't list them here. Suffice it to say that our aircraft delivered the attack on the Canal and returned without having been opposed by aircraft. All planes were recovered. The only failure of the attack was that the battleships scheduled to interpose themselves between us and the 'enemy' failed to arrive on time because they had mistaken the current off Cape Mala. This enabled the defending battleships to 'sink' the *Saratoga* because we stood on to recover aircraft as a peacetime safety measure.

"Later, at the critique, Admiral Pratt described the action as the most brilliantly conceived and executed exercise in the history of the navy, and made the trip north with us on the *Saratoga* to learn more about naval aviation.

"The subsequent history has, however, one important sidelight. Everywhere our carriers went in the Pacific, their tracks were dogged by Japanese tankers, one of which always seemed to be conveniently taking oil. From San Pedro everywhere the fleet went there were always swarms of Japanese fishing vessels.

"We learned that the Japanese feared our carriers more than anything else, and were feverishly building carriers themselves. There is no question that the Yellow Man copied the White Man's tactics and learned to execute them brilliantly. What you saw in the Coral Sea and what we know about Midway, is the culmination of this great transformation.

"Behind this brief sketch is the story of extraordinary development in every line, with great contributions by many others than those whose names I have mentioned. Behind it, too, is the story of the development of American aviation which was ready when the war came."

In this letter Mr. Wilson describes what was probably the first proper use of carrier forces ever at-

tempted. This fleet problem formed the pattern for
variations that were used in attacking other carriers at
sea, attacking battleship, cruiser and destroyer squadrons, a consolidated fleet, and fleets of warships and
transports in harbors. All this was, of course, tried in
practice. But the Navy's practice tactics, worked out as
carefully as if they were real battles, have proved to
be right in every particular when our forces used them
in Lae and Salamaua, at Tulagi, against a Japanese
fleet on last May 7th (1942) at Misima, and on the
following day, the finale of the Coral Sea conflict.

Many exercises, of course, followed the fleet problem off the Canal in 1929, and the earlier sea-borne
air raids on Hawaii in 1928. One of these came in
April, 1931, when the *Lexington* was called out of
Guantánamo Bay, Cuba, on an errand of mercy. An
earthquake in Central America had leveled the capital
city of Managua, Nicaragua, nearly 900 miles away.
Medical assistance, supplies, and serum were badly
needed.

At 30 knots the *Lexington* made a 715-mile dash
almost due west across the Caribbean. At 2:30 P.M.
on April 1, 1931, while still 150 miles from the Nica-
raguan shore the carrier launched five planes carrying
four doctors, three hospital corpsmen, 400 pounds of
medical supplies and 1,200 pounds of rice and beans.
The airplanes flew the 370 miles to Managua which is
220 miles inland and at an altitude of about 2,500
feet on the Central American plateau lands, in four
hours.

On April 2, while lying off Greytown, Nicaragua,
the *Lex* launched a second relief flight of six planes.
All eleven airplanes returned to the *Lexington* the
following day and the carrier made the transit of the
Panama Canal to the Pacific a day or so later.

It should be pointed out that this launching of aircraft, heavily laden, for operations from the sea to a
point well over mountainous terrain was almost a du-
plication of the war problem encountered when the
Lexington's squadrons—this time carrying 1,000-
pound bombs and 21-inch 1,750-pound torpedoes—
flew up and over the jungles of New Guinea, threaded

their way between the 18,000-foot peaks that dot the New Guinea highlands and after 125 miles of cruising dropped down to blast a Japanese troop transport formation in the twin harbors of Lae and Salamaua.

The *Lexington* was commissioned on Oct. 3, 1927, her sister carrier the *Saratoga* having been put into service in April that same year. Their exercises since those dates not only enabled the Navy to evolve the carrier tactics that today make our fleets the most powerful in the world, but also they have had a profound effect upon all American naval design. For the carrier emphasized speed—speed of the carrier itself, speed as the prime asset of its aircraft, and speed for the guardian and accompanying vessels. Range, too, suddenly became of vital importance for most of the Navy's earlier vessels could be run completely out of fuel by the *Lex* and *Sara,* just as the *Omaha* was run out of fuel by the *Saratoga*'s long fast-circling dash toward the Panama Canal in the 1929 Fleet problem.

Earlier American designs had been conceived around the battleship as the key vessel. Our battleships always had been relatively slow with power and speed sacrificed to heavy armor and heavy guns. The battleships were supposed to be great heavyweights—much like heavyweight boxers—slow, lumbering perhaps, but with great stamina and ability to absorb punishment and a terrific sock in their 14- and 16-inch guns.

With the advent of the carriers all this was changed. The new cruisers had to be able to step with the carriers at high speeds for thousands of miles at a time, and so did the new destroyers. Speed began to be the goal for the entire fleet team.

No summary of the carriers would be complete without reprinting the summation of some of the *Lexington*'s "firsts" that were gathered by a group of us the night on which the great old ship finally sank. We foregathered in the wardroom of one of the smart new cruisers that had been doing planeguard with us throughout the Coral Sea campaign. From the *Lexington*'s own records that had been sent over before the crew was ordered off, we obtained the following information:

From the day of her commissioning until she was sunk the *Lexington* steamed 345,000 miles or about the equivalent to 14 round-the-world voyages. Since the outbreak of war on Dec. 7, 1941 she covered 43,-311 miles before her end on May 8, 1942. She spent 112 days at sea following Dec. 7th.

During her career 57,700 landings were made on her flight deck. And 4,700 of these were made between Dec. 7th and May 8th. The first man to alight on her deck was Commander A. M. Pride. The last plane to alight was flown by J. E. Mattis, RE (Radio Engineer, a petty officer's rating) who belonged to the ship's torpedo-plane squadron.

The *Lexington* had nine commanders. Her first was Rear Admiral Albert War Marshall, retired, who was in charge of her fitting out following her launching in the fall of 1925. With the rank of captain which he had held for several years, he took command on Dec. 14, 1927 and held it until June, 1930.

Her last commander was Capt. (now Rear Admiral) Frederick C. Sherman, who took command on June 13, 1940, and fought her brilliantly through every war engagement in which she took part.

It is perhaps noteworthy that every man who commanded the *Lexington* rose at least to the rank of rear admiral. And Admiral Ernest King who was the *Lex*'s third skipper is now Commander in Chief of the United States Navy.

On the night of the sinking I went scouting through the 800 odd *Lexington* men who were on that cruiser I mentioned earlier. I was trying to find someone who had been aboard the *Lex* from the time she was commissioned to her end. And I finally found John B. Brandt, chief boatswain's mate, who had been assigned to aviation duties aboard her.

For a special issue of the cruiser's paper dedicated to "The Minute Man Ship," I had Brandt write a short piece he called "Looking Astern." This special issue of the paper was for Navy personnel only and contains information that never has been officially released. But I am able to reprint here Brandt's story, which commenced with an editorial note that he re-

Martin T3M

ported as an apprentice seaman to the *Lex* on Dec. 8, 1927, and remained on duty in her ever since. He wrote:

"When I reported to the *Lexington* she was still not commissioned but we soon put to sea from Quincy, Mass. At that time I was just a taximan (one who assists pilots in taxiing their planes on the flight deck) but had the honor of pushing the first plane aboard up the deck. I am still assigned to the V2 division.

"The planes in those first days were nothing to brag about, but I liked to fly anyhow. The rear cockpits of the T3Ms (Martin torpedo planes of the 1927 era) were drafty but the sightseeing was good. Commander Ellyson—holder of the Navy's No. 1 pilot license—the ship's first executive officer made his last and fatal flight from the *Lex*'s deck. He crashed at Washington, D.C.

"This isn't a history, by any means. Perhaps I should tell of a couple of the high points in the *Lex*'s career. For instance, in the winter of 1929 the Pacific Northwest had a very severe cold spell. Because of the freezing conditions the hydro-electric power supply of Tacoma, Washington, was cut off. Whoever thought of using the *Lex* for such a job I don't know, but we steamed up there and tied up beside the Coleman dock. For three months her power plant furnished all the electric power that was needed for the community with some to spare.

"That tremendous power came into play again in 1934 when it was decided to see what the old girl could do in a speed run. We left San Pedro and 72 hours and some odd minutes later we were anchored off Honolulu.

"Perhaps my most vivid memory is that of the search for Amelia Earhart. Well, I remember it because it cut off a good liberty. It was July 3, 1937 and we had just anchored off Santa Barbara. The first liberty party was in the launch when word came to proceed on the search. We shoved off for San Pedro and took on some fresh provisions, then to San Diego for the squadron personnel.

"Before long we were in Hilo, Hawaii, where we got some fuel and additional provisions. For 27 days after that we covered 25,000 miles in the cruise. The chow was beans and more beans. The rationing was so strict that even the matches were doled out. Miss Earhart was not found.

"The dear old *Lex* was first in everything. Every war game the fleet had, she came through in finding the enemy first. She set another first when on May 8th she became the first U.S. carrier to be lost in battle."

It was hoped by the *Lexington*'s officers shortly after the sinking that the crew could be held together and placed aboard one of the country's brand new carriers which thus could become *Lexington V,* carrying on the name in another carrier. The hope of holding the crew together was based chiefly on the idea that a now almost completed new carrier could be renamed the *Lexington*.

This project was dropped when the same yard that built the first carrier *Lexington*—the Fore River Yard at Quincy, Mass.—demanded the right to pass the name on to one of the new carrier hulls now building on its ways. The demand was made in the name of the workers at the yard in a telegram dated June 16, 1942, and signed by W. H. Horton, president of the Independent Union of Fore River Workers, and W. G. McDermott, chairman of the Employee Members of the War Production Board.

The telegram related that this new hull at the moment was merely designated "CV-16." Secretary of Navy Knox granted the demand saying that the yard workers promised "all the speed and all the skill in our power" in asking for the right. CV-16 had been earmarked for the name "Cabot" but this will be given to a later ship of the same design, the navy announced.

The new *Lexington* will be one of the Essex class carriers of 25,000 to 26,500 tons displacement and will carry more than 80 aircraft. She is due to be commissioned in 1943, the building having commenced in July, 1941. It was impossible for the Navy to hold together the valuable veterans of the old *Lexington* to await a ship that will not be delivered until next year. Consequently they are being given new assignments at sea that will split them among other carriers already commissioned where their experience and skill will count immediately.

3

CARRIER TACTICS

Air operations aboard a carrier are undoubtedly the most spectacular flying done anywhere today. Remember that aboard the *Lexington* more than 100 airplanes were flown off and on, repaired, stored, refueled, rebombed and rearmed in an area approximately 300 yards long by 35 yards wide. The landings and take-offs were made with a precision that required working to inches. And the penalty for mistakes was usually the loss of an airplane—over the side or a chewed tail —or death from a whirling propeller.

When the proper approach has been made an officer on the *Lexington*—while I was aboard this responsible duty was in the hands of Lieut. Aquilla Dibrelle— waves the incoming plane down. As it sinks to the deck and is seized by the arresting gear it is immediately pounced upon by the plane-handling crews. The hook is released and returned to its retracted position by one man. Another who watches this operation, signals to the pilot to open his throttle and "rev" up his engine, thus supplying taxiing power.

Four or five other men seize the wing tips and the tail, and guide the plane on down the deck. The deck itself is painted off into various zones. In each zone there is a traffic signal-man who takes over the control of each ship as it passes into his territory. These men stand to one side or the other—their special duties are indicated by the color of singlet and skullcap they wear. The plane traffic men wear yellow, for example. They beckon on or stop the pilot, and signal the plane to be swept off to port or starboard, according to the stowing arrangements.

These arrangements are always made according to a predestined plan. No matter in what order the planes came aboard the stowing is arranged so that the big torpedo bombers—heaviest tactical airplanes operated off our carriers—are stowed at the stern. Next in line toward the bow are the dive bombers and scout bombers which are exactly alike so far as their exteriors are concerned. The fighters finally are stowed far forward. The reason for this particular arrangement is two-fold. First, the fighters might be needed for defense of the ship at any moment and consequently have to be near the bow over which take-offs are made. Second, the fighters, being the smallest and lightest planes in ratio to the power of their engines, make the shortest take-off run. The scouts need a little more run for take-offs and the torpedo planes when loaded need as much as they can get.

The actual alighting area takes up only the first 20 percent of the deck at the stern—about the first 180 feet. Planes touch down and roll to a stop in measured distances of 10 feet. Each landing is a full-stall landing, and the hook picks up the arresting gear to bring the planes to an abrupt halt. Often this is accompanied by a screech of rubber tires and occasionally the collapse of a gear. This "shock" landing is one reason why Navy planes must be more strongly built than Army shore-based craft, though the additional weight, distributed throughout the plane's structure, reduces its performance.

The ship's airplane elevators constantly take planes needing special service or overhaul down to the hangar decks, even while other craft are landing or taking off. At sea most of the carrier's planes—and the *Lexington* carried more than 100 all told—are stored on the flight deck ready for immediate launching. The reserve craft are carried in the hangar decks where motors are changed and major repairs made.

Take-offs are as spectacular as the landing procedure. I marveled constantly at the skill with which the deck-handling crews threaded their way amid the stored craft. Long before the take-off every engine would be warming up, its propeller flashing as the

throttle was steadily opened up. Packed as tightly as
they were on deck, there was only a matter of a foot or
so between wing tips, tails, fuselages and propellers.
The torpedo planes stand with wing tips folded over
their back like so many sea gulls until approaching
the take-off line. The other planes would be fitted
in with wing tips overlapping.

For both take-offs and landings, of course, a carrier is turned into the wind. The air officer on the
bridge has two flags, one white, one red. "Prepare to
launch" is the order when he raises the red flag. The
first plane is taxied into launching position and there
waits, its pilot eyeing the bridge officer. When word
finally comes from the captain to commence launching,
this officer removes the red flag and substitutes the
white. As soon as this is done the control passes to the
launching officer on deck, who steps forward with a
small white wand in his hand.

With a rapid twirling gesture of the wand—not unlike the movements of a symphony orchestra con-
ductor leading his musicians to the crescendo of a
movement—the landing officer directs the pilot to open
the throttle and "rev" up the engine. A glance down
the deck to see that all is clear, and the wand points
straight ahead, giving the pilot his clearance. The motor is opened full out, the plane begins to roll and the
tail to come off the deck.

Fighter, scout, bomber or torpedo plane make exactly the same kinds of take-offs. They get their planes
into flight position as quickly as possible and hold
their wheels down until there is no more deck. The
last few feet of the forward deck curve slightly downward and ordinarily it is here that the plane is fully air-
borne for the first time. The same level flight is held
for perhaps 300 yards to allow the plane to accelerate
well above stalling speed before the first turn is attempted. A slight turn to starboard is made to get out
of the track of the ship and then once more the aircraft
straightens out into the wind and climbs away to whatever duty it has been assigned.

Immediately after the first plane has been moved
into the starting line the next plane in rotation begins

to move up. By the time the first plane is over the bow the second is in position and having its motor opened up. After half a dozen planes have gotten away there is a steady line of planes taxiing up to the starting point and going off—which is the secret of the speed with which these operations are carried out. The torpedo planes with wings still folded over the pilot's head roll up to the take-off line. As they arrive the pilots start putting the wings down and they are locked in place as the motor is revved up. This is done, of course, from inside the cockpit and without assistance of the deck crews.

For the men on deck this moving of planes is perhaps the most dangerous. Pilots must concentrate their attention on those directing the plane movements. Deck men are expected to get out of the way. They duck beneath wings, avoid propellers, and work in hurricane blasts from the props of the moving craft with an agility and skill that is amazing to see.

Until the Navy standardized landing and take-off procedures a few years ago each pilot made his approach and landing in the way that seemed best to him. In those days, pilots told me, there was a high accident rate, most of which, however, consisted of minor damage to airplanes. There is one classic carrier story they recounted, of the old timer who made what he called the "sneaking bird approach."

This consisted of flying along only 10 to 15 feet above the wake of the ship until almost overhauling it. Then he would zoom the 35 to 40 feet up to deck level, come in just over the fantail and alight.

"Why, Charley," his brother pilots would tell him, "that's the craziest way of coming aboard I ever saw. It's backwards; it shouldn't work at all."

But Charley always stopped such jesting by pointing out that he never had an accident and never damaged a plane. And because this was true he was allowed to continue. The standardization, however, brought up the general level of accuracy to the point where a carrier landing today is routine with well-trained fliers. Every move from the moment the landing circle is entered, is made according to a precision plan.

This includes slowing the plane down to proper speed, preparing the engine, gear, hook and flaps at the right moments, and approaching at predetermined heights.

All the time I was aboard the *Lexington*—for weeks prior to the Coral Sea battle and during the tense days and hours of the fighting—not a single accident occurred. The only time there was a crash landing —and on this occasion the plane hit the deck and then bounced off into the sea—the pilot had been wounded in the right shoulder by a Jap bullet. This rendered his right arm (the stick hand) useless. This boy, Lieut. R. F. McDonald, and his gunner were fished out of the sea a few moments later by our trailing destroyer. Three weeks later, his arm in a plaster cast, he came limping aboard the transport which brought many of us home and greeted me with high spirits. Today he is again well and flying.

It happened that my quarters were in "the admiral's country," immediately under the flight deck and just ahead of the forward airplane elevator. The hinged steel flap which covered the groove at deck level when the elevator was flush with it was on the deck just above my cabin. Every aircraft that took off had to run across this metal flap. And each time, there was a loud metallic "whang," as the flap slammed down on the steel plate of my ceiling.

I used to lie abed, still half asleep as the pre-dawn scout and fighter patrols took off. Even half asleep, I could count each craft, and finally I got to the point where I believed I could distinguish between the bangs made by different types. When I went down to the wardroom for breakfast I could always tell just exactly how many planes had taken off. I won so many arguments on this point that finally my reports were accepted as official.

"Is it too noisy for you there, Stan," I was asked repeatedly.

"Well, no," was the answer to it. "It's the same for the Admiral as it is for me." The point was that I was sleeping in part of the quarters occupied by Admiral Aubrey Fitch and his immediate staff who made the *Lexington* their flagship.

The pilots flew, did practice shooting, bombing and torpedo work almost daily. When not in the air they were attending lectures, instruction classes, and brushing up on navigation. This went for those who had 300 hours and for those with 4,000 hours (we actually had this range of experience in our flight personnel aboard the *Lex.*) And the same constant training routine—which would have been a grind except that the men universally enjoyed their training—was applied to every other department of the ship.

I used to spend a lot of time sitting on the various gun platforms gathering a sun tan, and watching the crews which were on duty at the guns for 24 hours a day. One thing that the Navy drives home to its anti-aircraft gunners is this: "You must be ready every second because your opportunity for firing at an enemy aircraft is limited to the few seconds it is within range. Always expect the unexpected."

On the *Lex*'s previous cruise our ship had been attacked by 18 Japanese bombers and the gunners had had the opportunity of shooting at live targets. They discovered the difficulties of hitting planes in flight. Their interest in learning all about gunnery, and in training exercises, had been sharpened. These boys were forever practicing ranging on targets, loading and firing, and sighting.

Our own airplanes, during daylight hours at least, were continually in sight, on patrol or other duties. The 5-inch gun crews, particularly, were forever "practice firing" on these craft. The boys themselves called the exercises—when no shots were fired—"dry runs." They needed no urging from their officers, because enough of them had seen battle and understood the tremendous responsibility each gun crew shouldered. As a matter of fact each crew out of its 12 hours of "off duty" time, daily spent one hour with a dummy loader down on the machine deck of the *Lex*.

A dummy loader is an exact duplicate of a 5-inch gun breech, with all the various loading appurtenances including fuse-setting, loading, and gun-pointing devices. They used this to go through the continuous motions of pointing, setting shells and loading. The purpose was to smooth out the teamwork and speed up the flow of shells to the breech in order to increase the rate of fire of the big guns. The crews used real shells, and went through the whole sequence of loading, laying and firing, as hard as they could go. They sweat buckets doing it for a 5-inch shell and powder casing weighs 60 pounds and must be manhandled. It was strenuous sport, but it had the effect of working the boys into wonderful physical condition and built them into close-knit teams. The extraordinarily high rate of fire our twelve 5-inchers put out when we were under attack later showed the improvements derived from all this training.

All the gunners assigned to the light automatic cannon—20mm and 1.1 inch—daily practiced to increase their accuracy by skeet shooting. Lieut. Moore, of the gunnery department, explained to me that this was done to give these men the feel required for "leading" their targets. Shooting at a Jap airplane, Moore said, is exactly the same as shooting at a clay pigeon. To hit it you must fire well ahead because the plane is moving so fast. The secret of good gunnery, he believed, was to give the men plenty of shotgun work. To provide targets, spring "guns" tossed clay discs away from the *Lex* and the gunners, using shotguns, fired at them as they spun past.

Moore used to show me the scores made by the young gunners, many of whom were new recruits, the first time at sea. A comparison of their first records to their last disclosed remarkable advance in marksmanship.

In addition they fired daily with their own weapons. Usually the 5-inch guns were used to shoot time-fused flare shells up into the air, ahead of the *Lex*. The shells would burst, throwing out a parachute from which dangled a magnesium flare. It would sink slowly downward. As soon as it was within range the light weapons would open up on it in rotation. Inside of two weeks after leaving Pearl Harbor these gunners were able to tear the small parachute to shreds, or shoot the flare to bits in a few rounds.

This shooting was practice not only for the gunners

but also for the loading crews who fed shells to the gun breeches in clips of five and ten. During these shoots the boys also practiced changing hot gun barrels, and substituting various types of ammunition—tracer, armor-piercing, explosive, etc.

A simple practice given the 5-inch gunners was to have one gun fire a shell set to burst at an unknown height and direction. The rest of the guns on the ship had the problem of ranging the bursts, calculating its height and timing their shells quickly enough to get several shots off before the smoke from the original shell was dissipated by the wind.

As a special treat, every few days one of the scout planes would go aloft and at the end of a 4,000-foot cable would tow a cloth sleeve target. It would be towed high—10,000 feet or better—at first for the five inchers to shoot at with live shell. Then the towing plane would descend to levels where the 1.1 inch and the 20mm guns also had their chance at it.

The same kind of daily gunnery practice was carried out by every ship in our force. Cruisers and destroyers would suddenly open up with their guns and shoot for perhaps an hour at a time. The first time I saw this I thought surely the cruiser off our port quarter had sighted a Jap aircraft. It fired a single shell and then instantly afterward it seemed to break into flame from stem to stern as all its guns opened fire.

The motto: "Fly, bomb and shoot," was vigorously carried out by the squadrons too. The scouts and fighter planes were constantly firing at towed targets. Almost every day we would drop a sled over the stern, pay out a thousand feet of line, and tow it back on our wake where it bounced and skidded. On this small jittery target the dive bombers and scout bombers laid thousands of light flash bombs in practice attacks. From the *Lex* we could see the accuracy of each dive and the flash of yellow light as the bomb burst either on the water or on the target.

While the pilots dived and zoomed, coming in close to the *Lexington* or speeding away at water level, the gunners followed them with their pieces, making their own "dry runs." Particularly did they follow the torpedo planes that made approaches on us without of course launching torpedoes. This emphasis on the torpedo-plane attack paid off dividends in victories for the various gun crews as they shot Jap torpedo bombers out of the air on May 8th.

For every minute spent in the air the pilots of the various squadrons spent from five to ten minutes in classrooms setting up a problem and discussing its various solutions. These men were and are professional soldiers. They went at their jobs as a civilian does at his trade. Their purpose was destruction of Japanese airmen and ships, and everything dealing with the subject was of intense interest to them.

Not only were they concerned with destroying the Jap, but with the possibility that the enemy would reach them too. Theirs was a most dangerous profession and woven through all their discussions were ideas for precautions or protective measures. They knew that every time they went out, some of them might not come back, but they wanted to reduce losses to the minimum that skill and efficiency could make them.

Tactics for the use of their planes were often sketched out on blackboards exactly as a good football coach sketches out the plays for his team. They also sketched out the tactics likely to be used by the enemy and his counter strokes to their blows.

Many of these men already had been through two actions against the Japs on earlier cruises. This experience plus information handed to the services from other ships and other pilots, was all passed on to every individual. The purpose of these discussions was to prepare the pilots for instinctively correct action against whatever type of Japanese planes might be encountered, or whatever kind of ground defenses might be used to hold them off.

Although the destruction of Japanese planes was primarily one for the fighter squadrons, it was also important for the scouts, dive bombers and torpedo plane pilots to be well versed in air combat. The latter groups had to expect to defend themselves against Japanese fighter assaults. Tactics had a part in these discussions, but most of all gunnery efficiency was

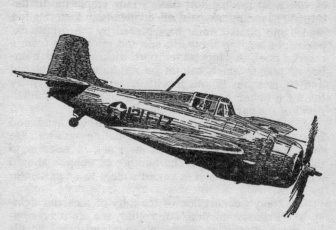

Grumman F4F

stressed. The leaders who headed the discussions repeatedly said: "There's no use getting a Jap in your sights unless you hit him with your first burst, and keep on hitting him as long as you fire."

To me, attending many of these lectures strictly as an observer, it was obvious that the Navy today has carried the old-time emphasis on good shooting in all its warships right into its air squadrons. Gunnery, the squadron leaders used to say, covers many a fault in execution of flying tactics.

To gain their performance advantages the Japs have given up armor and self-sealing fuel tanks, the lecturers said. The Grumman F4F fighters used aboard the *Lexington* had both these protective assets. In a knock-down drag-out fight the Grumman will take more punishment than the Zero. This, plus our advantage in hitting power, balances out the enemy's superior points, they argued.

The problem of the carrier fighter is very different from that of land-based fighters, the lecturers repeatedly explained. First, the fighter squadron is to the carrier what the belts of thick armor are to the battleship. They are the carrier's defense. Lost fighter planes and pilots cannot be replaced by the simple expedient of sending another plane and pilot down from a reserve pool. A ship leaves port with a limited number of planes which cannot be reinforced or replaced until it is again in touch with friendly shores. Every loss of a fighter plane and pilot diminishes the "thickness" of the carrier's armor plate.

A shipboard fighter must fight with his head and must be a cunning, careful, calculating warrior. He must gauge the risk he takes in attack in relation to the menace to his ship. The number of fighters aboard any carrier can be and is varied widely to fit particular missions.

The Navy's conception of the duty of a carrier fighter is: "Primary mission, controlling the air over combat areas, destroying enemy spotters and other hostile aircraft, protecting friendly planes and vessels. Secondary mission, attacking enemy surface and subsurface craft, exposed personnel, and vital controls with machine-gun fire, light cannon or small bombs."

Lectures for the torpedo-plane pilots were among the most interesting I attended. These always took place in the wardroom between meals. Lieut. Commander Jimmy Brett, skipper of this squadron, held a skull practice as rigorous as the signal drills coaches give their football quarterbacks, except in this case every pilot had to take part.

The stage used to be set by drawing up two of the long mess tables and bridging a 10-foot gap between them with specially cut light boards. Over these Brett spread a painted canvas which represented the surface of the ocean. It was ringed in white bull's-eye circles at scale distances indicating 1,000 yards. An arrow laid on the canvas indicated wind direction. Velocities and speeds of enemy ships were shown by numbered discs. And Brett also had a whole fleet of metal scale models of the Japanese battleships, carriers, cruisers and other vessels. The scale was such that a big carrier would be about a foot in length.

With the use of models representing tankers, transports, supply ships and warships a whole enemy fleet train could be laid out on the canvas. Once this was done Brett would call the pilots around him and say:

"Suppose you wanted to attack that first carrier. Where would you lay the smoke screen, and where would you make your torpedo approach?"

Several men would be invited to answer this question in turn. Each would give his solution and explain the reasoning behind his selections. Then a general critique would be held and ideas and suggestions from all the flyers given. Various phases of the problem would be discussed including arrangements for timing the attack and the getaway for each plane. Pilots would have to go through the orders and directions they would give over the radio if they were in charge of the assault. This was just part of the program to make every man fit to command.

Certain specific problems would be set up again and again and reasons for various actions rehashed and re-explained.

I recall that on the night of May 7th, after we had sunk the Japanese carrier *Ryukaku* near the island of Misima, the torpedo-plane pilots held a general discussion of the day's activity. The miniature ocean was laid out and Commander Brett placed the Japanese Fleet just as he and his pilots saw it when they began their attack. The fighters and dive bombers, in fact every airman on the ship, crowded round, stood on benches to see over shoulders and listened carefully.

The whole battle was reviewed, including the parts played by the dive bombers, in order to give those pilots who were not there a picture of the action, and to clarify possible errors. Alternatives that might have been tried were discussed and those elements correctly done were singled out and praised. Pilots reported Japanese defensive tactics. These were discussed and conclusions concerning them were drawn. In this way everything possible to be gleaned from air-versus-ship operations was absorbed by the men.

Problems confronting torpedo-plane pilots are quite different from those of the fliers who attack from above. The torpedo pilot flies a comparatively slow plane; he must come into the center of the enemy and to within a thousand yards of the ship he is to attack. He must stay close to the water because his torpedo would be damaged if dropped from too great a height. Basically the torpedo-plane pilot violates all the aviation precepts because he's a "low-slow flyer." His problem is to get into position by a route that will give the enemy the least number of shots at him at angles and ranges that make the shooting most difficult.

The dive bomber on the other hand comes screaming down from 12,000 feet or higher in an almost vertical descent. His problem is to get away after having dropped his bomb. In this the explosion of the bomb—whether a direct hit or not—is a help to the bomber pilot. The blast if anywhere near the target disconcerts the gunners at the moment when the diving plane is at its most vulnerable point—the pullout of the dive. Ordinarily dive-bomber pilots like to stay low and zigzag until they are clear of the enemy.

I was surprised and delighted when I went aboard the *Lexington* to find that Lieut. Commander Jimmy Thach, who had been the fighter skipper on the previous voyage, had clipped an article of mine from the *Chicago Tribune,* written last year after coming out of England. It was an account in which I told of the ineffectiveness of anti-aircraft fire in Europe. Thach had been interested because it explained why such guns missed their targets most of the time. The gist of it was that ordinarily planes were within range of these guns for seconds only and were gone before gunners had opportunities to correct their aim. Thach, who had led the *Lexington*'s fighters at Lae and Salamaua, had reported after this engagement that my analysis was correct and he had been using the article and its illustrations to make the same points with his pilots. Through this article I had become known to many of the *Lex*'s airmen before I came aboard and as a consequence we had many discussions about the air fighting over England and the tactics used there.

They were naturally interested to hear how their contemporaries in the R.A.F. and Luftwaffe fought their battles—just as interested as I was to hear their accounts of the U.S.N. fliers versus Japanese airmen in the Pacific. Thuswise we were able to satisfy our mutual curiosity.

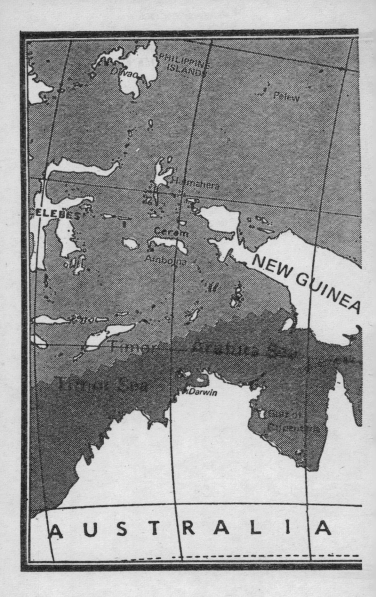

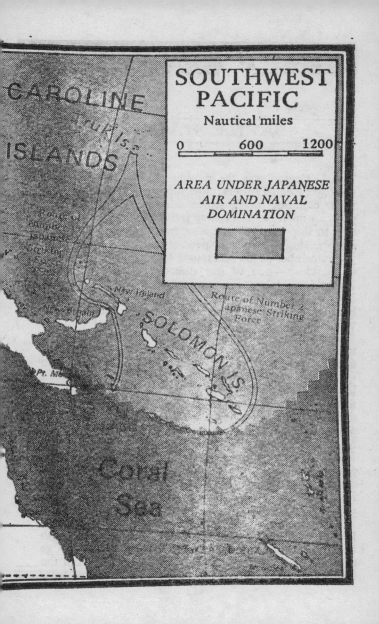

CAROLINE

Truk Is.

ISLANDS

Route of
Single
Japanese
Striking

SOUTHWEST PACIFIC

Nautical miles

0   600   1200

AREA UNDER JAPANESE
AIR AND NAVAL
DOMINATION

New Ireland

Route of Number 2
Japanese Striking
Force

SOLOMON IS.

Pt. Mb

Coral

Sea

4

BATTLE STATIONS

The *Lexington* was the mother ship to her brood of destroyers and cruisers. She supplied them with fuel, food, clothing, ship's stores and practically anything you can mention. Necessary transfers were made from ship to ship—tons and tons of fuel for example—without breaking the cruising speed of the entire flotilla.

I remember in particular one fine evening—May 6th to be exact—one of our destroyer attendants came alongside to take on a store of fuel. The *Lex* herself had swallowed into her enormous tanks the entire load of a big oil tanker that afternoon. And now she was redistributing it among the fleet.

This destroyer came alongside shortly after dark, tossed its mooring lines fore and aft to the *Lexington* and pulled in close to our starboard side. The two vessels, the huge matronly *Lexington* and the slender, low-slung destroyer became one. Our flight deck, 50 feet off the water, was high above even the bridge of the destroyer. It was a dark night as the smaller ship pulled in close while we rushed through the abysmal black, and was nestling against our flank.

The crews rigged a mail line and the destroyer passed over to us a list of things required by its ship's company. It would take about two hours to pour oil into her and meanwhile the other items were gathered and put aboard.

Shortly before she was scheduled to break away I wandered up on our signal bridge and stood with Capt. Sherman looking down at the destroyer's bridge and decks. The moon was beginning to rise from the horizon on our port side; this only intensified the dark-

52

ness in which the destroyer was coursing beside us. She was completely hidden in our shadow.

As we stood idly talking someone on the destroyer's bridge called across to us and asked: "Is the moon up yet?"

A voice from our deck called back: "What do you want to know for—you couldn't see it if it was."

"Perhaps there *is* something to Kate Smith's song," chuckled Capt. Sherman in his quiet way.

Just then the two ships changed course slightly on another leg of their zigzag and the rays of the moon slid past our Island and lighted one tiny corner of the destroyer's bridge.

One of our signalmen leaned over the rail, cupped his hands in round his mouth and began to croon: "When the mmmmmm moon comes over the mountain. . . ."

(One of the less serious moments of our war.)

Capt. Sherman began telling me that requests for all kinds of things constantly were being made to the *Lexington* by other ships in our unit. They expected, he said, the *Lexington*'s ship's supply department to carry practically everything buyable ashore.

"For instance," he said, "this destroyer alongside us asked for one ounce of block rosin along with other stuff tonight."

"Did he get it?"

"Oh, yes," the skipper replied. "We had it. Someone wanted it for his violin bow."

I had long since ceased to be surprised. The *Lexington* was so big and so perfectly equipped and supplied that practically anything could be produced at a moment's notice from her stores. Practically anything —that is, except the "five feet two inches of blonde" that a cruiser once ordered—and hard liquor, as the United States Navy still doesn't enjoy repeal. The noggin of black rum, "Nelson's blood" as it is known to the British (where it is served daily to all while in the tropics), is unknown to our Navy.

Only a few days earlier Commander Gilmore arranged for one of his junior officers to show me through the supply and catering establishments of the ship. He had explained the *Lexington* could stay at sea and fight for months without calling anywhere for stores or ammunition, and sent me around to have a look at the whole vast organization.

Our first stop was at the bakery. Here expert bakers worked 24 hours a day making bread and confections of all kinds. One would never suspect that our salts are as rough and tough as they have proven to be if you saw the delicacies in the way of pies, cakes, cookies and confections they consume while at sea.

The bakery itself was most modern. Electric power ran huge dough-mixers and cake-beaters. Electric ovens, controllable to within half a degree, did the baking. The place was spick and span, full of stainless steel mixing boards, bins, racks for the bread, and pans, pots and bread moulds of all sizes and shapes. Like every other department in the ship the walls, ceiling and floor were steel plates painted a spotless white and kept immaculate by countless scrubbings.

Don't for one minute low-rate the bakers either. Most of them had battle stations on anti-aircraft guns. Some were in the 20mm, some in the 1.1 inch, and some were stationed at the ammunition wells and hoists. On the day the *Lexington* met her end the bakers got their day's bread into the ovens early and then ran to their gun posts as the "battle stations" alarm came over the loud-speaker system. The baking thereafter was done by the ship's electricians by remote control. For when the bakers found they were unable to get back to take the bread out in time they telephoned to the electricians and had power to the ovens cut off.

On the same deck with the bakery the ship's butchers have a glistening white tiled butchery complete with chopping blocks and all the knives, hooks, meatgrinders and gadgets of the finest butcher shop ashore.

Each morning the butchers drew the meat supply for the next 24 hours from the enormous refrigerated stores section. The meat would come up in whole sides of beef, mutton and pork. It would be left to hang until the cold evaporated and then sliced into the proper cuts before being delivered to the several kitchens scattered about the ship.

The kitchens rate by rank. For instance, there is a small galley that cooks only for the admiral and his staff—about a dozen officers in all. Then there is another galley cooking for the captain and his personal staff—another half-dozen officers. There is a galley cooking for the wardroom mess where 130 odd senior officers are fed. A fourth galley cooks for the junior officers' mess—about 60 ensigns. Fifth comes the chief petty officers' mess. They are the Navy's "wily ones" noted throughout the service for the goodies they have on their menus. Last there are seven galleys to do the cooking for the men.

The Navy has introduced the cafeteria to the Raging Main. Gone are the bad old days when everything was cooked in one huge galley from which food for each separate mess—maybe 20 men at a time—was drawn in huge pannisters. Today each man takes his combination stainless steel tray-plate to the serving counter in the particular section of the ship where he lives. He passes down the serving line of steam tables and is served exactly as he would be ashore in any good cafeteria. Last of all he draws his coffee and silverware and sits down at any table that's vacant.

Meals are served three times a day and there is a 2-hour period for each meal. A man can eat any time during these 2-hour periods. Furthermore, he can eat as much as he likes, going through the lines as often as he likes. And there is so much variety that a man has quite a choice of foods at any meal.

Feeding of the men is considered so vital in the Navy that there is an involved system worked out to insure the men obtaining a well-balanced diet of proper food, the best quality of food, having it well prepared and well served. The menus are made out for a ship one week in advance by the ship's supply officer, who submits them to the ship's doctor, who in turn checks the meals to see that they contain vitamins and calories in correct proportion unit and number. After the doctor okays the list it is passed to the captain who assures himself that there is a wide enough variety of foods. If satisfied he signs the list whereupon it becomes an order and cannot be varied.

In the United States Navy you cannot cut down the men's rations and give the usual quantities to the officers. Nor can the officers have any foods the men cannot also have. So if the men are reduced to rations of beans for every meal, you may be sure that the officers too are eating beans for breakfast, lunch and dinner.

In every department of the ship there is an ever-boiling coffee pot. From these pots any man can draw himself a mug of "Java" at any hour. Because the ship had 16 boilers all these pots scattered over the great vessel were known as "the 17th boiler."

In addition to the regular rationing arrangements, the ship's canteen or "service" provided food. Men could purchase ice cream, soft drinks, malted milks and soda fountain concoctions, candy, cookies, as well as all kinds of clothing, toilet articles, presents for sweethearts and families, individual radios, and a thousand and one jimcracks. As a matter of fact the service did a rushing business at all times, especially in tobaccos.

Tucked away into corners of the ship were libraries where all sorts of volumes from technical tomes to detective and adventure stories could be secured. Keeping the library was the particular care of the ship's padre, Commander Markle. He told me he tried to keep the latest and best books—best-sellers and good technical volumes—on the shelves. Since the war, he said, there was great interest in travel books, exploration, etc.; all the books that gave any information about the country and the peoples of Japan, China, Malaya, the Dutch East Indies, New Guinea, Australia, New Zealand, New Caledonia, and all the Melanesian and Polynesian groups. Not until he needed them did he realize what a dearth of these volumes there was, and he had standing orders ashore for new purchases that gradually were being filled.

Commander A. J. White, senior ship's surgeon, had a remarkably fine modern hospital and surgery right forward in the ship at the waterline. He showed me through the place, quietly proud of his X-ray equipment, operating room, dispensary, first-aid treatment rooms and laboratory. I mentioned that only very big cities had hospitals as completely equipped as this.

"Well, we are a city, with this difference," he said. "We have a higher health record than a city and therefore the percentage of normal patients is very small. But we must be ready, for in a single ten minutes we could have 500 wounded or injured in here."

In anticipation of this possibility he had a staff of surgeons and physicians assisted by a large number of men trained as pharmacists' mates. Much of the time these men were more or less idle but they were retained for any emergencies that might arise.

At the time I went through, there were two patients in the isolation ward with measles, and one surgical case, an appendectomy in the hospital's surgery.

Commander White told me that experience in this war had shown more than 50 percent of the naval casualties were burns. Preparing for just such casualties, he had arranged for and stored a plentiful supply of tannic acid jelly. He explained there was a later, newer treatment recommended for burns but that the jelly could be applied by anyone, and quickly—speed being an important factor in burn treatments.

"We've cached more than 200 first-aid kits with a good supply of jelly and other essentials all over the ship and have trained someone in each general area to give first aid," the Commander continued. "On a ship one doesn't know where casualties are likely to occur and we want the men to get immediate treatment on the spot. For this reason we scatter our doctors and trained Red Cross men all over the ship during battle."

The doctor explained further that the main hospital supplies were also split up and stored in widely separated parts of the ship, so that no explosion, fire or damage at one section could destroy all of the hospital necessities. All preparations have been made, he assured me, to move patients into various sections all over the ship where temporary hospitals could be set up if the number of wounded required it. Only a short time later I saw how the Commander's foresight was justified by events that caused us to move our wounded three times in a matter of a few hours.

To walk down through the passageways in the men's quarters at any time of the day or night was to step into a bedlam of music, announcements, news dispatches, plays, and what have you, all coming from hundreds of individual radios. Half the crew was off duty all the time and the result was that several hundred different radios, at several hundred different bunks and tuned to widely separated stations, were always giving forth.

Near Hawaii the boys listened to American stations on Oahu. As we went south these faded out except for some of the boys with excellent short-wave radios who kept in touch with the mainland programs. When we got into the Coral Sea we could listen to New Zealand, Australia and Japan. It was a standing joke among the boys to keep track of the latest Japanese claims particularly concerning the sinking of the *Lex*. As we were steaming south the score was already at three claimed sinkings.

"We know we're on a good ship," they used to say, "it has to be good to go down three times and still be round and about."

The ship's authorities made no objections to these radios. It was felt, in fact, that the men should be encouraged to have them for entertainment. The officers said the men worked hard, studied hard—the whole ship was forever poring over some new course or other—and consequently needed what relaxation they could get.

There was one restriction though—each radio brought aboard had first to be tested to determine that it did not put out any electrical field that might be picked up by enemy detectors, and that it put out no electrical field that might interfere with the *Lexington*'s own delicate radio equipment. The tests were made by the radiomen aboard and were constantly rechecked by radiomen aboard other vessels in our task force.

Practically the only other entertainment on the ship

was provided by tournaments and competitions in various games such as "acey-ducey" (the Navy's universal name for backgammon) checkers, chess, bridge and cribbage. Each department on the ship played off for its champion and the champions then played in the finals for the ship's championship. In these tournaments rank didn't mean a thing and as on other cruises enlisted men won most of the titles. This time our finals never were played off—the *Lex* met her doom when the competitions were only halfway through.

Let me quote again from the *North Star,* the cruiser paper dedicated to the U.S.S. *Lexington,* published the day after the sinking. On page four of this immortal publication the following item concerning the "acey-ducey" tournament was printed:

"The 'all hands' acey-ducey contest held on board the good ship *Lexington* has been postponed until the new commissioning, expected to take place some time in the near future.

"While the contest lasted it was touch and go especially among the crew with intense feeling rampant between gunnery and air departments, closely emulated by the entire ship's company. In the officers' country the Jay Ohs (junior officers) were running off their finals. They interrupted the play when all hands were suddenly seized with an urge for a bath in the Coral Sea.

"At the moment it is impossible to say who was actually ahead, because Chaplain Markle, the tournament promoter, is 'visiting' on another ship in the force and only he has complete records.

"It is known, however, that the wardroom Minutemen have completed their contest with Lieut. Franny Farrington the undisputed champion. Lieut. Farrington finally overcame his sagacious opponent in the finals, Dr. White, in a match which was 4 to 0 the whole way. Dr. White seemed certain of winning after sensationally sweeping aside such opponents as Lieut. Commander Ramsey, c.o. of Fighting 2; and Lieutenant Bob Moore, assistant gunnery officer.

"Lieut. Farrington, a dark horse of Torpedo 2, came slipping from behind a smoke screen and let go his

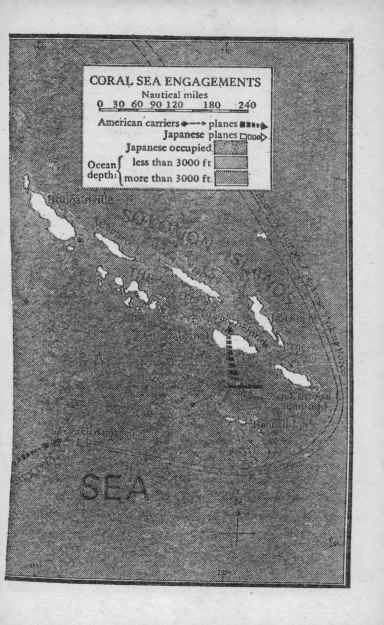

CORAL SEA ENGAGEMENTS

Nautical miles

0 30 60 90 120   180   240

American carriers ●--→ planes ■■■■▶

Japanese planes □□□▷ ▷

Japanese occupied

Ocean { less than 3000 ft
depth: { more than 3000 ft

Bougainville

SOLOMON ISLANDS

Malaita

Guadalcanal

SEA

acey-ducey at close range before Dr. White could recover from his victory over Lieut. Moore.

"Capt. Sherman expects an early resumption of the tournament."

The deck crews aboard the *Lexington*—and there were hundreds of men who handled the ship's planes— acquired a beautiful mahogany color from exposure to the sun during the weeks we were operating in the tropics. These boys stayed on deck throughout the whole day. Much of this time, however, they would be able to lounge, read, or keep a dozen baseballs flying back and forth in games of catch and toss.

While working, each man wore a singlet of a special color and a matching skullcap. These, as we said earlier, denoted the special jobs they were assigned to. When not working, that is when not launching or landing planes, they usually slipped the singlets off their shoulders and rolled their skullcaps up so that chest, back, and arms were exposed to the sun. The singlet would become just a roll around their necks.

This constituted no letdown in alertness, however. While playing thus on the deck these men were as close to their battle stations as they could get. With the sounding of the alarm on the loud-speaker system they would be at their duty posts in a dozen steps. And while they were scampering to them they would flick down the singlets, shrug their arms into the sleeves and with a single movement of the hand roll down their skullcaps. This left them clothed according to regulation and ready for anything the next moments might bring.

The boys who lounged, read or studied on deck were equally ready for instant duty. With the sounding of the gong they would jump to their guns, sweep their cushions, books, deck chairs, etc. into the safety net rigged along the edge of the *Lexington*'s flight deck. This left the decks clear for ascending or descending aircraft.

On our fighting ships at sea there is no fuss and feathers like you see in the movies or about training establishments. The gold braid is packed away once the ship leaves port.

The enlisted men wear blue jeans—pants and a loose jacket. The Marines stick to their khaki but make a concession by wearing a light open-weave sun-tan shirt in the tropics. The officers wear just a sun-tan shirt and trousers, putting on a black tie for lunch and changing to whites for dinner.

Many of the men in the crew wear shorts in the daytime on or below decks. The officers never wear anything but their khaki slacks. In their off-duty periods, however, they can come on deck in swimming trunks and sun bathe. There are specific health regulations encouraging all ranks to get a reasonable amount of sun. Yet great care is taken to prevent either officers or men from getting a burn because technically it is a crime to "become unfit for duty through personal neglect."

All the ship's normal activities, once we left Pearl Harbor, were punctuated by the dawn and dusk "battle stations" order. This order requires every man aboard ship to drop any job he may be doing at the moment and jump to his battle posts. Pilots stand by their airplanes, gun crews by their weapons, signalmen at their posts, ammunition handlers man the magazines and shell hoists, damage crews are at their firefighting apparatus and their stations. Every man on the ship has a special place where he is assigned in periods of battle, and there he must go when the double gong "bong-bong," "bong-bong," "bong-bong" is heard, followed by the very musical trumpet call to "stations" over the ship's loud-speaker system. Even while the call is still sounding you can hear throughout the ship the patter of men's feet as they race to their posts.

These calls sounded every dawn and every dusk and might be sounded at any time of the day or night. Once we got well to the westward we never knew when the calls were practice or the real thing. My own station was on the signal bridge where Capt. Sherman conned his boat and controlled the flying, landing and general activities of the carrier. Every time the battle stations call was sounded I dropped my loafing, writing or gossiping and tramped up to this open deck 25 feet above the flight deck from which one could see everything happening on and around the *Lex*.

The reason for battle stations at sunrise and sunset is because these are potentially the most dangerous periods in any 24 hours. The light is fading or growing. Submarines, tiny little dots on the sea, can see the flotilla plainly at such times yet lookouts aboard big surface vessels are virtually blind during these periods of changing light.

At dawn in particular, everyone on the *Lexington* and on our escort vessels was on the alert. We had traveled several hundred miles during the night into waters that might not have been scouted the evening before. There was no way to know in advance what forces might be close until our planes had reported "all clear." In times when the weather was cloudy with rain squalls and visibility was poor, there were long periods in which we had to stay on the alert never quite sure what might be just over the horizon. We had to be ready for anything at such times.

We left Honolulu as a single carrier battle force, with the *Lex* as the flagship and center of the formation, and had with us almost a dozen other warships— cruisers and destroyers. As soon as the *Lexington* cleared the twisting, narrow and tortuous channel leading out of Pearl Harbor our escorts that had been to sea for a couple of hours nosing about to be sure the waters were clear of Jap submarines took station about us.

The cruisers came in close. The destroyers nosed ahead, behind and on either beam, constantly listening for submarines as they zigzagged. They reminded me of a pack of hunting dogs sniffing out game for a sedate hunter.

The *Lexington*'s planes ranged the air constantly during daylight hours. We moved, as a matter of fact, within a double screen of planes that covered the sea and skies for more than 200 miles in all directions of the compass. One of these screens was directed high against enemy airplanes and possible sights of enemy fleets. The other screen operated closer in and at low altitudes chiefly watching the water for sights of Japanese submarines.

Our departure from Honolulu was a lazy, lackadaisical one. We just drifted away over the horizon apparently engaged in some routine maneuver. We disappeared in a direction almost opposite to that in which we intended going. This apparent aimlessness was continued until we were 50 miles or more from land, well out of sight of any islands. Then and only then, did the ships close up, turn on their southerly course, and gradually pick up speed.

From that moment we never sighted land until we were in the Coral Sea. We threaded our way through myriads of Pacific islands keeping a track that deliberately avoided them. Our purpose was to stay out of sight of prying eyes on the shores, for ours was a secret mission, and it remained secret too until we pounced for the first time on Japanese ships.

5

BOUGAINVILLE —
THE FIRST ACTION

All the training, the theorizing, the practice problems, the tactical conclusions and aircraft exercises that had been lavished on the *Lexington* and her crew over a 15-year period, came to their first war test on last Feb. 20th. It happened when the *Lex,* as the main unit of a single carrier task force, penetrated more deeply into Japanese waters than any other surface vessel up to that time.

That first engagement was unsought. It developed out of a bold attempt by Vice-Admiral Wilson Brown, who was commanding the striking force, to run in within 200 miles of Rabaul, the principal harbor on the island of New Britain. He proposed to deliver a surprise air attack on Japanese shipping concentrations anchored there.

New Britain is northeast of New Guinea and is considered one of the New Guinea group. Since World War I it has been governed by Australia under League of Nations mandate until the Japanese moved in late in January.

Our naval intelligence learned that the Japanese were making Rabaul a major base for their operations in this area. Rabaul has a good harbor and because of this fact was the capital of Australian New Guinea. It had also been headquarters for the copra planters throughout New Guinea and the Solomon Islands. There were a few hotels and a few business houses had branch offices there. Of military fortifications there were none.

Rabaul in fact was a backwater of which the world

had hardly been aware prior to 1936. In that year Vulcan Island, in the center of the harbor, reverted to its ancient volcanic activity and a series of terrific explosions and eruptions occurred. Volcanic ash covered the town of Rabaul to a depth of about four feet, but there were no white casualties. A few natives lost their lives when they refused to take to the hills with the rest of the population.

The harbor is very beautiful. Fringed with cocoanut palms and bright-leaved shrubs, scarlet bougainvillea and hibiscus and heavy-scented frangipani, it forms a deep gash amongst the surrounding hills. It is well protected and has deep-water anchorage for an enormous fleet of ocean-going ships. One mile out of the tiny settlement of Rabaul, travelers are in thick jungle. There are no roads in that country, all communication being by boat around the coasts. In the surrounding jungles the natives still live an undisturbed primitive Stone-Age life.

These facts were well appreciated by the Japs. The taking of Rabaul meant merely the arrival of the first Japanese ships. Not a shot was fired in defense of the town. Australian reconnaissance aircraft operating from the town harborfront discovered the approaching Japanese warships and transports while they were still several days' sail away. Lacking strength to hold off the invader they gathered the women and children from the plantations in the area and flew them out to safety. When the Japs arrived they found the place evacuated, the men having moved back into the jungle after the women and children had departed. All this happened toward the end of January.

Soon thereafter Admiral Brown was given reports from the Australian reconnaissance patrols indicating daily arrivals of new transports and supply ships. Obviously the Japs were concentrating there for another move on southward. He decided on a daring blow. He would head his force round the eastern end of the Solomon Islands and steam right up the passageway between the great Japanese naval and air "Pearl Harbor" on the island of Truk and the new enemy base at Rabaul.

His object was to reach a position along the northern coast of New Ireland, a slender sickle of land extending like a new moon across the northern approaches to Rabaul. New Ireland is about 125 miles due north of Rabaul harbor. If the *Lexington*'s force could gain its northern shore it might hide there, partly sheltered from Jap air patrols, and be able to launch its own air-striking units against the Jap shipping anchored and unsuspectingly in the roadstead.

At dawn, on the morning of Feb. 20th, after several days and nights of hard steaming, the *Lexington* was within 400 miles of her goal. The whole force was moving in fast, tensed for the effort that was plotted out to the last detail. Everyone in the little fleet knew they were in Japanese waters and every mile was taking them closer to battle, to unknown and unforeseeable dangers.

All around the *Lexington* her long-range scouts were scanning the waters, the islands and the skies for enemies. It was necessary to steam on another 200 miles to get within safe launching distance for the heavy dive bombers and torpedo squadrons that were lined up and ready on the flight deck. This would require 8 more hours of 25-knot steaming. So it was hoped that the attack could be launched shortly after lunch that day.

Over breakfast there was a lot of speculation on the day's outcome. The airmen looked forward to the coming trial with confidence. This was exactly the sort of mission they had been fulfilling in their practices and they were anxious to have an opportunity to carry out the operation with live bombs, real torpedoes and, above all, to have Japanese vessels as their targets.

Between 9:30 and 10 o'clock that morning scouts radioed that a Japanese plane was shadowing the fleet. The Navy calls such planes "snoopers." Capt. Sherman sent off four fighters—in two pairs—to find and destroy the Jap airplane. For the job, Lieut. Commander Jimmy Thach, skipper of the fighter squadrons on the *Lex*, chose Ensign Edward R. Sellstrom as his wing man. The second pair were Lieut. (jg) Onia B. Stanley and Ensign Leon W. Haynes.

Kawanishi

"The area was full of cumulus clouds, low-hanging, with heavy tropical rain squalls dotted over the sea where nimbus cloud had developed," Lieut. Commander Thach told me later.

"We climbed up through these clouds until we came out on top. Once in the clear our pairs split and taking different sections of the sky we began to quarter the area. After some minutes I spotted the Jap through a hole in the clouds.

"It was a big four-engined Kawanishi flying boat. (The Kawanishi is a Jap copy of a French flying boat built originally for passenger and mail service across the South Atlantic between Dakar and Brazil.) This baby, I learned afterward, has a wing span of 132 feet, which is more than Pan American Airways trans-Pacific clipper ships.

"I pointed him out to Sellstrom and we both went right down on him as he was in the clear 5,000 feet below us and about 5,000 feet above the ocean. The Jap evidently saw us coming for he flew into one of the cloud banks. But now we knew what cloud he was in and we circled through the edges of it.

"This time we got into the vapor deep enough to hide us from anyone outside but we were still able to look out. A few minutes later the Jap came out of the rain below us, this time at about 1,500 feet.

"I waited after seeing him, wanting to give him plenty of room to get well into the clear before starting my dive. My object was to allow him to get far enough out so that he couldn't duck into the cloud or rain after I commenced my dive.

"When I thought he was far enough I went after him. As I approached and while still at long range, the Jap started to shoot at us and I could see his tracer passing. We were still out of range of his light machine guns which indicated that he was firing with 20mm cannon. These were mounted in the turtle back on top of the fuselage.

"We continued in and made our firing run and I saw that I had hit his fuel tanks, for gasoline was spraying astern of him. We turned, came back and made a second run from the other side. As we closed in the big Jap plane seemed to be spitting fire from half a dozen places.

"Our bullets ignited him for he suddenly caught fire. Great white sheets of flame from the streaming fuel spread out behind him and he began spinning down into the sea.

"Besides his 20mm on his back this fellow had machine guns in the tail position, 20mm guns firing forward, and evidently unmounted machine guns which they fired out of the cabin windows, just as the Germans do with their Heinkels and big Condor bombers.

"We'd hardly knocked this Kawanishi down when the scouts said there was another one up top. We hurriedly climbed again and were searching, when radio control on the *Lex* told us that this one had been dealt with already. One of our scouts caught this second one.

"This is a good story too," Thach chuckled. "That scout was just a mile or two faster than the Jap boat which could fly at more than 200 knots (225 miles an hour). Our pilot chased the Jap, but his scout plane couldn't climb up to the enemy's level. So he flew just underneath the Kawanishi and gradually edged up as close as he could.

"The crew in the flying boat opened a bomb door and began firing down at our men with machine guns. The scout's rear gunner turned his twin guns straight up and fired into the Jap until it started to burn. That's meeting the situation, isn't it?"

That made two Japs out of two seen, Thach said, and as there were at least 10 in the crew of each of the flying boats it meant the death of at least 20 Japanese airmen—for none even attempted to escape by parachute. Nevertheless, Thach explained, the Japs had done the most vital part of their work—reporting the presence of the American fleet by radio to their base.

The fighters returned to the *Lex*, alighted, were refueled and rearmed. As they sat down to lunch it was generally agreed in the wardrooms that there would be a fight that afternoon. The Japs could be expected to make some sort of an effort to attack our ships, probably by aerial assault.

Admiral Wilson, however, made no effort to change course. The force kept on boring in. Capt. Sherman then prepared for the anticipated attack, calling his crew to battle stations. The problem confronting the Captain was a pretty one. He believed the Japs would attack but did not know the direction, the height, nor the time when they would come, nor had he any way of knowing the number of aircraft that would be sent against him. However, he disposed his fighters and scout squadrons so that they would give warning and be in position to fight with maximum strength when the enemy appeared. While the fighters stayed within about 20 miles of the ship at all times, the scouts went a long way out—their mission was to watch for the incoming attackers even if they were high, and to report them by radio.

That afternoon it was when Edward (Butch) O'Hare, in a now epic conflict, shot down five Japanese bombers. Most of the published accounts have failed to do justice to the captain of the *Lexington* for the extensive preparations just mentioned and to the other fliers who were in the air battling the Japanese when O'Hare performed his remarkable feat.

But let Commander Jimmy Thach, who directed the whole battle and was in the thick of it himself, tell the story:

"Six of us were in the air," Thach began. "Six other fighters who had just been relieved were almost down to the *Lexington*, when the first Japanese planes were sighted. I was at 10,000 feet and the six planes about to alight were ordered to climb right back to me. O'Hare was then on the deck of the *Lex*.

"The enemy consisted of nine twin-engined bombers flying in three vees of three. When first seen they were 12 miles out at 12,000 feet flying in a slight dive toward the 10,000-foot level. These were land-based planes. We discovered later that they were fast—able to do over 300 miles an hour—and almost identical to the Army's Martin B-26s.

"They had guns in the turtle back in the tail position, and in the nose—machine guns and 20mm cannon.

"In a running fight Lieuts. Noel Gayler, Walter Henry, Rolla Lemmon, and Ensigns Edward Sellstrom and Dale Peterson singled out and destroyed one each. I too got one. Each time one caught fire it would drop its bombs harmlessly into the sea because they were still too far from the *Lex*.

"This fight continued right into range of the ship's anti-aircraft curtain, but our fighters stuck with them regardless. Two that we damaged were finished off by anti-aircraft fire from the ship. The ninth and last, in a crippled condition, turned away and tried to escape.

"A second enemy formation had been reported while we still were milling around with the first one. Six ships on deck, including Butch, were sent up to intercept them.

"Six of us in that first fight still had gas but the group that had been recalled at the last minute had to return for more fuel.

"This left us pretty well split up, and we were scattered widely as a result of the fight anyway. The new Jap group, another nine flying in three vees, was 60 miles behind the first lot which meant that none of us could see them yet.

"The six, including O'Hare, spread out to find and intercept these second raiders, climbing as they went. It happened that Butch and his wingman saw them first. They sounded the alarm and went into attack, beginning their dive 12 miles out. Here we had a bad break because O'Hare's companion found that his guns wouldn't fire. That left Butch there alone.

"The rest of us were heading his way, climbing up toward the oncoming Jap bombers, but we all knew we could not intercept them before they reached the bomb-dropping position."

Explaining the ensuing fight to me O'Hare said:

"I knew my wingman had dived away, but there wasn't time to sit and wait for help. Those babies were coming fast and had to be stopped. In the first run I fired into two, the two trailers in the last vee. I had to pull up to let them fall away.

"I had fired at the starboard engine in each ship and

kept shooting each time till they jumped right out of their mountings. This caused both these planes to veer round to the starboard and fall out of the formation.

"I then crossed to the other side of the formation. I fired into the port engine of that plane and saw it jump out. I pulled away slightly while this third plane skidded violently and fell away, then went back in and fired into the trailer of the middle vee, still shooting at the engines.

"The same thing happened again. It seems as if all you need to do is to put some of these .50-caliber slugs into the Jap engines and they come all apart and tear themselves right out of the ships. The engine fell out of this fourth plane, too, and I could see the plane commence to burn.

"By this time the Japs, still in formation, were right on top of the release point (the place where bombs aimed at the carrier would be dropped). They *had* to be stopped any way at all: there were five of them still. I came in close, shot into the fifth one till he fell away and then gave the remaining four a general burst until my ammunition was exhausted."

All this happened in a space of four minutes. During those four minutes Thach and several of his original group of six had turned and with wide-open throttles were boring down on the diminishing Japanese formation.

"As we closed in I could see O'Hare making his attack runs with perfect flight form, exactly the way that we had practiced. His shooting was wonderful—absolutely deadly. At one time as we closed in I could see three blazing Japanese planes falling between the formation and the water—he shot them down so quickly.

"How O'Hare survived the concentrated fire of this Japanese formation I don't know. Each time he came in, the turtle-back guns of the whole group were turned on him. I could see the tracer curling all around him and it looked to us as if he would go at any second. Imagine this little gnat absolutely alone tearing into that formation.

"Just as O'Hare got his fifth machine, we were within range and took over the fighting. We collected two more and shot up the other two. They staggered away losing height."

Back on the *Lexington*'s deck, the plane-handling crews, the Admiral and his staff, Captain Sherman and his staff, and pilots of the bombers and dive bombers had been watching this show, although they had had a few moments of their own.

Out of the first formation the leading plane was struck by anti-aircraft fire while still several miles away. The damage seemed to have been loss of the left or port engine. The Jap pilot with desperate courage and great skill retained control of the bomber and made a suicidal attempt to crash into the *Lexington*.

With his starboard engine wide open he came down in a swooping dive toward the *Lex*'s stern. He flew across a destroyer, then over the cruiser line. As he lost altitude he came within range of the small machine-gun cannons on the fleets' vessels and they all poured their fire up at him. But still he kept on coming. Lower and lower, close and closer.

Finally, when he was down to a height of no more than 300 feet, the 1.1 inch and 20-mm fire from the *Lexington* seemed to really take effect. The nose of the bomber began to come up, the speed to diminish. While still 200 yards behind the *Lexington*'s zigzagging stern, the bomber finally stalled in the air. Its wings ceased to carry its weight and the nose dropped in a precipitate dive into the sea. An instant later only a huge pillar of black smoke marked the grave of the bomber and its crew.

Some of the most remarkable motion pictures taken in the Pacific recorded this incident from the *Lexington*'s rear deck. Stills taken from this film show clearly the intent of the Jap pilot, the condition of his ship, and the final stall and dive.

While this was going on O'Hare began his attack. The surrounding skies seemed to be full of planes falling from the first group of nine and from the formation further out. We lost two fighters in the engagement. One making an approach was hit on the engine with a

20mm shell. The engine quit and the pilot made a dead-
stick landing near a destroyer which quickly picked him
up. The second loss involved both plane and pilot.

Hardly had the skies cleared from the initial combat, when the four Japanese planes that had survived
O'Hare's guns, reached bombing distance and released
their projectiles at the *Lexington*.

Capt. Sherman standing on the bridge was watching
this formation closely. He saw the bombs fall away
from the enemy planes and momentarily judged their
probable course.

"Hard aport," he directed the helmsman. As the big
ship, now traveling 25 knots or better, commenced its
swing the Captain still kept his eyes on the falling
bombs. But he evidently decided the *Lexington* was
in the clear for he suddenly turned his back on the
bombs and in a quiet voice ordered the navigating
officer to bring the ship back to her course. With
hands clasped behind him, he walked to the opposite
side of the bridge to watch his fighters finish off the
remaining Japanese planes.

Remember the ninth plane in the first formation? It
had slid away damaged and disappeared over the horizon. But that is not the end of the story. Scout Pilot
Lieut. Edward Allen saw this ship 30 miles away
from the *Lexington* as he was returning from patrol.
Turning after it he gave chase in his SBD which had a
top speed of about 240 miles an hour.

Under ordinary circumstances the bomber could
have stepped away from Allen's plane, but the dam-
ages sustained in the fight near the *Lex* had slowed it
down so that it was doing no more than the little scout.
Allen found that by careful trimming he could gradually creep up to within gun range of the bomber.
At first machine guns from three or four emplacements
fired at him as he came in close.

Allen fired back, using the two .30-caliber weapons
in his nose. The recoil and rocket effect of his guns
firing slowed him down a mile or two an hour allowing the Jap plane to pull ahead again. Allen would stop
shooting, retrim his ship, and slowly creep up to within range once more. Again he was met with machine-

gun fire, this time not so much. He fired again and once more dropped back.

This seesawing and shooting was repeated for an hour, over a distance of almost 200 miles, before Allen's diminishing fuel forced him to break off and head back toward the *Lexington*. He reported that when he last saw the Japanese plane it was flying on, wobbling and recovering almost as though there was no hand at the controls. He said that the machine-gun fire directed at him ceased, and he believed he had killed or wounded all the crew.

Of the two of the last nine bombers that went wobbling away one is believed to have crashed. Another scout saw a damaged Japanese bomber fall into the sea some 30 miles away from the *Lexington,* and reported it had probably been fatally shot apart near the carrier but flew on for this distance before finally crashing.

Lieut. Commander Thach told me the encounter had taught him and his men a lot. It had given them a close look at enemy fliers and enemy aircraft.

"Those Japs came in with great determination. The first lot went right for the *Lex.* They never hesitated a second, despite our attack, until their leader was shot down. Then there was an apparent momentary uncertainty, that might have been, however, because of the heat of the assault they were subjected to. The second nine never faltered and came right on in to the bitter end, even though O'Hare was eating them up behind and we were coming in from ahead.

"The morale of the Japs was shown by their ability to hold formation and keep their line headed toward the *Lex* without maneuvering defensively in any way. Also, they did not drop their bombs and try to get away when we closed in. They held on to their bomb loads until they were shot up or burning or beginning to fall. Another thing, none of them attempted to leave their burning planes by parachute.

"O'Hare's firing was a real record. We figured that he used only about 60 rounds to each of the planes he knocked down. That, of course, is deadly shooting. To knock down five planes with one load of ammunition is something that only a fighter pilot can appreciate. I don't suppose shooting like that has ever been seen before in the air.

"It also showed us that the only real defense for a carrier or any other vessel against air attack is an airplane. We're beginning to believe you must meet the attackers with at least plane for plane. It did show that the defending pilots have to be the best men procurable."

In addition to the two Kawanishi flying boats shot down in the morning the *Lexington*'s men shot down 16 of 18 bombers that attacked in the afternoon. The anti-aircraft gun crews of the *Lexington* were given credit for two of these. In all, 12 members of Thach's squadrons were credited with a clean "kill," or an assist, or both in this fight.

While the air fighting raged around the ship, Commander White and his assistants were engaged in doing an emergency appendectomy down in the operating theater. The doctor complained to me later that this prevented him from watching the ship's fliers give a practical demonstration to all aboard of "how to deal with Japanese aircraft."

The Navy recognized this day's work by awarding the following decorations:

To the Captain, now Rear Admiral Frederick C. Sherman, a gold star to add to the Navy Cross he won as submarine commander in World War I. Rear Admiral Sherman's decoration was in reward for the outstanding manner in which he co-ordinated and timed the employment and relief of his combat patrols so that 16 enemy bombers were downed, and for handling the *Lexington* so that she escaped damage.

To Lieut. (jg) Edward H. "Butch" O'Hare the Congressional Medal of Honor and promotion to the rank of Lieutenant Commander (two jumps) for destroying five and damaging a sixth Japanese twin-engine bomber.

To Lieutenant Commander Thach for the destruction of one Kawanishi bomber, one twin-engined bomber, and assisting in the destruction of a third, the Navy Cross.

Other Navy Cross Winners:

Lieut. Noel A. M. Gayler
Lieut. Walter F. Henry
Lieut. Rolla S. Lemmon
Ensign Leon W. Haynes
Ensign Edward R. Sellstrom
Ensign Dale W. Peterson

Distinguished Flying Crosses were awarded to the following:

Lieut. Commander Donald A. Lovelace
Lieut. Albert O. Vorse
Lieut. Robert J. Morgan
Lieut. (jg) Howard F. Clark
Lieut. (jg) Onia B. Stanley
Ensign John H. Lackey
Ensign Willard E. Eder, Jr.
Ensign Richard N. Rowell

6

SMASHING THE JAPS AT LAE AND SALAMAUA

As already mentioned, our fleet had lost its greatest asset—surprise—in the proposed raid on Rabaul. Admiral Brown decided it was pointless to carry on further and ordered a change of course that took the whole force in a southeasterly direction. The little carrier force rounded the Solomon Islands and then continued southward.

In the waters just north of New Caledonia the Admiral kept a rendezvous with tankers, and several days were spent in transferring gasoline and oil to the various ships. The *Lexington* picked up mail from the tankers, and in turn acted as supply ship for food, medicines, etc., to the smaller vessels in her group. The mail from home was the biggest and most important item as far as the crew was concerned. These letters and papers had come through since they had left Pearl Harbor.

It is truly remarkable how the Navy gets mail to its men. Fighting vessels can go to sea and remain out for months yet somehow the mail finds its way to them, arriving aboard at all sorts of odd times and often in odd ways. All the natural ties to home and family seem to be intensified by overseas service and the men develop the greatest interest in a few odd facts, a bit of gossip, a look at the home town newspaper.

The refueling period is a popular time for writing letters home. Usually refueling requires several hours, even with the speedy new secret methods for pumping oil from a tanker into a warship that the Navy now

uses. Aboard the *Lexington* the men were told the
dead-line for getting mail to the censor to have it passed
in time to go off with the tanker, and all over the ship
during these hours gobs could be seen penning messages to families, wives, sweethearts and friends. Mail
from a crew the size of the *Lexington*'s can snow under the censors—even though all the senior officers of
each department examine the outgoing mails.

There was never a moment at sea when vigilance
could be relaxed. The air patrols were out regardless of
weather, and all day long there was a constant coming
and going of planes. Pilots on a carrier pile up an amazing total of flying time. They average at least five hours
a day—the minimum for scouts and fighter pilots—
and in a matter of three weeks a man in these squadrons adds another 100 hours to his log. Not even the
airline pilots fly as much in normal routine, although
for years these commercial airmen were putting in more
time than any other airmen in the world.

About the end of February the *Lexington* met another single carrier force of about a dozen ships including one of our new carriers commanded by Rear
Admiral Frank Fletcher (now Vice-admiral). The
second carrier must be unnamed here for reasons of national security. These two groups joined and together
represented a powerful modern air striking force. The
world today recognizes a carrier force as the most powerful naval force that can be put to sea, but at that time
the Coral Sea and Midway battles in which the carrier
came into its own had yet to be fought.

A fleet slowly patroling these waters is not on aim-
less maneuvers. It actually is holding open our supply lines between the United States and Australia. It is
plugging the natural route the Japanese would follow in
making a foray against either our shipping or against
the Southern Pacific islands held by the United Nations. Specifically, the Fleet's presence there protected
New Caledonia, the Fijis, and the Tonga group.

This situation has now changed considerably because
United States Army and Marine Corps units have moved
into many of these islands, built airports and armed

them with land-based bombers. The former need for the fleet to be continually there has been somewhat relieved.

By early March the Japs had pushed on from Rabaul and established a big airfield at Gasmata on the south coast of the island of New Britain, and had also established themselves on the mainland of Australian New Guinea at Lae and Salamaua. This is the northeast shore, and these two roadsteads are the most important entries to that area of New Guinea. Here, as in Java, Sumatra, Borneo and Malaya, control of the coasts and ports means control of the country because there is no internal communication system.

The Japs had found in Lae and Salamaua two fine airfields used by New Guinea Airways. This company supplied freight and passenger transportation from the coasts up to the very rich Bulolo and Eddy Creek gold field, 80 to 100 miles inland and respectively 4,000 and 8,000 feet above sea level. New Guinea Airways carried more freight over this route in the years from 1929 up to the beginning of the war than all the rest of the freight airlines of the world.

The small town of Salamaua is built on a 3-mile-long narrow isthmus which is joined to the mainland by a 100-yard neck of low sand. The bay formed by the finger of land affords good anchorage for vessels after they enter through the coral reefs which guard the entrance.

The town consists of the administration buildings, a hotel, stores and two trading companies' warehouses.

In the official guide to mariners we find: limited supplies can be had from the stores, and sometimes fresh vegetables, bananas, etc., can be obtained from the stores. The water supply consists of rain water from cisterns and a few springs.

There is a radio station and hospital near the airfield.

Steamers arrive from Sydney every three weeks, and motorpower boats carry freight and passengers from Salamaua to Lae, which lies 18 miles to the north along the coast.

The small village of Lae stands 3 miles from the mouth of the Markham River and besides the airport the government has established an agricultural station there.

Before the establishment of N.G.A., the 82 miles over mountainous tracks was an 18-day trek, with native porters. Each native could only carry 60 pounds which included the food he would eat—15 pounds of rice on the way in and 15 on the way out—so he could only deliver 30 pounds at the gold fields.

The country was surveyed and it was finally decided that the costs of building roads were absolutely prohibitive. As a matter of fact it was found impossible to maintain a native labor force at the fields because two porters were needed for every man who worked in the field, and the porters would only be able to take in the food required.

So precipitous is that country that the rivers reach the coast by sheer falls—leaving no other means of transport except the airplane. In the early days temporary airfields were put down inland and all kinds of adventurous pilots with unsuitable machines came up. Freight used to be 50 cents a pound for the 40-minute haul from the coast. But these planes couldn't bring up sufficient weights to allow the transport of machinery so the big mining interests got together to form their own air transport.

They wanted planes capable of carrying four tons of weight with low landing and take-off speeds. Also they required all-metal planes because of the heat and damp of the coast and the wide variations of conditions as the planes went into the interior highlands. The Germans supplied them with tri-motored Junkers Ju-31s and also with a single-motored version of the Ju-31.

It was on these fields that the Japs now were basing bombers and fighters. They were flying out to sea and along the coast in early patrols and had their links in overseas flights back to Rabaul, and then on to Truk. Planes were also coming into Lae and Salamaua from the Dutch East Indies. It was obvious to the Australian patrol planes that made daily visits to within sighting distance of these ports on their reconnaissance flights, that the Japs were moving in occupation troops and a naval fleet for another step in their southern push.

From December 7th, the Japanese had advanced "according to plan." Now it was America's turn. . . .

The clouds, high, white and fleecy, hung over the towering, wild peaks of southeastern New Guinea. Those ramparts of rock climbed 14,000 to 16,000 feet into the tropic skies, effectively guarding Japanese-held Lae and Salamaua from any inland assault. And Japanese seaplane squadrons patrolling the northeastern shores of Australia and the Islands of Melanesia for 500 miles in all directions reported there was no sign of enemy planes or vessels.

Thus it was that the Japanese, with vigilance relaxed, filled up these two harbors with their warships, tankers, supply vessels, and transports. They were preparing for an advance from New Guinea against the Australian mainland. Lae and Salamaua, only 20 miles apart, were being used as jumping-off points for the invasion forces.

The preparations were proceeding leisurely. The Japanese commanders knew that the nearest soldiers, fleets, and aircraft of the united nations were at Port Moresby. This harbor, still under allied control, was 1,500 miles away by sea, all the way around the southeastern tip of New Guinea. Clearly there could be no surprise attack from there.

And yet, out of those innocent appearing clouds, on the early morning of March 10, came avenging airmen of the United States Navy in the first war raid in which any of our seaborne air hornets had taken part. Out of the wilderness skies of central New Guinea—a land where live the only people still dwelling in stone age conditions—came dive bombers, torpedo bombers, and fighters that smashed this Japanese force in 20 action-crowded minutes.

This raid demonstrated perfectly how naval air strength has—to borrow a term from the family bridge circle—finessed the ancient concepts of sea fighting. The airplanes taking part delivered in this short assault on the two harbors as much actual weight of

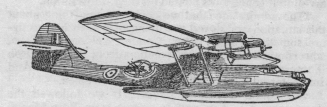

Consolidated Catalina

explosives against the enemy as could the broadsides of a fleet of a dozen heavy battleships in the same period.

This great story proves that the American spirit of originality and willingness to dare is not lost. Official Navy announcements mentioned briefly that the *Lexington*'s fighting pilots, bombers, and gunners had taken part in an action at New Guinea. But the inside story, the airmen's story, is told here in its amazing detail.

I shall now take you to sea at a period when the Australians and Americans were reeling under the successive Japanese victories in Malaya, Singapore, Sumatra, Java, and in the Philippines. It was a time in which the Japanese had been continually on the offensive. They had held the initiative, and had not been checked on any front.

Their naval units, aided by carriers, had seized northeastern Dutch New Guinea, and had spread along the northeastern coast of Australian New Guinea, taking one seaport after another until early in March American and Australian flying patrols had noticed the growing nucleus of vessels in Lae and Salamaua harbors. All these patrols were being carried out by Consolidated Catalina and land-based long-range bombers that followed the sea routes, avoided combat and continually hid in cloud cover, to escape Japanese eyes.

When the *Lexington* and another carrier under Admiral Brown appeared in New Guinea waters the Army's intelligence units passed on their information.

"The admiral decided we could do something about this situation and asked the flying men with him to figure something out," Lieut. Comm. Weldon Hamilton, who commanded the dive bombers from the *Lexington* in the raid, told me a few weeks after it was over. "And so we got our charts and dope on New Guinea.

"We found a curious picture. If we followed the coast around to Lae and Salamaua from Port Moresby, we would have traveled a good 1,500 miles. But if we could fly almost due north from Port Moresby, and hop right over the mountains, we would have to cover only 100 miles.

"The catch, of course, was the fact that the mountains were as high as 16,000 feet. Furthermore, there were no charts—and I mean absolutely none at all—that accurately showed the mountains of that wild inland country. Remember, most of it has never been trod by a white man. The black tribes there are among the most ferocious fighters found. They fashion stone axes and make knives out of human leg bones, and absolutely are back in one of the primitive ages. They're the kind of savages that pierce their noses with rings and go almost naked."

Such were the problems. Nevertheless, it was decided to go ahead regardless of the risks.

"I had read many books on Papua," Commander Hamilton related, "and while we were flying I remember speculating to myself upon the cannibal tribes living there below us and watching for the neat looking clearings and their thatched village huts that stood out against the heavy dark greens of the jungle.

"Our first 75 miles inland was a twisting course over heavily timbered steep mountains. The peaks rose on all sides of us right into the heavy clouds around them. At first I had been picking spots where I might have made a landing if engine trouble developed. But now there was nothing but jungle to see, not a place for an emergency landing anywhere.

"I took a good look around at our planes—strung out at intervals planned to allow each group plenty of skyroom—and I remember thinking how petty the tribal wars in that New Guinea jungle were compared with the one in which we were engaged. I also wondered what those savages who saw us must have thought at seeing such a number of great rumbling birds. I'll never know, of course, but the thought amused me at the time.

"While we were still 25 miles away from Salamaua harbor we could see the shipping lying at anchorage," Lieut. Commander Jimmy Thach, who led the *Lexington*'s fighter units that day, recalled in telling of the raid. "The land fell rapidly away beneath us and we came down in a long, fast dive.

"Our motor noise must have warned the Japs because we could see them begin to scramble before we got in. Instead of remaining behind to try to protect the unarmed merchant ships, the Jap war vessels, as they always do, slipped their cables and tried to head out into the open sea. They seem to leave the crews of the transports and auxiliary vessels to shift for themselves whenever an air attack is made."

The fighters and torpedo planes came down first, in accordance with timing worked out in advance. The torpedo planes picked out the largest transports and cruisers for their attentions, and the fighters went roaring around the harbor looking for Japanese defense planes.

"We were such a surprise to them," said Lieut. Noel Gayler, one of the fighter pilots, "that there was only one Jappie airplane in the air. He was a seaplane fighter with a rear gunner, and I must say he was a good little fellow. Lots of guts.

"He went after our torpedo planes that were down almost on the water, fanned out to take in a number of different targets. And he was doing a good job. He slid in and out among them, forcing some to bank away, and firing his front and rear guns in all directions. His harassing was of the best."

I remember my own surprise at Gayler's observations. I failed to note a twinkle in his eye as he spoke in his slow, quiet way. There was a pause, then he resumed:

"But that little Jappie made a mistake. Tut-tut. Too bad. He left the torpedo planes to pull up and challenge four of us [the fighter unit]."

Gayler ends his story at that point. But Gayler's friends will tell you that this young man (he came out of the Coral sea battle the navy's leading air ace with eight confirmed victories) eased out of his dive for half a second. His machine guns spat momentarily and, as the navy boys said, "Our Jap pal joined his ancestors."

This ended the opposition, except for a little anti-aircraft fire from a few ships and from a battery of heavy guns set up ashore. And while the torpedo planes began a systematic smashing of the anchored ships the dive bombers went after the fleeing cruisers and destroyers.

"I selected a fine cruiser," Commander Hamilton said. "It looked from 8,000 feet like a giant speedboat racing for the open sea. It was really pretty; alive.

"But I was too enthusiastic. I hadn't allowed for the wind at lower levels. It drifted me in my dive over the target and my bomb hit the water alongside. But the man right behind me saw my error and corrected for it. His heavy bomb plunged through the cruiser's after deck and the tremendous blast smashed the stern portion to a tangle of débris. This fellow sank within a few minutes."

The planes turned Salamaua into a shambles, and up the coast, a seven-minute flight in a dive bomber, the squadrons from the second carrier were performing equally effectively at Lae.

"Those fighter pilots were superb," Commander Hamilton said. "When they found there were no Jap planes in the air they made dummy runs with the torpedo planes and dive bombers to spread the anti-aircraft fire. Then they amused themselves by trying to drop fragmentation bombs among the crews of the anti-aircraft guns aboard the ships and ashore."

In telling of his reactions during the battle of Salamaua Commander Thach said:

"Imagine my astonishment to see the Japs running in all directions to escape our bombs and bullets. The romantic writers who spent years misinforming us by telling of Japanese immunity to fear and of the universal Japanese desire to be killed fighting for their emperor, should have seen the interest those Japs showed in remaining alive."

Only one airplane was lost of the total that attacked both harbors. That was at Salamaua where a scout bomber was damaged by the anti-aircraft fire. Its pilot, Ensign Johnson, made a good landing in the water of the harbor with his wheels up during the fight. Presumably he had a good chance of getting ashore safely and now should be a Japanese prisoner of war.

The toll of shipping destroyed when the last airplane was called away included the confirmed sinkings of five transports or cargo vessels, two heavy cruisers and one light cruiser and one destroyer. A minelayer, two destroyers and a gunboat were left burning and probably were lost to the Japanese. A seaplane carrier and a gunboat were severely damaged by bombs. Fighters at Lae shot down a second seaplane fighter, matching the one downed at Salamaua.

The return trip, with all the planes lightened by having dropped their bombs or torpedoes, was made swiftly. The vigil of Commander Bill Ault, chief of all the flying squadrons of the *Lexington,* who had kept watch from above the mountains, was soon over, and he then trailed the formations back to the carrier to watch for any pilot who might have engine trouble.

The *Lexington*'s crew, and that of the other carrier as well, had made a great ceremony of the airplanes' departures. Because this was the first war raid by the pilots, virtually every one aboard the carriers who could be spared from pressing duties cheered them off and anxiously awaited their return.

"We could hardly believe our good fortune," the executive officer of the *Lexington* said as we discussed this raid long afterward, "when we began counting the incoming planes. Group after group swept past us with all its planes exactly in formation. You can't know how much that means until you have had your own friends go off on perilous duties and see them come home to the ship safely."

After dinner that night back on the *Lex,* the pilots and flying officers gathered for a grand critique in which one of the main conclusions was: The enemy's anti-aircraft fire even at short range is no great hindrance and is not likely to take a heavy toll. The second point made here was general satisfaction that the conclusions they had arrived at in practice maneuvers during peace years had proved correct in actual battle.

As the fleet had moved up northward on its voyage to the Gulf of Papua a week earlier, one of the little two-seater Seagull float planes from one of the cruisers had failed to return. Because the fleet was on a battle mission with no time to hunt for the missing airplane no effort had been made to recover it.

But now as they moved back along the same general track, Admiral Brown began asking about this missing plane and its crew. The decision was that the pilot had missed his rendezvous and probably had alighted on the sea when his fuel was depleted. The Admiral then demanded of the navigating officer and Lieut. George L. Raring, the *Lexington*'s meteorological officer, to get together. Taking into consideration the plane's probable alight point and the winds during the ensuing week, the Admiral asked that the probable drift be calculated. When this was done he changed the course of the fleet to pass through the area where the plane might be, assuming it still was afloat.

At dawn one morning, the seventh after the little Seagull was lost, lookouts noticed the silhouette of a plane sitting on the sea on the horizon. Hardly was the report made when the plane was seen to start up, climb off the water and fly toward the ships. It circled overhead, gave the correct identifying signal and then asked its cruiser to take it aboard. It was the "lost" plane with both ship and crew intact. It had drifted some 300 miles.

The pilot, recognizing the approaching fleet as his own, didn't wait to be picked up. He had sufficient fuel left for a little flying and proceeded to make a routine "return from reconnaissance" landing. When the little plane was hoisted aboard this cruiser, the pilot and gunner stepped out and reported themselves aboard as if nothing out of the ordinary had occurred. They had suffered some from the heat and from seasickness but rainfall had supplied them with ample water and their emergency rations had sustained them.

As a result of the attacks on Lae and Salamaua and the destruction of the Japanese forces there the following fliers won decorations. Lieut. Noel Gayler, received the Gold Star—equivalent to a second Navy Cross, the first having been won at the Battle of Bougainville.

The Navy Cross was awarded to:

Lieut. Commander James H. Brett
Lieut. Commander Robert E. Dixon
Lieut. Commander Weldon Hamilton
Lieutenant Robert F. Farrington
Lieut. Evan P. Aurand
Lieut. Harry B. Bass
Lieut. (jg) Mark T. Whittier
Lieut. (jg) Robert B. Buchan
Ensign Norman A. Sterrie
Ensign Anthony Quigley
Ensign Richard F. Neely
Ensign Harold R. Mazza
Ensign John A. Leppla
Ensign Marvin M. Haschke

and Distinguished Flying Crosses were awarded to:

Lieut. Edwin W. Hurst
Lieut. French Wampler, Jr.
Lieut. (jg) Richard B. Forward
Ensign Curtiss Hamilton
Ensign Tom B. Bash
Ensign Lawrence F. Steffenhagen
Gunner Harley E. Talkington
Aviation Chief Ordnanceman, Naval Aviation Pilot
    Melvin H. Georgius

7

CASTAWAYS AMONG CANNIBALS

Though the public seldom hears of them, small and large forces of our Navy are constantly patrolling the seas on specific or routing missions. While Admiral Brown's two-carrier force was smashing the Jap ships at Lae and Salamaua some United States cruisers and destroyers were cruising on stations "plugging the sea gap" south of the Solomons.

Though on this occasion these cruisers saw no trace of the Japanese, some of the pilots of their scout planes began a period of adventurous action that has no parallel. They encountered dangers on the sea, and some met a whole series of benign, reformed and educated cannibals. One group of them spent 18 days as the guests of the descendants of an old cannibal king, Mooyo, on the island of Rossel which has a black history behind it.

Two of the airmen alighted in a sheltered pool on the afternoon of March 10. The others alighted on the island on the morning of the thirteenth. The parties spent several days there before either was aware of the other's presence. And even after the natives had brought reports and finally messages from one party to the other, it was several days more before they finally came together.

As a matter of fact that small force of patrolling cruisers lost—for a time at least—more airplanes than did the Admiral's two great carriers in their vicious and destructive assault on the Japs at Lae and Salamaua. Only one scout bomber out of the 108 that took part in the raids on the New Guinea harbors failed to return safely to the *Lexington* and its companion carrier. The cruisers, however, without sighting a single Jap, lost five scouting seaplanes in a period of two days.

All five of these planes were lost when for various reasons the cruisers and aircraft failed to make contact after the planes had left on scouting missions. This was an easy thing to do at sea where much of the flying is done by dead reckoning—by watching a clock and compass—especially since the scouts are out for as much as five hours at a time. Furthermore, they are enjoined to radio silence lest they reveal their own and their cruiser's position to unfriendly ears.

These little scout planes that operate from the cruisers are all equipped with a huge central float and floats at each wingtip. They are small and extremely rugged, designed both for rough-water alighting and for catapult take-offs. Ordinarily they are fired off from the cruiser's catapult with a charge of gunpowder that in a 90-foot run lifts their speed from zero to 90 miles an hour.

The planes on these cruisers are older types of biplanes with open cockpits, the forward one for the pilot, the after cockpit for the gunner-radioman. Their motors are small—450 horsepower air-cooled radials—and while the plane has sufficient fuel for hours of cruising, its operating speed is slow in comparison to a fighting plane's. Ordinarily these little scouts fly at about 130 miles an hour. Sometimes they are armed with a light bomb, but their main job is to allow their crews to observe and report observations back to their ships.

Pilots of these crafts are really the "Eyes of the Navy." They enable their captains and superior officers to look out for several hundred miles in all directions. In recent years these scouts have come to be an absolutely essential arm for all the vessels in the Navy large enough to carry them, some now even being placed on destroyers. In a ship versus ship fight they spot for their vessel's gunners like observation planes do ashore.

Probably the best and most detailed story I got at first hand was that of Ensign William I. McGowan, a tall slender young man, clean cut, and alert. He told his tale with a story-teller's appreciation of its high

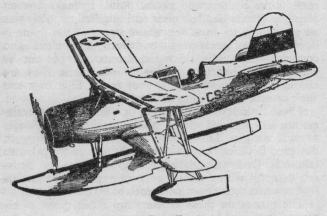

Seagull

points and humor. McGowan and his radioman, Miller, and the crews of four other Seagulls (the little cruiser patrol planes) spent the time on the formerly sinister island of Rossel. His story was related to me as I was bound toward the United States with the rescued crew of the superb old *Lexington,* following her sinking in the Coral Sea fighting on May 8th. McGowan's ship had aided in the rescue.

The young ensign's tale begins on March 10th and he tells it about this way:

"Our cruiser (I may not mention the names of any of the cruisers in this story, because these craft are still active in the Pacific, most of them probably having seen service in the later fleet-and-air success at Midway Island) fired us off during the forenoon of March 10th.

"We flew our patrol as instructed, saw nothing and when the time to pick up our ship had arrived, proceeded to the rendezvous area. To my surprise there was no sight of it. I then began to fly a searching pattern. Still finding no trace and having covered a wide area around the rendezvous point I decided something had delayed the cruiser so I alighted at once rather than run my fuel tanks dry in the air.

"We spent several hours drifting and listening on our radio for some indication from our base ship. We heard nothing and so late in the afternoon decided to take-off and fly to the nearest land. This happened to be Rossel. I put the ship down inside the outer coral reef which practically surrounds the island, and after taking stock of the shore, began taxiing in. Miller assisted by standing on the top wing and pointing out the coral heads to be avoided. We beached on a sand shoal about 60 yards off shore.

"Not knowing exactly what to expect from the natives we waited in the plane for some time with our automatic and free machine gun ready. (All Navy planes carry a sub-machine gun for the crews to use in emergency landings of this sort.) About 10 minutes after we beached a group of about 30 natives appeared on the near-by shore. Some waved their arms in what appeared to be a friendly gesture indicating they were not carrying weapons. We returned the signal and tried to indicate that two of them should come out to the plane. About six came wading toward us.

"The natives were short, of rather compact build. Their skin varied in shades from *café au lait* to a dark chocolate brown. Nearly all wore a rather elaborate five-pronged long comb in their bushy hair. Many wore a polished bone or shell ornament in their pierced ears and noses, as well as a variety of highly colored ornaments attached tightly to greatly stretched ear lobes. All wore a single skirt-like garment consisting of a piece of cloth secured around the waist with a belt or fold reaching to the knees. Some were crudely tattooed, often wearing their name printed in crude inch-high blue letters across their chests.

"The leader of this group, Mungi by name, greeted us with a 'Hello airmen.' We were much surprised at this and pleased to learn he spoke a good grade of pidgin English. We talked to him for about 30 minutes and were told there were no white men on the island, no towns, but that there was a mission some distance away. We decided to go there hoping to find someone who could give us information. Mungi balked at first at the idea of leading us there but after receiving gifts—pencils, paper and a flashlight lens—he agreed to guide us and furnish boys to carry our gear."

At this point I asked McGowan if he knew anything of Rossel's history. He replied that he did not so I went to the ship's library and found there a magazine I had seen earlier that gave much detail about the Island's cannibal days. The writer of the magazine piece had lived on the island for two years and pointed out that Rossel had a particularly unsavory reputation because during the latter end of the last century the natives captured, killed and ate all except one of 327 shipwrecked Chinese. Many other instances of cannibalism were attributed to these Rossel tribes.

The banqueting on the Chinese was carried out by King Mooyo. The wretched victims were aboard the French ship *St. Paul* which was wrecked on the reef bordering the island in 1858. The captain and eight of the crew left in a small boat for New Caledonia to get assistance. But aid did not get back to Rossel until four months later. Then the French warship *The Styx* called. Its officers found only one Chinaman alive to tell what happened and his story was that Mooyo had put all 326 of his countrymen on a barren coral ait just off the main shore.

He provided food and water for their sustenance. But whenever he held a feast for his tribe—which was often—he brought over a number of the Chinese to provide the *pièce de résistance,* until soon only one remained.

The last instance of killing a white man occurred in 1892. The victim, Lucien Fiolini, an escapee from the French penal colony of New Caledonia, reached Rossel in a small craft from the isle of Nou. When the natives were asked why they killed him they gave as reason: "He caused disharmony in the community through his assiduous attentions to the women of the tribe."

The article described the island—easternmost of the Louisiade Archipelago—as volcanic, rugged and mountainous. It is about 20 miles long by 10 wide. Waters around it are treacherous. The native population consists of about 1,200 men, women and children. The writer described the island as infested with crocodiles, snakes, scorpions, mosquitoes and sandflies. The forests contain hundreds of beautiful orchids and other blooms rare to civilization.

"I didn't know a bit of this," McGowan laughed when we finished reading the piece. "I'm glad I didn't at the time. I was suspicious enough of the natives as it was, until they unmistakably showed us they were friendly. If I'd read the piece beforehand I might have felt worse."

The boys moored their plane, dismantled the machine guns and toted the ammunition ashore. Then they took out parachutes, rations, canteens, machine guns, Very pistols and had the natives carry them up to a near-by house. The codes and chart board were burned and destroyed.

McGowan went on to describe the trip to the mission. He and Miller took only their pistols, smoke grenades and canteens and began a walk of six or seven miles that took them four hours. In his own words: "We had to proceed quite slowly—at times having to watch each step to avoid spraining or breaking an ankle as the roots and rocks were so slippery it was hard to obtain solid footing.

"We were welcomed at the mission by Satepan, the native missionary. He explained to us in pidgin that he and three other missionaries on the island had come over from Misima, 100 miles to the north northwest. Then he gave us a very good dinner consisting of delicious ripe bananas, fried pumpkin, boiled chicken, boiled yams and potatoes. We did very well by this repast as we had not eaten since breakfast at 5 A.M. that morning."

After dinner McGowan asked Satepan if he had a map. I still remember the way McGowan's eyes went round as he told of his utter amazement when Satepan produced an Upper Air Chart of the Southern Pacific (U.S. Navy Hydrographic office publication).

"You can't possibly guess where Satepan got that map," McGowan grinned. "He got it by way of a bottle. Yes—really! He found a bottle on the beach one day with a note in English in it. It had been dropped into the ocean thousands of miles from there by some American hydrographer. Satepan sent this man a letter telling him where he found the bottle and the hydrographer sent him back the map as thanks. Of course it was a godsend to us for we couldn't have gotten a better map for our purposes."

McGowan and Miller returned to their planes next day and spent the daylight hours trying to raise any United Nations forces on their transmitter. There were no results. All they got was news, broadcast from Sydney. Meanwhile they stripped down the plane taking out all possible gear, compass, clocks, etc. At that time they had in mind the possibility of making a sea trip to New Guinea in a native boat—but fortunately never tried it.

The second afternoon, McGowan continued, was spent bathing in a creek near Satepan's mission with the same supposed cannibals with whom he had been ready to do battle when he arrived at Rossel. Discussions with them over the possibilities of getting out of their predicament followed, the young ensign recalled, in about this pattern:

"I would ask a question in English, addressing Mungi. It would be a simple question such as: 'Could we kill a chicken for dinner tonight.' Mungi would turn to the others, deliver a brief exhortation and then pause dramatically. Instantly there would be a tremendous uproar from the 25 or 30 native men gathered around. Some would frown and shout, others would wave their hands wildly while talking at the tops of their voices. This would continue for a couple of minutes.

"Suddenly there would be a silence. Mungi would turn back and in English reply: 'Yes.'

"I always wondered what in the world they all found to say on such unimportant matters as we brought up."

On March 13th, while on the way to look at a native canoe—they were considering the chance of making a voyage to Misima where two Americans were reported to be operating a gold mine—they were met by a native boy who said that four very large airplanes had landed on the other side of the island.

"We thought this was just a tall tale told in the hope of getting presents," McGowan goes on. "Later, however, another boy came with exactly the same story. This time the planes were described as exactly like our own. I became practically sure the planes were from some United States cruisers—especially when the native described their wing insignia—so I wrote a note to the crews."

It so happened that the four planes *were* from American cruisers. Their crews consisted of Lieutenant J. M. Brandt, and Ensigns Leland L. Wilder, John H. Graves, and Joseph B. Young. with Radiomen Horne, Lucas, Hulegerd and Owen. They too had missed a rendezvous with their ships on March 12th. The four planes met at the rendezvous and finally alighted when the cruisers did not appear.

They drifted all night on the open choppy sea in an 18-knot wind. Lieut. Brandt described this: "Our rations and life boat were placed in a readily accessible position because it seemed that at any moment the plane would capsize or wrench apart. Almost immediately on landing, Lucas and I became very seasick and were both intensely thirsty from the heat of the sun and engine during flight. We each had two malted milk tablets for supper with a small sip of water."

During the night Brandt's plane drifted close to one of the other three in the group and they were able to discuss their plight back and forth from cockpit to cockpit. They decided it would be permissible to send off a radio message next morning telling where they were going to sit down. They considered waiting on the water one day longer in the hope that the cruisers would hunt for them, but the planes were getting too much of a beating.

"Every few minutes," Brandt said, "a wave would

wash over one wing and the swirling water would twist the wing structure and put a tremendous force on the wing tip floats. About midnight the plane slid backwards down the front of a wave, dug the tail into the back of the next wave and the water folded the port elevator down under the horizontal stabilizer and against the stabilizer strut.

"At daylight next morning (March 13th) I crawled back on the stabilizer and straightened the elevator as best I could by hand.

"As the sun rose we could see one plane a mile behind us and the other two about five miles ahead. At 6:15 I took off and the plane handled surprisingly well in the rough sea and with only one elevator in operation.

"In the air the lieutenant sent his radio message and listened for 10 minutes. There was no answer. The other planes then took off and all four flew to Rossel, 130 miles away. They circled the island and finally alighted in a small bay near a deserted copra plantation after making a survey for enemies, a town or for a probable place of shelter.

"A few natives in red loin cloths, an occasional village consisting of three or four grass shacks, and a small herd of cattle was sighted in a cocoanut grove, before we alighted," Brandt continued.

"The plantation belonged to a Mr. Osborne and his wife, the only whites who had been living on the island. They had left in January, natives told the young airman. The house, a red-roofed comfortable bungalow, stood on a hill 250 feet above the plantation.

"Leaving four men to guard the planes, the other four of us set out to look for fresh water that seemed of paramount importance at that time," Brandt said. "We found it—fresh rainwater—at the house, and by the time we got back to the planes several natives had gathered. From them we heard that three days earlier another plane had landed on the island 'just around the point.'"

The airmen learned later that the natives have no ideas of distance. A journey which they say will require only a few hours of walking might take days.

At any rate Ensign Wilder's plane was partly refueled from all the other tanks and he was sent over to investigate Tagula, 25 miles distant. Wilder was soon back having been frightened off by the appearance of natives in a large war canoe. Coming back from Tagula his ship ran out of fuel just after he alighted at the entrance to the bay. He had to paddle ashore.

During the afternoon Brandt and another pilot started out with guides to find the other flyers about whom the natives talked but were near collapse after an hour's walk through jungle swamps, streams and up and down almost vertical rocky trails. They wrote a note and sent native runners ahead to McGowan and Miller, and then started back to their planes.

Toward dusk the airmen walked to Osborne's house "to survey the food situation," as Brandt said.

"Osborne had evidently foreseen the possibility of aviators being stranded on the island. He had left word with the natives that he might never be back and for them to help any white aviators in trouble. We found that he had 15 or 20 head of cattle, 15 ducks, 7 or 8 chickens and a turkey. We also heard from the natives Osborne's 28-ton boat the *Yela Gili* was hidden in a bay on the other side of the island. When we made this discovery we decided to eat off the land and save all canned rations from the aircraft for a possible boat trip to Cookstown or Townsville.

"At the house we were amazed to find that a native named Tapy who was apparently Osborne's house boy and right-hand man, had laid out mattresses on the bunks and was in the process of spreading sheets on each mattress. He brewed some tea and broiled up a chicken that was as tough as rubber, but the broth was good. The house also contained a small bag of sugar, a bag of tea, two pounds of flour, one quart jar of tapioca, three jars of sago, and a bag of salt."

One of the fliers remarked later he was absolutely astonished to find Osborne's belongings and particularly his food and stock untouched by the natives although he already had been gone for weeks. The native boys refused to touch this food at any time, living entirely off their own produce, fishing, or their own fowl. Evidently the missionaries or Osborne had instilled in them a real sense of respect for a white man's property.

"On the 14th there were hard tropical rains all day. We had asked the other pilots, whom we had decided were McGowan and Miller, to meet us at Osborne's house in the note we had sent on. When they did not appear we concluded they had either not received the message or had also heard of the *Yela Gili* and were traveling toward it. It was decided that two pairs of us would start around the island in opposite directions hoping to find McGowan. Graves relieved Tapy of the cooking and served us up some dumplings with left-overs of the chicken," Brandt added.

The morning of the 15th Wilder and Brandt started out on what was to be a grueling five-day trek. On this day, which was Sunday, they were dumfounded to have their native boy Tapy inform them after a short walk that he would rather not work on the Sabbath Day. He got two other boys to lead them on, however.

By dark they had not arrived at the mission where McGowan was supposed to be so they sent a messenger on with a note to ask the other two airmen to wait for them and above all not to set off in the *Yela Gili* before the eight men from Osborne's could be taken aboard. The messenger was sent off in the dark with a flashlight, and a dollar bill as a present. We learned later that he located McGowan about 1 A.M. the following morning at another mission house further along the north coast.

"Wilder and I stayed in a little grass hut set up on poles six feet off the ground," Brandt went on. "The natives feasted us on cocoanut and a boiled green banana each. Two of them insisted on sleeping across the doorway to protect us. On another occasion on this trip when the mosquitoes were very bad at night we were astonished to awaken about 2 A.M. and find that one of our native boys was staying up all night to keep a fire going and smoke drifting into our hut to keep the mosquitoes away from us."

On March 16th they arrived at Satepan's mission, found definite proof of McGowan's presence in some of the things he had left behind. Satepan also told

Brandt: "McGowan left for the *Yela Gili* two days before and you should reach him in two hours."

Brandt said he and Wilder weren't able to decide whether this remark was a reflection on McGowan's jungle speed or downright flattery of us. (We were traveling with our feet in bandages and going very slowly.)

On the 17th of March they reached the *Yela Gili* to find it a most seaworthy little schooner with two Diesel engines, each on a separate shaft and on deck four 55-gallon drums of Diesel oil. The boat was 65 to 70 feet long. Nogo, its captain, received the boys with faint hospitality. Brandt wrote in his official report of these incidents, and a short talk with him disclosed the following information:

"1. Nogo had a hangover from chewing too much betel nut.

"2. He would go ashore and get some kai-kai (food) and the native engineer.

"3. He was the first native we encountered who seemed unfriendly evidently because he feared we were going to steal his boat, which was almost correct, but we had offered him several inducements.

"4. From a chart of the island we found on the boat we discovered we had traveled three quarters of the way around in the wrong direction. If we had gone the right way we would have found the boat in one day instead of five."

Brandt and Wilder stayed one day on the boat and on March 18th they had decided to seize the boat if necessary and prepare it to make the voyage to Australia.

"Shortly after noon," Brandt relates, "a very odd coincidence occurred. I was sitting daydreaming about being rescued. I was planning in my mind just what I would do if I suddenly saw a rescue plane in the sky. I would rip off my skivvy shirt and tie it to a pole that was at my side. Then I would climb up the mast and at the same time call to Wilder who was in the cabin to bring a mirror that was stowed in a cubbyhole there.

"I was so engrossed in my thoughts that when a patrol bomber did appear at that instant over the mountain it seemed the natural thing to happen and I was hardly taken aback by surprise. I carried out my little plan and Wilder came up with an Australian flag in addition to the mirror.

"Either the mirror attracted the pilot's attention (he was about 7 miles away) or he spotted the boat, for he turned 90 degrees from his course and headed directly for us. He made another turn 200 feet above the boat and then continued on out of sight.

"We were dumfounded as well as brokenhearted for the pilot made no sign of recognition or acknowledgement. We hoped he might have stopped on the other side of the island to pick up the rest of our party and would return for us next day. On the other hand we thought: 'What if he saw the Australian flag and our long beards and thought we were just two old copra traders who did not want to get bombed.' (We learned later that our second thought was correct.)"

Wilder telling of this later said that Nogo, the captain, never reappeared. But he did send them two helpers, one of whom, Tom by name, came out three times daily and boiled up a mess of rice, cocoanut and squash.

"This with a few bananas and oranges was our steady diet for three days and we were very grateful for it despite the fact that we had to snap a worm out of the rice every now and again."

During the next two days they received messages from the boys at Osborne's house saying that a Catalina—skippered by Squadron Leader F. B. Chapman of the R.A.A.F.—had found them and that repair crews were being brought so the planes could be refueled, checked and flown out. A day later by dingy, a mountain trail, a canoe trip down a river and finally an outrigger ocean canoe they reached the Osborne plantation.

During the trials of Brandt and Wilder our friends Lieut. McGowan and Miller had reached the *Yela Gili*, decided it was a good seaworthy boat and then treked right on to Osborne's place, where they joined the six men who had remained there. McGowan described the journey thus:

"We climbed mountain sides that seemed to be very nearly vertical, waded through alligator-infested swamps sometimes shoulder-deep in the water and knee-deep in the mud. After several hours of this our path led out onto the shore along the beach on the southern coast of the island. While we were walking along the beach we spotted a PBY flying an easterly course paralleling our route. Though we signaled with a Very pistol he failed to spot us (we learned later this plane was an R.A.A.F. Catalina searching the reef for evidence of our seaplanes).

"When he went by we felt a little sunk but not too badly as this was the first indication that patrols were covering the island and we hoped that he would see the planes on the beach at Osborne's place. We made the last part of the trip by outrigger canoe paddling about three miles along the coast."

McGowan said he found Osborne's house about what he had expected from the native's description—an iron-roofed substantial frame house on a hillside overlooking a 60-acre cocoanut grove. Half an hour later and after they had exchanged greetings with the six men, he and Miller were served a meal of "rump roast, and potatoes with *salt*, which was just about the most tasty I ever enjoyed." (Graves and his party had killed one of Osborne's cattle the day before.)

"Next morning the men were lounging near Osborne's house when Tapy was sent up a tree to "catch-'em cocoanut." Tapy shouted that he heard an airplane. We could hear nothing but taking no chances of again missing the plane we got our pyrotechnic gear ready for signaling. Tapy kept saying he heard a plane and pointed northward in the direction of the hill behind us. About 15 minutes had passed by when suddenly a PBY came roaring down the coastline at an altitude of about 100 feet. We set off our smoke grenades and fired our Very stars giving him a real fireworks display.

"Almost at once he turned inland and flew directly over us. We then signaled him with our blinker lights and shortly after, he landed in the lagoon directly offshore from us. While he was circling Graves and I ran down to the beach, got one of our seaplanes started and as soon as he landed we taxied out to where the Catalina was anchored."

McGowan, Young, and the four radiomen rode over to Tulagi in the Catalina. There the decision was made to fly in gasoline and repair crews so that the Seagulls could be flown out. McGowan and Young came back on the 21st with a crew of half a dozen Australian mechanics and one officer, having left the four radiomen in Tulagi for minor medical treatment.

During the next week the work of examining all the planes, checking engines and making repairs to Brandt's elevators was carried out. The Aussies came out with tools but virtually no materials. When they needed rivets they took a piece of copper tubing and sliced strips out of it. From these strips they cut rivets that served their purposes very well. They also showed ingenuity in handling two of the engines which were dismantled, and in finding ways and means of rerigging the biplane wings. All in all the Aussies impressed the pilots with their ability to find makeshift means of doing any job required.

"During this time we lived well," Brandt told me later. "Our food consisted of vegetables brought in by the natives in exchange for the meat we gave them from two cows we slaughtered. Each time we killed a cow we cooked up a quarter of it and gave the rest to them.

"We had to eat our meat in two days otherwise it spoiled in the heat. Besides the veal, we prepared and ate six chickens, six ducks, the one and only turkey, and two large fish we caught off the reef."

On the 27th a Short Sunderland (a big four-engine flying boat) came in from Port Moresby with part of the gasoline required and a lot of food for the men. The rest of the gasoline was scheduled to come in by flying boat from Australia. That same day the four radiomen who had gone to Tulagi for medical attention came back in a Catalina, and were all sent to Port Moresby in the Sunderland. In their place the pilots kept four Australian mechanics plus Miller who stayed with McGowan.

The officers on the Sunderland also brought the pilots directions to fly their airplanes out to Port Moresby, Townsville, Brisbane and finally to Sydney. The airmen were overjoyed at the prospect of getting to a big city and in fact were jubilant over the chance. Only a little more fuel was needed to allow them to start the 440-mile trip to Port Moresby.

While they were sitting down to breakfast the morning of the 28th two cruiser seaplanes from their own striking force arrived at the cove. At this point they were really unwelcome visitors for they carried an invitation to the beachcombing airmen to come back to work. And so our castaways bade farewell to the Australians who returned to their base. Our own pilots shortly afterward flew the five planes back to their own ships, arriving aboard in time for lunch.

What the pilots really thought about this sudden change of plans was expressed in the plaintive note attached to the end of Lieut. Brandt's written report. He closed: "We had to return without our radiomen but they had a wonderful month's vacation in Australia."

lost farthest probably first of their largest and eldest
ap. In the earlier attack, this force was probably
started directly south from Truk toward the north-

8

TULAGI: A FLEET
IS DESTROYED

Toward the end of April the Navy began to receive reports from long-range planes based in Australasia and from our submarines that indicated the Japanese were preparing for a move of some sort in northern Australian waters. In spite of our destruction of Japanese shipping at Lae and Salamaua and the constant pounding of Rabaul and other New Guinea harbors by Army bombers from northern Australia during the preceding seven weeks, the enemy was building up troops, equipment, transports and navy forces in these areas.

It was clear to anyone who had access to our reconnaissance reports that they were getting ready to make another southward thrust. Although we did not understand their full plan of action at the time later events showed they had apparently worked out an involved program that included movements of four powerful sea fleets—two of them striking units with aircraft carriers as their chief weapons, and two occupation forces.

Although this is ignoring the proper chronology of the action I want to tell at this stage what a reconstruction of the events showed the Jap plans to be. This reconstruction was not made until after the final Coral Sea battles in which we decisively smashed three of the fleets mentioned above, in fighting that spread over five days and more than 100,000 square miles of sea.

We believe now that the Japanese striking forces came out of Truk—which is equivalent in importance and permanence to our own Pearl Harbor. Both these forces were led by aircraft carriers—there being at least four and probably five of their largest and newest types. The smaller striking force was a prong that started directly south from Truk toward the southeastern tip of New Guinea. It most likely was intended to seize and hold the Jomard Straits, the only deep-water passage into the Coral Sea between that tip of New Guinea and the Louisiades. Two carriers, five cruisers and a dozen destroyers formed this arm.

The importance of holding the Jomard Straits can be seen in a glance at the maps inside the cover. Whoever does not hold this passage must route its transports, supply lines, and reinforcing elements at least 700 miles around the coral-girt Louisiades.

But in order to do the job in a thorough manner the Japs did not depend on this first prong alone. They sent a second and larger force consisting of three carriers, three battleships, a number of cruisers and more than a dozen destroyers, in a long looping southeastward sweep that passed into the Coral Sea between the Solomon Group and New Hebrides, and then curled back in a northwest direction toward the Jomard passage from the south.

These two powerful spearheads were expected to protect, proceed and prepare the way for the invasion forces. These were gathered in two concentrations. The first was at DeBoyne Island just north of the Jomard passage. The second was in the harbor of Tulagi, on the island of Florida in the British Solomons. Each of the occupation outfits consisted of a number of cruisers and destroyers, seaplane tenders, transports, troopships, supply vessels, and fleet auxiliaries.

Command on the *Lexington* at this time had shifted from Vice-Admiral Wilson Brown, Jr., to Rear Admiral Aubrey Fitch. And the *Lexington*'s force—one carrier, several cruisers and destroyers—had rejoined a similar one-carrier unit that was commanded by Vice-Admiral Frank J. Fletcher. Being the senior officer made Admiral Fletcher Commander in Chief of the whole Carrier Striking Force.

The junction of these forces came about April 30th. On that day two of the *Lexington*'s scout planes surprised a Japanese submarine on the surface. They dived on it and dropped three bombs. Although the pilots believed the sub was sunk they could report only that a huge patch of fuel oil spread over the ocean after it crash-dived.

This was the *Lexington*'s first brush with the enemy in several weeks. During this period the ship had been refueled, new stores of all kinds been put aboard, the crew had been given a few days ashore, new pilots and new airplanes had been added to the ship's main "batteries"—its air squadrons—and a large number of brand-new recruits had been poured into its various departments. These recruits, freshly enlisted and just out of the naval-training centers, comprised about 20 percent of the total complement as I said in earlier chapters.

We were a confident crowd, ready and anxious for more action. We had already felt out the Japanese and found them far from the supermen their victorious East Indies campaigns had suggested them to be. And now our constant aerial patrols began to bring in information that told all the old hands action was not far off. Their almost daily report told of seeing Japanese snooper planes ranging the area. Usually our scouts would be from 150 to 200 miles out from the *Lex* flotilla when they sighted these snoopers. Their presence indicated the enemy was interested in the waters into which we were steaming.

Besides increasing the vigilance of everyone aboard these reports acted as a wonderful tonic for the morale of the crew. Weeks of inaction had tended to take the fun out of their constant practice and study, and the unchanging daily routine had become monotonous. Even the pilots who had to work hard all the time were spoiling for a fight. Word of the Japs' presence raised their spirits just as the sight of his quarry's spoor quickens the big-game hunter's pulse.

I began to spend a lot of my time in the *Lexington*'s radio room where I was learning the routines of the airmen aloft when they communicate with each other or with the Fighter Director—the central radio control for all the *Lexington*'s airplanes. The various airplane circuits were connected to amplified loud speakers in the radio control room and sitting in comfort I could hear the pilots out on their patrols far over the horizon.

Much of this conversation when the airmen were at extreme ranges was too dim and blurred by static to be understandable. But when the planes were closer in we could hear every word the pilots said and when I closed my eyes and followed some one conversation I had the sensation of being in the airplanes with them. In the beginning, it took me some time to be able to interpret what I heard, because almost everything was said in code that consisted largely of Navy fliers' slang.

Each scout, or each pair of fighters when in the air were identified by girls' names. For instance, Lieut. Commander Paul Ramsey and his wingman might use "Agnes." Other names the pilots perhaps fancied were "Lilly," "Katie," "Mabel," and "Joan."

Listening to the radio conversations one would hear remarks like:

"Agnes to Lilly. A plane at 17,000, bearing 130, five miles. Having a look."

"Lilly acknowledged. Will be around."

An enemy formation report would instantly bring a call to battle stations and immediately afterward the carrier would take over radio direction of its own scouts. When identifying aircraft the pilots if possible would name the type of Japanese planes, calling them Mitsubishis, Nakajima, Zeros, Kawanishis to indicate the probable type of mission they might be on.

The reason the pilots were allowed to talk freely to one another in the air or back to the carrier under certain conditions, was that in these conversations only a limited amount of transmitter power was used. Most of the time the range of these inter-plane conversations was barely to the horizon. All the planes carried in addition long-range transmitters that could be used to talk over a distance up to several hundred miles. Most of the conversations I heard in the radio room, however, came in on the low-power circuits and had to be greatly amplified for us to understand them at all.

Our double carrier force was moving northward toward the Solomons on the afternoon of May 3rd, when one of our far-flung scouts located a concentration of enemy shipping in Tulagi harbor. We did not know then that the two-prong striking forces were on their way north where the Japanese invasion fleets were going to concentrate.

That first report came in by radio this way:

"Joan to carrier. Concentration enemy shipping Tulagi Harbor."

The scout used his high-powered long-range transmitter for just this one message. His job was done, even though Japs might catch him and shoot him down.

As it happened they didn't. This pilot made his observation cautiously and successfully used the towering cumulus clouds that fill the skies in these areas day and night for cover. The result was that apparently the Japanese never saw him at all, never suspected his presence and consequently were unwarned that our carriers were in the vicinity.

The pilot came back late that afternoon and made his full report first to his air officer and then directly to Admiral Fletcher. We continued our normal cruising until dark. Then as soon as the brief twilight had faded the fleet turned and commenced a high-speed run directly toward the island of Florida. This indicated to every man in the flotilla that they were heading for trouble and going in to force battle on the enemy.

Dinner was quickly finished that night and as soon as the dishes were cleared by the messroom attendants a general pilot meeting of all air squadrons was held. First the particulars of the Solomon Islands and specifically of Tulagi harbor were dug out. *Sailing Directions for the Pacific Islands,* Volume I, U.S.N. Department, Hydrographic Office, says as follows: .

"The Solomon Islands lie between the New Hebrides and the Bismarck Archipelago, and extend over an area 600 miles long in a northwest and southeast direction and up to 100 miles wide. They consist of a double row of large mountainous islands attaining heights, as in the case of Guadalcanal and Bougainville, of 8,000 and 10,000 feet.

"In addition there are a great number of smaller islands and small coral islets.

"In appearance the islands present many similar

characteristics, consisting of a chain of lofty mountains for the most part covered with dense forests and rank undergrowth, here and there giving place to long grass and ferns. The slopes incline gently to the sea, and the shores are lined with mangroves in places.

"The larger islands are well watered by numerous streams at the mouths of which as well as on the swamps and sandy shores of uninhabited coral islets crocodiles abound.

"Some of these islands are entirely of volcanic formation while others are calcareous, but there are also many cases in which both these formations are combined."

"The same standard seaman's reference book says of Florida Island:

"This is the largest of a group of volcanic islands lying to the westward of Malaita Island. It attains an elevation of about 1,366 feet and is well wooded, with occasional grassy tracts bare of trees. This variety of surface presented by sharp peaks and rounded hills and apparent want of order in their features, affords a pleasing contrast to some of the other islands.

"It consists of two islands of a combined length of about 22 miles, in a west-northwest and opposite direction, separated by a narrow channel Utaha Passage. Olevuga, Buena Vista, and several other small islands lie northwestward of Florida Island. The eastern portion of Florida Island lies some 13 miles northward of Guadalcanal Island, there being numerous shoal patches and reefs between them. Three deep channels run through this foul ground, namely Ngela, Sealark, and Lengo channels.

"Westward of Tulagi harbor there are no off-lying dangers. The 100-fathom curve runs parallel with the coast about three miles offshore, the general depth across to the Guadalcanal coast being from 200 to 400 fathoms.

"Tulagi harbor, the principal port and seat of government of the British Solomon Islands Protectorate, is situated about midway along the southern coast of Florida Island. The island is well populated and the inhabitants (the natives) are quiet but lazy. The villages are large and built chiefly on the slopes of the hills."

Tulagi is only a tiny settlement and the only representatives of Great Britain there are a resident administrator and a dozen native police. It was undefended, and its only asset was a wharf where a small island steamer from Sydney called every six weeks, to pick up copra gathered from surrounding plantations and to drop supplies for the 300 to 400 whites who lived in the Solomon group.

(The Japanese had moved in there without opposition only a few days before.)

The pilots were given all this information plus photographic copies of maps showing the harbor and the surrounding islands. Their attention was called to Guadalcanal Island because the plan for attack would send them right up over the island in their flight to Tulagi. Information available indicated that Guadalcanal is 70 miles long, extending almost due east and west by 50 miles wide. The terrain is densely wooded and mountainous, with peaks ranging up to 6,000 feet. On its northern shores there are 12 to 14 large cocoanut plantations, mostly owned by overseas companies with only a white overseer in residence.

Admiral Fletcher proposed to move the carriers in close to Guadalcanal during the night. One stood in near shore whence its planes could be launched against Tulagi harbor. The other carrier remained at sea where its air squadrons were available as reinforcements if needed, and principally as a guard against the Japs launching a surprise rear attack from carriers possibly in this area. The airmen were told that they would "come down" out of the mountains onto the Japs so that they could remain hidden by the peaks until within 12 miles of the harbor.

Our scout pilot had been able to count 15 vessels in the harbor. He was certain they included three cruisers and some destroyers. The rest were a miscellany, he reported.

After a general conference each squadron had its own meeting. Timing, direction and flying speed as well as fuel and bomb loads were given out. Everyone was told that the carrier would be in position to launch by dawn and it was suggested that everyone hit the hay early. And the young pilots, knowing that they must be at their best in the morning, turned in quietly and went to sleep. I gleaned the story of what happened during the attack from fliers who participated in the combat. The events of the next few hours are better told in their own words.

Everyone on the ship was awakened and summoned to his battle station by the general quarters gong and trumpet call, long before dawn the morning of May 4th. We had always stood dawn and dusk "battle stations" but now we were going to launch a blow ourselves and instead of a mere precaution this time it had a vital meaning.

No land was in sight. The ships were still speeding over a starlit sea. Nevertheless the airplane crews were warming up engines, and pilots were pulling on their gear in the ready-room or getting their breakfasts in the wardroom.

"We are coming in close to Guadalcanal," the pilots were told, "and from the point where you will take off it will be a 120-mile flight due north to Tulagi harbor. Don't forget the heights of those Guadalcanal peaks. It'll still be dark by the time you are coming in close there, so give them plenty of clearance."

The attacking planes were launched at 6:15 A.M., the first group being 18 Douglas SBDs (scout bombers). These were followed in a matter of seconds by the same number of heavy dive bombers—Douglas BDs— each carrying one 1,000-pound bomb. Last off, a few minutes behind the leading scouts were 18 Douglas TBDs (torpedo bombers) three place craft each carrying a 21-inch almost 2,000-pound torpedo.

The scouts spread out in pairs and beat a swift patrol for 50 miles over the sea in all directions around Florida, Guadalcanal and Malaita Islands, without going near Tulagi harbor. This was done as a precaution against the possible arrival in the area during the hours of darkness of an enemy carrier. The night that had hidden our own approach might also have blanketed an oncoming enemy fleet.

Douglas TBD

None was found, however, and the scouts returned to join up with the dive bombers at 15,000 feet as they approached Tulagi. These scouts were each carrying one 500-pound bomb and when their scouting duties were completed they became light dive bombers inasmuch as their planes were identical in every way with the heavy dive-bombing craft.

The torpedo planes flying at 160 knots climbed barely high enough to get over Guadalcanal's 6,000-foot peaks. The sun's first rays flashed off their wings as they passed over the jungle gorges and the rocky heights. Then they pushed their noses down in a screaming dive to get back to water level and into the proper position for launching their "tin fish." Their approach had been so timed that as they flashed out across the 12-mile wide channel separating Tulagi harbor from Guadalcanal, the dive bombers were just arriving in position overhead.

"You take 'em low and we'll take 'em high," Lieut. Commander William O. Burch, leader of the dive bombers, said over his command radio to the torpedo planes as the attack commenced.

This attack had come so unexpectedly that there were no Jap crews at the anti-aircraft guns. Literally the first warning was the low drone of motors coming across the water mingling with the high-pitched throaty roar of the first dive bomber coming out of the heavens.

"We found that harbor a busy place," one of the dive-bomber pilots reported when he returned to the carrier an hour and a half after his take-off. "Everything was in there from cruisers to rafts. Lighters were carrying troops and equipment from the troopships to the shore. One of those troopships was at least a 20,000 tonner, and the others in the six to eight thousand ton class."

Before the dives began from the three-mile height specific targets were assigned to individual pilots by their squadron leaders—the largest transport, the three cruisers—one being a heavy cruiser type—the three destroyers alongside a seaplane tender, and another destroyer anchored alone were marked for first assaults.

"Down we came," another pilot put in. "Not a gun was fired and we had sitting targets. The only annoyance was the fogging of my sights as I went through a warm layer of atmosphere on the way in. We couldn't miss. We held the dives to 1,000 feet, dropped our stuff and were away before the first guns opened on us."

Sitting back on the carrier with the ship's officers and the fighter pilots who didn't go out with the first waves, one heard over the intercom the calm voices of the squadron leaders selecting targets and announcing that they were on their ways. Static and motor noise from the fighting planes' radios was so great that one couldn't tell when they ended their dives. The first pilots back to the ship, however, told what they had seen.

"That whole harbor was being churned up when I looked last," one of them said. "There were huge columns of smoke, water and debris and the sound of heavy explosions could be heard above our engines.

"Just as I was leaving, the torpedo planes were coming in low and fanned out. I could see the white trails of their torpedo wakes all over the harbor. I saw two torpedoes explode against a ship and the resulting blast and water splashes completely hid it. Two others that missed ships went off on the beach. There was complete hell in that harbor and the Japs were running to cover."

"At least two heavy bombs fell smack on the deck of the heavy cruiser," the last of the dive-bomber pilots related. Huge flames licked 200 feet into the air and the ship staggered under the impact. It began to settle at once. Explosions amongst the smaller craft tossed lighters into the air, spilled men into the water, and shattered to splinters the light wooden auxiliary vessels.

"Torpedoes struck the grouped seaplane tender and the three destroyers. When the smoke cleared away one destroyer already was under water, a second was turning over and the tender was seen to be in trouble."

An alert scout-plane pilot, having dropped his "little" 500-pound bomb, saw a Jap seaplane fighter take off from one end of the harbor. Diving on the seaplane he opened fire and loosed a hundred rounds of ammunition. The Jap plane went into a slipping dive and crashed. Then the same pilot noted five other seaplanes moored close ashore and shot them up too in a series of diving runs up and down their line.

The pilots re-formed into squadrons as the last of their bombs, torpedoes and ammunition was exhausted, and when noses were counted they found that not one was missing.

The carrier had continued to steam in closer to Guadalcanal while the planes were fighting, so the return journey for the fliers was only a little more than 80 miles, or about half an hour's flight. The formations were as tight and as full when they came in sight as when they left. The pilots broke into the landing circle, came out of the formation one at a time and alighted, hot, thirsty and happy.

But the first men back demanded the utmost speed in refueling, rearming and rebombing their planes. They said that while much damage had been done, some of the Japanese warships had steamed up, had slipped their anchors and fled to sea. They wanted to return and get "the entire bag," as one squadron leader put it.

The group was ready to go back into the air by 11 A.M. when 54 planes took off. As they crossed Guadalcanal they fanned out over the waters surrounding Florida to hunt down the fleeing Jap vessels while others went to finish the work in the harbor.

"Mazie to carrier" came a call from a dive-bomber squadron leader 20 minutes after the second take-off. "You should see this harbor. Ships damaged in the first raid have now sunk or run ashore and are burning. The seaplane tender and destroyers have disappeared—sunk. One cruiser and a transport are just leaving the harbor. We'll take them."

The planes caught the two in the harbor mouth. Direct hits seen by more than a dozen pilots and heavy bombs that exploded in the water close beside it, sank the transport in a matter of seconds. The cruiser was hit astern, came to a stop and appeared to settle.

Anti-aircraft fire from shore installations, and from a destroyer and a cruiser that had gotten away to sea and were steaming parallel to one another with an interval of about three miles between them, was heavy. Down the squadrons went in a combined torpedo and dive bombing attack. Both vessels went into what the pilots call their "snakedance"—zigzagging and twisting.

Six TBDs dropped their fish but the cruiser avoided these by making a quick turn after the missiles had been dropped. All six churned on parallel to the Jap ship without hitting it. But the dive bombers went screaming down on the same vessel as it held its straight course to avoid the torpedoes just then passing up its sides, and paralleling its course. Seven heavy bombs dropped on and beside it, where they had the effect of mines on the hull. It lost way and began to heel over.

Part of the reason for the failure of the torpedo-plane attack was the bold interference of a Jap seaplane fighter. Its pilot dived in amongst the torpedo planes, turning and firing in all directions to divert them. Several scouts pounced on the Jap plane but found it so maneuverable and so well flown that, although they were three to one, the unequal fight went on for minutes before a burst of fire finally downed it.

This Jap plane crash-landed near an island. The pilot tried to climb out of his cockpit but slumped dead or unconscious. The rear gunner jumped overboard and was last seen making a strong wake as he sped ashore in what was unquestionably world swimming record time.

Returning for the second time to the carrier the pilots considered their job not yet completed. They complained of the seaplane fighter interference, and reported some Jap ships still in the harbor as not yet sunk. Lunch was served to them while the planes were serviced for the third time that day, and again at 3:30 P.M. 18 dive bombers escorted for the first time by two teams of two fighters each, were launched to finish the work. This time no torpedo planes were sent off.

Six of the bombers caught a damaged cruiser just outside the harbor mouth and sank her. The other 12 dive-bombed three obviously damaged ships, but not all the pilots found it necessary to use their missiles here. They searched the shores, went down to fly around the harbor at 50 feet above the water, seeking a target for their bombs. But now there were more bombs than targets.

The fighter pilots found three Japanese float biplane fighters in the air. Quickly shooting them down they too looked around for a target on which to use up their ammunition. They cruised out to sea where they found a lone destroyer, sole surviving vessel of the entire concentration, making off under forced draft.

The leading pair dived on the destroyer's anti-aircraft gun crews. Heavy bullets from the planes' .50-caliber machine guns cut down these men as they tried to run for cover. The second pair shot up the bridge. After that second attack not a Jap crewman or officer could be seen. All not killed must have been hiding below decks.

Next the fighters made runs in close to fire at the torpedo tubes, intending thus to put the fighting power of the destroyer out of action. Satisfied that this too was accomplished the pilots began diving close to fire into the hull. They saw their hard-hitting armor-piercing bullets apparently cut the thin hull and deck plates like butter. Then they systematically began to shoot into the vessel's boilers and machinery, in the hope of completely disabling her.

There were immediate results. The plunging destroyer began to slow down. Steam and smoke poured out of her hatches. Oil seeped out of the hundreds of tears in the hull where the slugs had ripped ragged holes.

The planes returned to their carrier but from this last raid not everyone got back. Two fighters, for instance, noticing one of our torpedo planes which had been sent out on an earlier raid, began to follow it. As their fuel tanks emptied they realized the torpedo plane was going in the wrong direction and that all three were lost.

Eventually, just before dusk, the two fighters flown by Ensigns Elbert S. McCusky and a companion whose name I never was able to learn, arrived back at Guadalcanal and announced by radio that they were making forced landings on the southern shore. They settled their planes into a broad boulder-strewn section of the beach which was washed by the surf. To cushion the shock they put their landing wheels only halfway down, tightened their belts, and made the slowest possible stall landings into the shallow water.

"We were able to walk away," McCusky related weeks later when telling of the experience. "As a matter of fact neither of us was hurt. We got out of the planes and waded ashore, to find ourselves surrounded by natives wearing only g-strings and armed with stone axes and knives made of human thighbones. It looked like a tough spot.

"But those boys were friendly. It was getting dark and we wanted a fire to signal a destroyer that might be sent for us. We couldn't talk to the natives but with signs we made them understand what we wanted.

"The native warriors used the oldest known method for creating a blaze," the pilots went on. With grunts and groans attesting their efforts they whirled a thin pointed stick whose tip was inserted in a hole in another stick. By revolving it at high speed between the palms of their hands, this friction created a spark. The spark was caught in half a cocoanut where a nest of shredded dried bark had been prepared. A few puffs and a blaze appeared, soon to be nursed into a roaring beach fire.

"We opened one of our parachutes and, using the cloth to screen the blaze from the sea, we sent Morse code signals," the ensign continued. "Soon one of our destroyers was edging cautiously into the bay and launched a power boat.

"Trying to destroy our planes was a tough job. We machine-gunned them hoping to ignite the fuel tanks, but they were dry. Finally we stripped the radio and other gear and smashed the instruments with rocks. We took the breach mechanisms out of our machine guns and carried them off and finally with all of our remaining ammunition for the sub-machine gun, shot up the planes.

"We were satisfied that the Japanese could find nothing of value in them and we freely 'gave' the wrecks to the natives who were overjoyed. The metal in the planes would be saved, every scrap of it, and used for knives, hooks, spearheads and other purposes. It was a treasure trove for them and we knew the tides would soon wreck anything they left."

The airmen had several narrow escapes getting through the heavy surf to the destroyer's longboat, but finally made it. McCusky went back ashore on a rope after having made it out to the boat once. His purpose was to damage the planes still further. But in the darkness the rope caught on the rocks and he was almost drowned before freeing himself from it and swimming ashore. Another man then took a second rope in and both came off together.

The torpedo-plane pilot was Lieut. Leonard E.

Ewoldt. He also made a forced landing in the sea near Guadalcanal when his fuel was exhausted. He had lost contact with the fighter planes and notified the carrier by radio that he was coming down some miles away. The destroyer which picked up McCusky and his companion that night failed to locate Ewoldt and his crewmen.

Though the fliers had seen several Japanese ships sink during the day they did not realize until later just how successful the day's attack had been at Tulagi. From shore watchers, whose reports came in later it was learned that the following ships had been sunk:

Three cruisers, 3 destroyers, 3 transports (one of approximately 20,000 tons and two of about 10,000 tons, 1 seaplane tender, 4 gunboats, and 8 aircraft destroyed. One destroyer (the one shot up by our fighters) was given as "severely damaged."

The observer also added: "Few of the Japanese who were on the ships survived. Most of those who were not killed by the explosion of our heavy bombs aboard, were drowned or otherwise failed to reach shore."

By sinking 14 out of the 15 enemy ships found in Tulagi, our fliers again demonstrated that combined dive-bombing and torpedo-plane attack is the most certain, destructive and deadly method yet devised for attacking ships.

Our own losses were merely three planes (two fighters and one torpedo plane). The two fighter pilots were back flying with their squadron next day.

9

THE EVE OF
THE CORAL SEA BATTLE

The official Navy communiqués on the Battle of the Coral Sea speak of our forces there losing a destroyer and a tanker in the conflict. This is true only by the strictest possible interpretation of the facts. Here is the story and you can draw your own conclusions.

Our twin-carrier striking force did not loiter after the action of May 4th. That night we turned southwest and steamed away from Tulagi just as hard as we had come up toward it the night before. This withdrawal was based on the sound military premise that secrecy and elusiveness is a prime requisite for all naval forces but especially so for a barrier force which has great speed (i.e., great mobility) and a long arm with tremendous hitting power (its planes).

"If they can't find you they can't hit you," was Captain Sherman's maxim. "The carrier is a weapon that can dash in, hit hard and disappear."

While maneuvering about the Coral Sea, we met the tanker U.S.S. *Neosho*, one of the big new fuel carriers built for the Navy. She had been launched in April, 1939, after being authorized with similar craft by a Congressional Act of May, 1938. The *Neosho* was commissioned on August 7, 1939.

This vessel, 553 feet long with a displacement of 25,000 tons, was commanded by Capt. John S. Phillips, U.S.N., and manned by a naval crew. Service aboard tankers is generally a non-fighting job but it is one of the most dangerous branches of the Navy's fleets in wartime. Long-range naval operations depend on such tankers for meeting the Fleet at sea to supply fuel so allowing the fighting vessels to remain in action zones for long periods.

The enemy knows this well and tankers are always No. 1 targets. Furthermore, tankers supplying fuel to fighting fleets often must steam across vast expanses of sea with no escort at all or with entirely inadequate protection. Worst of all they must penetrate, as did the *Neosho*, deep into waters that are really an ocean "no-man's land," where at any time an enemy might appear over the horizon.

In the case of the *Neosho* an escort was provided, the destroyer *Sims*, 1,570 tons, commissioned in August, 1939. This trim little featherweight was named after the late Admiral William Sowden Sims, U.S.N., who commanded American naval forces operating in European waters from April, 1917 to the end of World War I. The *Sims'* skipper was Lieut. Commander Wilford Milton Hyman.

My meeting with the *Neosho* occurred in the early morning of May 5. I rolled out of my bunk at dawn, the "clang, clang, clang, clang," of that hinged steel flap on the flight deck just over my head awakening me as the first squadrons of scouts raced down the deck for their take-offs. By the time I got 'topside it was full daylight. The *Neosho* was alongside the *Lexington* already passing aboard mail and oil. The speed of the entire flotilla had eased down from the normal 20-knot clip because we were waiting for Carrier II's fleet to rejoin us.

There was a second tanker waiting around to oil Admiral Fletcher's flagship, Carrier II, when it arrived. It was usual for new ships to arrive or leave the force and this morning I noticed that in addition to the two oilers, two Australian cruisers had slipped in and joined us.

The *Neosho*'s arrival meant another chance to get some mail back home and like everyone else on the *Lexington* I seized the opportunity, and beat out a series of dispatches covering the latest action. My stories went off with the confidential mail to the Naval censors at

Pearl Harbor. Naturally I made use of every occasion to get dispatches back to my paper whenever I could. Although mine was a correspondent's paradise, there was a thorn in my garden. I had to send my stories to the Navy without ever knowing what the censors did to them—whether they were killed, *in toto,* or whether they were going through untouched. In fact I was never sure they were getting to Pearl Harbor, or to the mainland at all.

Being accustomed to work at the end of a cable where my office can send messages, queries or condemnations in a matter of a few hours, it was trying to go suddenly to sea and find oneself cut off completely. I couldn't even cable, "Dear Editor, am I still with you?" Nevertheless the dispatches had to go regardless of how long it might take for them to reach their destination. The good feature of the whole thing was that there was no other correspondent with any of the ships in the fleet therefore I couldn't be scooped.

I paid no particular attention to the *Neosho.* First I was busy writing most of that morning; next, even while the *Neosho* was linked to us by oil pipes she was too far away to carry on any conversation with her officers or crew except through a megaphone. Of course there was a telephone connection from our bridge to theirs but that was for Navy business. We idly watched her crew moving about on deck, examining the hose connections frequently to see that they hadn't loosened, or working on the anti-aircraft guns she carried. Some were swabbing down the decks or painting, a never-ending chore on all Navy ships at sea. Many of them had stripped off their shirts and were sunbaking as they worked.

When the *Neosho* finally pushed off to oil other ships in the fleet, none of us realized what these men were going to be subjected to in the near future.

The *Sims* had been with our striking force for some days and late that afternoon when the *Neosho*'s capacious hull tanks had been drained the two turned out of the fleet formation and started southeast. From there on they were on their own, and were no longer connected with our carrier forces. Neither of them expected to have any further part in the Coral Sea actions. They were homeward bound and probably the crews were anticipating short shore leaves on their arrival.

The next we heard from them was on the morning of May 7th. It was a radio message from the *Neosho* saying that they had been attacked by Japanese aircraft. The *Sims* had been sunk and the *Neosho* had been hit several times but Lieut. Commander Hyman reported she would float indefinitely although she could not steam. The attack had occurred at a point several hundred miles from us for, following our parting, the *Neosho* was going east while we were headed west. The disaster overtook them some 36 hours after they had left us.

More messages continued to come in. We learned that the Jap planes were from an aircraft carrier—probably from one of the three carriers in the Jap's second striking prong that had come down from Truk and into the Coral Sea behind us. It is very likely that this carrier was one of those we sank in the great battle on May 8th when our two carriers met and defeated this powerful fleet.

It seemed that the *Sims* had been quickly sunk by a bomb that landed squarely on her fantail (after deck). The *Neosho*, however, although hit several times by bombs and torpedoes, stayed afloat because her tanks were empty and the buoyancy of those which were not holed acted as watertight compartments. The derelict nevertheless managed to pick up some of the *Sims'* survivors. Others floated away on rafts which they could neither propel nor control.

The sinking occurred at a point so far away from our position that the Navy dispatched a warship from a different and nearer area to their rescue. When it arrived it took off all the men found on the still floating hunk and then sank what was left of the *Neosho*. A search in this general area was made for the *Sims'* rafts. But I never have been able to learn how many were picked up.

Technically, I suppose, these two were lost in the

battle of the Coral Sea—but actually these sinkings were very remote from us. Also they were not taken from under the eyes of our aircraft or our protection.

The morning of the 5th, to return to our own story of that date, was bright and clear except for occasional patches of cloud and haze several thousand feet above us. These thickened into a solid overcast by afternoon and made the tasks of our scouts more difficult than ordinarily in these latitudes. Carrier II was approaching her rendezvous with us and our own scouts were flying a wide umbrella around both ships.

Suddenly over the *Lexington*'s radio we heard the voice of Lieut. Commander Jimmy Flatley, skipper of the fighter squadron of Carrier II. He was calling his own carrier from the air to report "a gangster." A few seconds later we heard his voice again identifying the plane as a Kawanishi, the four-motor Jap flying boat that is apparently their favorite craft for long-range scouting. We could see neither Flatley nor the Jap, both being above the cloud level.

At this point the *Lexington*'s fighter director Lieut. "Red" Gill broke in to ask Flatley: "Where is the Kawanishi?"

Gill was asking the question so he could direct his own fighters toward the Jap.

"Wait a minute, and I'll show him to you," Flatley replied.

I was in the fighter control room and ran up the steel ladder to the signal bridge to see what would happen. Everyone else on the deck and bridge was peering and trying to see the scrap which we knew was taking place somewhere above. For about a minute there was nothing to see except the featureless cloud base.

Then suddenly there was a glow in the clouds like a ball of fire. It increased and then there popped out of the vapor a huge plane, spinning madly and burning like a torch. The fire seemed to grow in intensity even as we watched it fall. It hit the water almost in the middle of the fleet and instantly exploded. There was a big flash of flame and then nothing but a huge pillar of black smoke. Jimmy had called his shot and delivered for the whole fleet to see.

So quickly had all this happened that none of us realized we had just seen a dozen Japs die a horrible death. A strange thing about airplanes—when they crash, somehow you have the feeling that it is the plane that is dying, not the men within it. In this case not one of the crew made any attempt to bail out. And strangely enough never once in all that sea fighting did any of our pilots see a Jap airman take to his parachute.

We speculated many times on the possibility that perhaps Japanese sea fighters do not carry parachutes. We know their land planes do, because we have seen photographs of Jap army crews lined up ready to go into the air and invariably these men would be wearing their chutes and chute harness.

"Maybe they don't give them parachutes so they can't be saved, become prisoners and give military information," some of our flyers suggested.

"We know they've got the silk to make them if they wanted to," another young ensign speculated. "But maybe they've sent all their silk to the Germans in exchange for engines and planes. Or perhaps they sold it all to us before the war opened."

A few seconds after the Kawanishi hit the water we could hear Flatley's voice again. This time he was ribbing the *Lexington*'s fighter pilots.

"A fine thing when we have to come over here and shoot these fellows down from on top of you. Why don't you keep your own nose clean."

A minute later we heard Lieut. Noel Gayler from our own fighter squadron call Flatley. He said: "That one nearly fell on top of me, Jimmy. I was climbing up through those clouds and when that ball of fire swept past me I couldn't make out for a minute what it was."

"That'll teach you not to fly underneath me. It's a dangerous place to be with Japs around. The air beneath me is always full of falling Japs," Jimmy cracked back.

Later I talked to Gayler aboard ship: "You can't imagine the surprise I got. I was flying through the cloud, climbing and not saying nuthin' to no-one, when this big burning Kawanishi came across in front of me. It disappeared before I recognized what it was but I'll tell you it gave me a start for a minute."

Although Gayler didn't say so it was really a close affair. If that big Japanese boat had clipped Gayler's plane, it would have meant curtains. Flatley knew this as well as Gayler, but as long as it hadn't happened he was prepared to tease him about it.

I had a talk that night with Commander Mort Seligman, the *Lex's* executive who is a long-time flying man himself. Seligman's duties on the *Lex* prevented him from joining her air squadrons, but he took part in the pilot meetings and in the discussions of air strategy that forever were under way in the wardroom.

"We are under a handicap out here. The limited range of our scouts makes it necessary for us to be forever on our toes. If we want to find out what the enemy is doing we've got to move up to within easy range of his land-based aircraft to find out," Seligman said.

"On the other hand, the Japanese, by using these 3,000-mile Kawanishi boats, can see a lot farther than we can. They range out over the ocean and watch every movement within some 1,000 miles of their bases. There's little we do in daylight that they can't know about. It costs them a plane every so often because we shoot them down every time we come across them. But with these clouds out here this isn't always possible because even though we know they are there we can't always find them.

"Once their day patrols have come out and they know their waters are clear for 500 miles around, they can relax. Even if they find us they have time to bring up air defenses before we can get in our poke. That limits our attacks almost to early morning only after an all-night fast approach. And it makes it very difficult for us to gain the advantage of the element of surprise which is a much more important factor in war than most people realize."

Positions were reversed in the Midway battles, we have since seen. Our own long-range flying boats from Midway spotted the enemy's occupation forces while they were still 700 miles out, and were able to attack them and turn them aside before they got anywhere near their objective.

Usually, after dinner, a number of the officers would gather in front of a huge map of the Pacific that was blown up to cover one end of the wardroom lounge. They would discuss ways and means, possibilities and prospects of the war against the Japanese. This was an almost nightly topic. Almost everyone who was not playing checkers, bridge or acey-ducey would come over and put in an oar.

The main question always was: "How can we get at the Japs?" And invariably the ideas flew thick and fast, and the pros and cons were thrashed back and forth. None of us, naturally, had any idea what the High Command had in its program nor the strength of men and weapons available for the job. But there were certain obvious factors which everybody understood. We knew where the Japanese were, and we knew what the problems of digging them out amounted to.

The main Japanese base was the island of Truk in the central Pacific. This is protected against a frontal advance from Hawaii by the long chain of the Gilbert and Marshall Islands, continuing northward to the islands of Wake, Marcus, and on to Tokio. They had also moved southward and were busy converting Rabaul into a southern bastion to protect Truk. Their efforts to move into the Solomons to cover the southward approach, had for the time being been frustrated by our shattering attack on Tulagi but no one on the ship was deluded into thinking that this was more than a temporary setback.

The Japanese occupations of Lae and Salamaua not only were advance bases from which Australia could be attacked but also were outposts to protect Rabaul. The Japanese use of aircraft knit this widely flung island network into a strong chain which they hoped would halt any moves we made.

Any open assault from the south toward Truk would be subject to flank attacks by land-based planes and submarines from the Marshalls or Rabaul.

In these informal, endless discussions, many agreed with my speculation that Rabaul was a key post and the first step in breaking the chain was to take it. Invasion and occupation of Rabaul would provide: 1. an advanced base of operations against Truk and 2. would remove the enemy in the area of New Guinea. It was the consensus of opinion that Lae and Salamaua were only satellites of Rabaul which would automatically fall or the forces there would be withdrawn once Rabaul had fallen.

After taking Rabaul the next move would be to invest Truk. Success here would dry up supplies for the enemy in the Gilbert and Marshall islands thus dropping them into our laps like ripe plums. Instead of being untenable for us, Wake Island would be easily taken and thereafter supported from the same bases that the Japanese now use for its support.

Japan would therefore be forced to fight from behind her inner island defenses—Tokio, Marcus, the Marianas, Guam, Yap, Pelew, Amboina, and Timor.

Our wardroom "strategists," with this attractive picture before them, then invariably would get down to brass tacks on "how to capture" Rabaul.

While we conceded that air raids served the purpose of destroying supplies, ships, defenses, and aircraft on the ground, and generally delayed the Japanese in their strengthening of the base, an all-out offensive would require occupation forces. We would need several transports full of troops trained as the Marines are for amphibious operations. We would also need at least four carriers, supporting vessels and the co-operation of General MacArthur's air forces based in northern Australasia.

We pictured the offensive as opening with three or four sustained, day-long air bombardments of the enemy airfields in these areas by MacArthur's big bombers. During this time the carriers, followed by their occupation transports, would move up into positions off shore. These carriers would be specially equipped with a preponderance of fighter planes so that they could take command of the sky when they slipped in on the fourth or fifth day after the bombardment began.

As soon as the bombardmen had taken a serious enough toll the invasion forces would be shoved ashore with the assistance of some six- and eight-inch gun cruisers and dive bombers as artillery support. The bridgehead would be chosen in a suitable position so that these ground troops could seize as quickly as possible one or more aerodromes. The carriers would still be in the area, to take care of any enemy fleet that was rushed down, and to put ashore strong fighter-plane forces. At the same time the army could fly in with bombers, troop transports, fighters and the full equipment of a modern air-borne army.

Whether this is ever done at Rabaul or not, the wardroom would agree as the picture grew in the minds of the men discussing it, that this is the method that will eventually be used against the Japs when we begin to wrest back from them some of the territory they overran so swiftly in the opening months of the war.

Since the time of these conversations the Japanese have been seeping into the Solomons and the Louisiades and have built further advance bases from which to protect approaches to Rabaul. The problem is today even more difficult than it was back in the first week of May when these discussions were taking place.

May 6th was a dull day as far as action was concerned. The tropic sun was beating down with fierce heat. Our scouts at this time were coming back from their patrols with faces and necks deeply tanned. Their flying goggles or sun glasses protected their eyes, parts of their foreheads and the tops of their cheeks. The result was when they took their goggles off they appeared to be wearing white masks—so great was the contrast between the tanned lower half of their faces and the unpigmented upper skin.

We were heading northward and our scouts were working out at extreme ranges, and those to the north of us were scouring the Louisiade Archipelago. The Louisiades—a collection of islands and reefs—are flung out from the southeastern tip of New Guinea for a distance of 200 miles. With the exception of Pana Tinani, Tagula, Rossel, and Misima, the islands are small. Of those named the three latter are high and mountainous. The main portion of the group is encircled by a barrier reef which is bisected by numerous passages, while

Rossel (where the cruiser pilots spent their 18 days) is surrounded by a separate reef of considerable extent, according to the *Pacific Islands Sailing Directions* for New Guinea.

A large portion of this archipelago has been unsurveyed and navigation in its vicinity is "attended with some risk" according to the hydrographic office reports.

The largest island is Tagula, 60 square miles in area. Only a few whites live in the islands, maintaining themselves chiefly by carrying on desultory trading with the natives for copra. There also are a few prospectors on Tagula who bring in a little gold for their efforts.

Misima is mountainous and densely wooded. It is about 21 miles long, lies in an east-west direction, and is five miles wide at its eastern end—the point of greatest extremity. Important gold reefs which were discovered in 1905 were being worked on a large scale by American interests up to this time.

We dug out the *Sailing Directions* in anticipation of passing along the southern side of these islands, and before the day was over we found a more immediate interest in it. During the afternoon a scout flying near Deboyne Island—one of the group—saw fifteen or sixteen enemy ships, among them warships and transports. They were concentrated in the lagoon there. And another scout who had been even further north had an even more electrifying report.

He said that far north of Misima he had seen an enemy force similar to ours. It was comprised of two aircraft carriers, five cruisers and at least a dozen destroyers, and was moving slowly southward approaching the Louisiades.

Evidently Admiral Fletcher decided to go after this force for with the coming of darkness he swung slightly to the northeastward and steered toward Rossel once again. About the time we changed course he detached the two Australian cruisers and one American cruiser to take up a position at the southern end of the Jomard passage where they could stand guard in case the Japs at Deboyne tried to slip into the Coral Sea during the night.

Our suspicion, that Admiral Fletcher intended to attack in the morning, was justified when all flight personnel were called into conference after dinner. Photographic copies of the charts of these islands were given to every pilot, and detailed instructions were gone over by the squadron commanders with their men, in preparation for attacking these enemy carriers, as soon as our scouts relocated them in the morning.

These talks were brief because the men knew exactly what had to be done and the favored tactics for doing it. As soon as the conferences broke up they sat around in small groups animatedly talking of the coming fight—a brand new subject because it was their first opportunity for an assault on a carrier. Also they knew they were going to meet up with the much talked of Jap Zero, single-seater fighter, the next morning for the first time.

From the tables came remarks like these:

"Don't forget now, no dogfighting with these babies." "I think if we stick to our pair combinations we should be able to handle 'em." "What do you suppose their performance really is like?"

The boys had heard that the Zero was outmaneuvering the P-40s in Burma and at Port Moresby. A lot of ex-Navy pilots were flying with the American Volunteer Group and some of the officers in our force were getting letters from friends with the Flying Tigers.

The scout pilots, who also fight in pairs, were faced with the problem of relocating the enemy fleet in the morning and expected they might run into the Zeros in their slow, less maneuverable planes. The dive bombers and torpedo plane pilots also were interested in the Zeros because they had never been up against these craft in earlier actions. They knew what our plans for defense of the *Lexington* called for and anticipated that the Japanese too would have a fighter plane screen around their fleet.

The refrain heard again and again was: "No matter how well you shot before, baby, it's how straight you are tomorrow that counts."

Lieut. Commander Ramsey (the man with the mustachio) was getting a fair bit of ribbing from the boys. One of them was saying: "I'll lend you my scissors,

P-40

Paul, to clip that mustache. You ought to get five anyway—that'll let you cut one side off." "I'd like to see
you come out from under that spinach," another
said; "I've forgotten what you look like when shaven
clean."

Paul, who was a checker expert and interested at
that moment only in trading his opponent, Lieut.
Moore, one man for four, merely looked up, grinned
broadly and raised his expressive eyebrows mischie-
vously.

By 10 o'clock these fliers had turned into rest in
preparation for an early take-off in the morning.
Though the men fully realized the danger they would
face in another few hours, they slept as peacefully as
they would have at home. I know they slept—I saw
them through the ever-open cabin doors.

There was no nervousness and there was no obvious

tension. They were in for a fight; they knew it, and they were prepared.

All night long the flotilla knifed its way at 25 knots northward. There was moonlight, and brilliant starlight from the Milky Way, now and then obscured by big floating clouds of the sort never seen outside the tropics. I went up to the flight deck and looked out to see the fleet drawn in close together. It was a wonderful sight, one I'll never forget.

Sliding along as we were, all ships holding the same fast clip and never varying for an instant their relative position, gave me a sudden realization of the immense forces exerted to drive all these ships through the black waters. As I looked across at one or another, I could see its outline chiefly through the white bone-in-the-teeth and the phosphorescence of its wake. Now and again dim light-signals were exchanged between the *Lex* and a cruiser, or a cruiser and destroyer, as we zigzagged onward.

Going below finally I dropped into the wardroom and had a cup of coffee with the Padre—Lieut. Commander C. L. Markle—before we turned in ourselves.

10

THE CORAL SEA VICTORY: MISIMA

The entire ship's company was awake on the morning of May 7th, for a good hour before dawn. We had been steaming northward at a steady clip all night long and every man knew that we were within range of an enemy force as powerful as our own. We had no way of knowing whether they had been aware of our presence the afternoon before—we rather suspected they had. And they too might well be planning to make the same sort of dawn assault we would attempt.

All the plans, however, for getting the dive-bomber and torpedo-bomber squadrons off early, fell through. Our scouts, off and ranging the surrounding sea in the half-light before sunup, could find no trace of the Japs. Their precision quartering of the sea still was bringing no results at 7 A.M. And they were beginning to get out toward the limit of their ranges—which also was toward the maximum limit of our squadrons' fighting distances.

"The Japs couldn't have seen us and run away," one officer told me. "We're in their waters and they'll want to press the attack first if they can. They probably missed us entirely and during the night turned aside to go in some direction that has taken them outside our zone of search."

His estimate, I thought, was probably correct—but it turned out that we were both wrong.

"Gangster near fleet," came a radio call about 7:30 from a fighter plane of Carrier II. "It's a Kawanishi snooper," the same pilot reported a few seconds later.

If we could see the snooper, certainly the snooper could see us. And unquestionably by this time his radiomen had reported our presence to the Japanese fleet and possibly to the land-plane base whence this long-range craft had come.

"Well we're in the soup," one of the boys opined. "The Japs know where we are and we haven't found them. If they're as good as they are supposed to be they'll be taking off right now to give us a pasting."

The fighters, after sighting the Kawanishi, were talking back and forth among themselves and we were following their progress aboard the *Lex.* Within a few moments we heard one airman say: "Well there he goes."

The locale of such fights, often at heights from 10,000 feet upward, is seldom certain. This time we discovered where the snooper had been flying when our own lookouts reported that a plane was burning and falling several miles away on our starboard beam. We could all see the ship and it seemed to be spinning slowly down from a great height. It took a long time to reach the sea and left a vertical trail of smoke like a comet. We could follow it right down to the water with our eyes. There was the usual burst of flame when it hit, and then more smoke. By that time, however, we had moved on and the smoke plume was behind us.

"At any rate we got into 'em first," was the deck crew's summation.

About 8 o'clock a long-range scout from Carrier II called his vessel:

"Jap fleet—one carrier, three heavy cruisers, six destroyers—180 miles, course 120, speed 20 knots. West-northwest."

Quick glances at our charts showed us the enemy was about 50 miles north of Misima. We were standing a little south of the island of Rossel. The scout's cryptic language indicated that the Japs were 180 miles from us, and that they then were steering a course of 120 degrees at a 20-knot speed.

From the scout's report it was evident that the Jap fleet had split up. On the previous evening the *Lexington*'s scouts had seen a flotilla of two carriers, five cruisers and a dozen destroyers. Possibly this force split during the night into two formations with one carrier to each group.

Much later we learned that Gen. MacArthur's bombers claimed to have sighted and attacked a single Japanese carrier on this date. It is possible that the land planes saw and hit the second Japanese carrier from this force. That could be very likely, if the second carrier which disappeared during the night had steered a westerly course taking it over toward Deboyne Island.

At any rate the carrier—the *Ryukaku* the Navy later said it was—which our scouts found that morning, had suffered no attack until our squadrons reached it. Furthermore, there were no Army planes around while this attack was on, and the *Ryukaku* sank before our last planes left the scene.

But to go back to the *Lexington* again, our pilots were all set for take-off at the time the Jap fleet's location was pinpricked on our charts. A few minutes were required for our navigators to plot the courses our squadrons should fly to intercept the Japanese, and to chalk this and some last minute weather information on the readyroom blackboard.

Our Meteorological Officer, Lieut. G. L. Raring, kept this weather information up to date and it was unusually complete. That morning I remember, he had the direction and velocity of the wind at 1,000-foot levels right up to the maximum heights to which our planes could climb. He also predicted that the overcast which spread over our general area would dwindle away to nothing by the time they were passing along the coasts of the island of Tagula, and they would find the Japs in the clear under perfect flying conditions.

Also on the blackboard were instructions to the pilots concerning the course and speed the *Lexington* would follow for the next three hours. This was information they would require when they started home, and Capt. Sherman always religiously adhered to exactly the speeds and compass headings he had given the pilots before they left. Such matters are vital to men going out to battle, because the ship might move 60 nautical miles from her position at the time of their take-offs during that three-hour interval.

Getting all this information to the pilots and stowing them into their aircraft required only 20 minutes. And not more than 30 had elapsed by the time the last of the air-striking group was speeding on its way. In all 76 airplanes were sent off. They consisted of 24 torpedo planes, and 36 scouts and dive bombers, most of which were carrying a 1,000-pound bomb load. A few of the scouts carried one 500 pounder and two 100 pounders. Finally there was a unit of 16 fighter planes to escort the others and to deal with the Japanese fighter-plane defenses.

Hardly had our attack squadrons cleared the deck when the scouts reappeared with landing gear and hook down. This was the unspoken signal that they wanted to come aboard. The first crew in reported that they had been in combat over the Japanese formation. Biplane float fighters had intercepted them and they were forced to shoot their way out. None of the scouts was lost and they managed to shoot down two of these interfering Japs. There was no sign, they said, of any of the Zero monoplane fighters from the Japanese carriers.

The bombing, torpedo-plane and fighter formations meanwhile were climbing up to cruising altitude. Flying through the overcast they leveled off in clear air. In a few minutes they passed the edge of the cloud layer, as Lieut. Raring had predicted they would, and from there on the trip was made in cloudless skies with visibility as wide as 60 miles.

"Lieut. Commander Weldon Hamilton, the dive-bomber skipper was at the front of his formation which had climbed up to 15,000 feet and was slightly ahead and above Dixon's scout-bombers who were at 12,000. Underneath these two groups were Brett's torpedo planes. The fighters had split up, four pairs in the high-level group flying slightly above and behind Hamilton, and the other four idling along with the torpedo squadron.

"Our course led us along the island of Tagula for 60 miles," Hamilton later told me. "From our height in the clear air this island with its coral reefs, its tiny

aits (islets) with the breakers combing over them like
whipped cream, was a sight to behold. The blue of the
sea, the green of the island and the cream and silver of
the surf and sand were truly magnificent.

"After we had passed Tagula we went northward to
bring us past the eastern tip of Misima. The flight up
to that point had been uneventful but now we were
within 30 miles of where the enemy should be. A few
minutes later we were over the area where we expected
to find them so I began to search the horizon with my
powerful binoculars.

"Visibility was remarkable, the sky cloudless and
eventually I found, almost 40 miles to the eastward, at
right angles to our course, a number of thin white hairs
on the blue sea. A careful look at these showed them
to be the wakes of the Japanese fleet we were seeking.

"I radioed to the other squadron commanders and
we all altered course, to fly toward them."

"Little was said over the air," Hamilton told me.
"When I first sighted the enemy I radioed: 'Bob from
Ham, Bob from Ham (he was calling Commander Bob
Dixon who was leading the scout-bombers) enemy
ships sighted 20 miles north of our present position.'

"I underestimated the actual distance. At that time I
could only see those white wakes in the light blue distance. Bob sent a message to Brett (Lieut. Commander
Jimmy Brett, torpedo-squadron skipper): 'Did you get
that Jimmy?' When Jimmy said yes but he couldn't see
'em, Bob said: 'I'll coach you in, boy.' He did that as
soon as he was able to sight the enemy. Remember
Bob was somewhat lower than I was and had no binoculars.

"When I was finally able to distinguish the ships I
recognized the carrier from the reflection of the sun on
its light-colored flight deck. I then radioed: 'I see one
flat-top bastard.' Then Bob saw it. Little else was said
that I remember until after the attack. There was some
fighter talking about Japanese seaplane fighters which I
did not pay much attention to.

"I came out of the sun and almost exactly down
wind and commenced my attack immediately after Bob

Dixon's squadron was finished. The Japanese had made a turn to the left as Dixon's crew attacked. They made a second turn while I was waiting for our torpedo planes to take station for their coordinated attack with us. I went down at the start of the third turn the carrier made. The torpedo squadron attacked at the same time.

"We began from 16,500 feet, and pushed over in our dive at 12,000. The Jap was exactly down wind as I nosed down, simplifying my problem tremendously. My bomb, which was the first 1,000 pounder to hit, struck in the middle of the flight deck's width, just abaft amidships. As I looked back the entire after portion of the flight deck was ablaze and pouring forth heavy black smoke. Pulling up I heard Bob's voice (Dixon's on the radio): 'Mighty fine, mighty fine.'

"Watching the rest of my squadron come down I observed some of the boys missing the carrier with their bombs. I called them on the radio saying: 'Use the wind boys, use the wind,' because their bombs were hitting down wind of the ship.

"My rear gunner told me later that a Jap fighter followed me in my dive and made three attacks on my plane after the pullout. But evidently his guns had jammed as my gunner never saw him fire. At that time I was a sitter as I did not know he was there and was busy watching the Japanese carrier exploding. My radioman believes he disabled the Jap but did not actually see him crash.

"During their dives rear gunners in my squadron definitely got two Jap fighters which attacked them.

"The assault on this Jap carrier should go down in naval history as a most successful coordinated dive bombing-torpedo attack. The two coordinating squadrons VB-2 and VT-2 did not lose a single plane."

The arrival of the squadrons over the Japs was also recounted by Lieut. Commander Bob Dixon who that day was leading his scouts as dive bombers. (These were the planes with single 500 and two 100 pound bombs.)

"We came over at 12,000 feet. Enemy fighter patrols

were in the air but they barely reached us as we eased off into our almost vertical dives.

"To be really effective against dive bombers fighter planes have to reach them before they get to the turn-over point. Ordinarily fighters can't stay with us in the dive because with our airbrakes we keep our speed at about 250 miles an hour. The streamlined fighters with noses down go right on past us and pick up speed toward 400 miles an hour.

"But these Japs wouldn't give up. They were Zeros and that means they were very clean jobs. But the pilots put their flaps down, dropped their landing gear and did everything they could to keep their speed slow. Nevertheless they would go on past us. But that didn't keep them out either.

"They would pull up, do a zooming chandelle and come right back in to fire at the next planes diving past."

The commander added that the result was a terrific free-for-all.

"The Zeroes stayed with us right down to the water."

"Naturally we went for the carrier first. It was obvious we had caught them by surprise. In the dive I could see a number of planes on deck and one was coming up from the interior hangar deck in the elevator.

"When we first saw the Japs," Dixon continued, "the carrier was steaming down wind. It immediately made a sharp turn to the port trying to get back into the wind to launch its planes. I could see it all clearly as I peered through my telescopic sight, lining myself up for the bomb release."

A dozen or more pilots told of that "fighting dive" the scouts made that day. Imagine a huge cascade 15,000 feet in height, with every few seconds a mighty salmon flashing down its course! Our dive-bombing pilots were following just such a track, almost like salmon flashing over an immense water fall. They were changing formation at the top to echelon—which means they were stringing out one behind the other. They would then push off, each man following his leader or taking his own special target during the approximate 40-second interval between the commencement of the descent and the recovery after dropping their bombs 1,000 feet above the water.

The Japanese fighters, to give them their due, were tenaciously battling, even during the 40-second dives, to distract the pilots throughout this aiming period. Often there would be a chain of diving planes with a scout bomber at the bottom, a Zero just above him, a second scout bomber on the Zero's tail, with a second Zero above the second scout. Above that there would be other similarly mingled chains of Jap fighters and our scouts.

The Japanese ships around the carrier had thrown up a heavy curtain of bursting shells from their anti-aircraft guns. All the planes, scouts, Zeros, and our heavy dive bombers, which by now were coming down from about 16,000 feet, went right through the shell curtain, in most cases without ever knowing it. Our pilots' eyes were glued to their sights and our rear gunners in both the scouts and heavy dive bombers were firing at the Zeros. The Japs probably were equally intent for they were using their 20mm cannon and machine guns every time they were lined up, even momentarily, on one of our planes.

Some of our fighters, sitting up at 16,000 feet where they were protecting the last of the dive bombers at their most vulnerable point (a few seconds before they turn over in their dive), reported that Commander Dixon's dive was perfectly made. They saw his 500-pound bomb—the first one dropped—hit the Jap carrier amidships, wrecking the flight deck and preventing the launching of any of the planes still aboard.

Right behind Dixon followed Ensign P. F. Neely whose 500 pounder hit near the carrier's port side. It was a near miss, but the blast from this bomb tossed two burning planes from the carrier's decks into the sea.

The third bomber, flown by Ensign Smith, scored a direct hit on the carrier's starboard anti-aircraft battery. The explosion of this bomb silenced this group of guns and blew three more planes overboard. The fourth bomber, flown by Ensign J. A. Leppla, was one of those attacked by the Zeros almost as soon as his dive steepened to the near vertical. His rear gunner John Liska, facing backwards and firing his twin .30-caliber machine guns, fought off this particularly persistent attack. In a duel with two of the Zeros that quickly overhauled the scout and closed to point-blank range, firing their cannon, Liska got hits that caused flames to burst from their fuel tanks. Both these Zeros crashed into the sea.

Ensign Leppla was busy during his dive, too. He saw a Zero go on past him and begin shooting at Smith's plane. Easing out of his dive slightly, Leppla got the Zero into his sights and shot that one down also.

The carrier was well into its turn by that time and besides Leppla had been distracted. The best he could do with his 500 pounder was to lay it close beside the carrier in a near miss. This, however, didn't satisfy him. He zoomed away, climbed back to 4,000 feet and dive-bombed one of the Japanese cruiser escorts with both his 100 pounders. One of these hit the cruiser on the stern, which invariably is the target at which dive bombers aim their bombs.

But let us return to this dive which was completed by the entire scout squadron in less time that it takes you to read these few paragraphs.

Ensign O. J. Schultz, fifth in line in that attack, secured a hit on the carrier with his bomb but was attacked by four Zero fighters as he recovered from his dive. His rear gunner whose name I never learned but who was, you may be sure, as much a hero as any of the pilots, broke up the attack by shooting one down and making it so hot for the others that they turned away. When that plane got back to the carrier 29 bullet holes were counted in it, but neither pilot nor gunner was wounded.

The scouts' dives had taken away the enemy's fighter protection aloft and the heavier dive bombers with 1,000 pounders in their belly rack had little opposition as they delivered their attacks. But the two or three minutes during which the scouts were attacking had enabled the Jap fleet to spread out so that each vessel would have plenty of water in which to maneuver and to get their heaviest anti-aircraft guns into action.

Coordinated with the commencement of the heavy dive-bomber assault, was Lieut. Commander Jimmy Brett's torpedo-squadron attack. The Zeros that had survived the battle with the scouts during the dive, now stayed down on the sea and flew out to intercept the torpedo planes now making their final approaches.

"Hey fighters, come and get these Zeros off me," Brett radioed to our Grumman pilots, as the first of the Japs began playing leapfrog across the torpedo planes now fanned out almost in a squadron-front formation.

Lieut. Baker and his wingman, whose contribution to the battle up to that point had been the downing of a Jap seaplane fighter, answered Brett's call. In two runs they shot down two Zeros and held off the rest to free the torpedo formation.

The first of the heavy dive bombers which we left a moment ago just starting their dives, was piloted by Lieut. Commander Hamilton. "Ham" had been over-carried by the wind in his dive at a Jap cruiser at Salamaua and had vowed before he started his flight that morning of the 7th that he would get a bull's-eye.

"My ambition in life is to put my big bomb clean through the deck and into the vitals of the biggest Japanese carrier I can find," Ham had been telling all of us in the wardroom mess.

"Hamilton did just what he wanted," Paul Ramsey later said. "I watched his dive and saw that he plunked his bomb into the exact center of the flight deck just slightly abaft of midships. There was a tremendous explosion, flames seemed to leap four hundred feet into the air."

Another fighter pilot, Lieut. Commander Flatley, skipper of Carrier II's fighters, told me later:

"I was sitting upstairs at 5,000 feet watching them come down. The heavy bombs began exploding at three- and four-second intervals. Fire, flames, and sea-water were being thrown hundreds of feet high, from each explosion. The 1,000-pound bombs seemed to be pattering down like rain and those big babies do four times as much damage as the 500 pounders.

"The sight of those heavy bombs smashing that carrier was so awful it gave me a sick feeling. Every second bomb was landing and exploding aboard the ship. Those powerful blasts were literally tearing the big ship apart. She burst into flames from bow to stern. I don't see how anybody aboard that ship could have survived."

While this split-second action was going on, Commander Brett, now free of the fighters was dropping his own "fish." He is a wily one. He used the smoke pouring out of the wounded Jap to screen his squadron's approach. They sneaked in from down wind under the smoke. When so close they couldn't miss they made an "S" turn so that their torpedoes finally dropped full into the starboard side of their victim. The Navy's remarkable photographs of this action show exactly how this was done and in many of these pictures Brett's planes can be seen following his trail.

One after another these deadly fish zipped in and blasted against the carrier's hull. Twelve actual torpedo hits were scored, literally tearing the whole side out of the vessel. Almost at the same time 16 bombs of the 1,000-pound size, plus three 500 pounders were slamming into her from above. The result was that this vessel disappeared in a giant cloud of smoke and steam almost as if a giant's heel had crunched her beneath the surface.

Back on the *Lexington* all of us were anxious to know the results of the attack. We were confident the squadrons would do a good job but this was, after all, the first such attack ever made on a carrier by American crews. In the radio room we could hear some of the pilots talking, but static was bad and much of it was inaudible. By watching the clock we knew they must have gone into action and our natural anxiety was heightened by this knowledge.

All the tension on the carrier exploded the moment we heard Commander Dixon's voice come in strong and clear:

"Scratch one flat-top! Dixon to carrier. Scratch one flat-top!"

It meant that the Navy could scratch one more Japanese flat-top (carrier), off the lists of the enemy's fleet. In other words the boys had done the job and the carrier was sunk—news which brought forth resounding cheers and applause throughout the ship from stem to stern and keel to truck.

All this action happened in such short order and the results were so final that there were pilots in both the torpedo and dive-bomber squadrons who arrived too late to get a crack at the carrier at all.

One torpedo plane, for instance, saw the carrier was finished and made off after a cruiser. One of his squadron mates who had dropped his fish against the carrier saw this boy and guessed his intention. The unarmed torpedo bomber joined up with the craft that still had its torpedo and both planes ran in as if making the attack together. Of course it was a "dry run" for the pilot who had no torpedo but it was not merely a bit of bravado. I saw the report this pilot made when he got back to us safely. It read: "I went along to draw some of the anti-aircraft fire which otherwise might have been concentrated too heavily on just one plane." Unfortunately the reports do not show that this torpedo hit its mark.

The gunnery officer from Carrier II was a rear-seat passenger with one of the scout planes that day. He had gone over to watch the effect of heavy bombs on warships and after the carrier had sunk beneath his gaze, he was astounded to see a heavy cruiser which was down by the stern, turn over and sink. His attention had been fixed on the carrier and he had seen no attack on any other ship in the Jap fleet.

When he arrived back on his carrier all the other planes had returned. The first thing this officer did was to ask which pilot or pilots had sunk the cruiser. No one seemed to know what he was talking about. But there was one way to find out—go through the individual pilot reports. You see when an airman is given a bomb or a torpedo on a raid like this, he is expected to tell just what he did with it when he comes back. These things cost the U.S. taxpayer a lot of money. And fliers aren't supposed to go off and just drop them anywhere without telling anybody.

A search through Carrier II's pilot reports failed to disclose any mention of an attack on a cruiser. The *Lexington's* reports were combed with the same result except for Ensign Leppla's 100 pounder which couldn't possibly have achieved this.

All the air-control officers by now were interested in the case. And all the men who had taken part in the raid were called up in both ships and asked if they had seen anyone hit a cruiser with either a bomb or torpedo.

Finally a young ensign went to his squadron commander and said:

"I'm terribly sorry, Sir. I'm the one who did it. I started to bomb the carrier but could see she was sinking. While I was flying around wondering which ship to give my bomb to this cruiser started to shoot at me. So I said: 'Right then, I'll give it to you.' So I did. It was only a cruiser, and I didn't think that worth while reporting."

This boy's attitude is typical of all the pilots, who realize better than anyone else that if they can kill off the carriers in an enemy force and so destroy its air defense and offense they destroy the fighting power of that fleet. The rest of the vessels may be picked off at leisure.

When Commander Dixon got back to the *Lexington* I questioned him about the fight. His main concern was for the safety of two in his squadron, Lieut. Edward Allen, and Ensign A. J. Quigley. Allen, a particularly close friend, who won the Navy Cross on Feb. 20th by his 200-mile pursuit of a Jap land-based bomber at the Battle of Bougainville, was hit by anti-aircraft fire in his bombing dive, and his plane went into the water.

We were able to give him better news about Quigley because the ensign had been in touch with the ship by radio.

He had been attacked by a Japanese Zero which scored a lucky hit on his left aileron, damaging it so badly that his aileron control was virtually nil. He at-

Zero A6M5

tempted to make the trip back to the carrier but after getting as far as Rossel he reported that he would have to land.

We had asked him at that time if he couldn't continue on to the carrier, which was then not far away. He replied: "Afraid not, my fuel supply is giving out."

The skipper told Quigley that Rossel Island was the best place for him to land, and that everything would be done to pick up him and his radioman, R. E. Wheelhouse. Some joker in a plane piped in to tell Quigley to "watch out for those brown-skinned beauties," and the last word we had from him was a cheerful: "Tell the boys we're going to do a stretch of beachcombing."

Quigley and Wheelhouse were rescued eighteen days afterward by a small Australian warship which was making a methodical patrol of the islands in this area, searching for marooned American flyers. Quigley described his experiences later while recovering in the Pearl Harbor naval hospital from malaria. He made a high-speed landing inside a reef off Rossel Island. "I was stunned a little," he said, "but the water coming in revived me. We got the rubber boat out and I took the chart board. We rowed for 45 minutes, but got nowhere because the current was too strong, then saw an outrigger and three of the wildest looking natives you can imagine."

Despite their looks, the natives took them ashore to the house of the local missionary, also a native, where they were the center of interest for some days.

Quigley spent some time aboard with the Australians while they continued their rescue work. "They almost drove me crazy," he said. "One day, they steamed up to a harbor which was reported to be full of Jap seaplanes. We were to support some Allied aircraft in attacking the enemy inside. Somehow the air attack force didn't show up, but the young Australian commander decided to steam into the port anyway and get after the Japs. The little ship dashed into the harbor—but the enemy had left, so there was no fight."

Commander Hamilton got back to the carrier with his engine vibrating severely and with bullet holes in his propeller—drilled by bullets from his own guns. He told the story this way:

"As I came through the anti-aircraft pattern and released my bomb, inadvertently I squeezed the 'Mickey Mouse' (the gun- and bomb-release trigger) a little too hard and my guns fired. Of course at the time I didn't know this but the plane began to vibrate violently and I assumed I had been hit by Jap fire.

"I throttled back as I pulled out and found I could amble along home at reduced speed. I took a look to see where I'd been hit as soon as I landed. Only then did I find that the synchronization gear on one gun had slipped and the prop was perforated by my own slugs."

As the planes started to return we could see by the

way some of them were flying that they had been damaged. And as they came into the landing circle I saw tears in their metal skins that later proved to be cannon shot holes in wings and tail fins on several of the ships. One came in asking to land out of his turn and the ship's physician, always on duty on the flight deck, was waved up onto the plane. And as this plane was taxied into parking position the doctor was standing on the wing cutting away the shirt of the rear gunner who had been drilled through his upper left lung. They put him into the special Navy wire stretcher and carried him below—the *Lex*'s first man wounded in action.

Practically everyone else in the squadrons had routine flights back to the carrier except Ensign Leppla and his gunner D. K. Liska. These two who already had accounted for three Zeros in this battle—and remember, they were flying in a comparatively slow scout bomber which should have been cold meat to any fighter—had flown about half the 180 miles of the homeward trek when they spotted a Jap seaplane fighter. It was then several miles off their course and interfering with no one.

But to these two boys, a Jap is a Jap wherever he is. Leppla turned after the seaplane and rapidly overhauled it. The Jap was waiting for them, and he too was a two-seater. The result was a short but violent air duel, that ended when the Japanese plane crashed into the sea. It gave Leppla and Liska a day's total of four.

When their plane finally alighted on the *Lex*, all of us went out and walked around it, examining it closely. Parts of it looked like my wife's colander. There were bullet holes in the wings, fuselage, the tail, the ailerons. It must have whistled a cheerful tune as the wind whipped through these holes while flying. The other pilots wondered how and why it answered to the controls. Its return at all is a testimonial to the builders of the ship and engine.

When I looked into the cockpit I found that other shots had gone through the plexiglas cockpit covers, missed the pilot and gunner by inches, and then completely smashed some of the instrument board. One bullet tore the heel off the pilot's right shoe, and another after coming through the plane and "buzzing round the cockpit like a bee" to quote Leppla, went through the leg of his flying suit and was found stuck in the knee of his trousers.

Our pilots were home in time for lunch which turned into a celebration. There was a good deal of satisfaction over many things, first the destruction of the enemy carrier and all the aircraft aboard her at the time; the sinking of a heavy cruiser and the shooting out of the air of 17 aircraft. All of this had been accomplished for the loss of three SBDs—the Douglas scout-bombers. The crew of one—Quigley and his gunner—being saved.

Another important point for all the airmen was the fact that they had encountered the vaunted Zero and found that even scout-bombers could handle it. The fighters got little chance at the Zeros which went down with the dive bombers and stayed down to hit at the torpedo planes. Only two Zeros as a matter of fact were credited to the fighters, the rest going to dive bombers, torpedo planes and scouts.

The weather deteriorated rapidly as we turned southward that afternoon. We got into rain squalls, low scud, and some fog. Visibility was at times zero, and at others lifted to only several miles—tricky flying weather in which carrier pilots work hard and run the risk of losing their carrier.

As we moved along I spent the afternoon talking with Commander Bill Ault who had gone over that morning in command of the *Lex* group.

"The failure of the Japanese anti-aircraft to take a higher toll of our planes was very gratifying. Their shooting, I thought, was quite good."

He then said that when he flew in toward the carrier at a height of 10,000 feet, he approached a cruiser steaming away. This vessel's batteries opened on him with all guns and the shell bursts were so close, the plane was bounced around and violently jerked about so that the control stick was slapped around in his hand.

"I made a gentle turn round this cruiser and the ship turned with me so that it kept broadside on all the time. This way it was able to hold every gun on me. The bursts from these guns stayed with me until I was out of range. Miraculously the plane wasn't hit, though the shooting could hardly have been better."

Late that afternoon with the early twilight of a rainy day beginning to descend, Ramsey, who then was aloft on a fighter patrol, radioed that he had sighted nine Zero fighters almost over the fleet in the rain. He added that he was going to attack although he had only three other planes with him.

His voice was coming to us in the wardroom through a big radio placed there and constantly tuned in on the fighter frequencies.

We heard him talking to his wingman and to the second pair of fighters in his group.

"Do you see them? There are five in the leading vee, then two, with two trailing. George, you take the center two and I'll take the last two. Have you got it? We'll deal with the others later. Let's go and get 'em."

There was silence for a while and then we heard another voice—that of Jimmy Flatley from Carrier II. He evidently had heard Ramsey's report and had joined in. After some indistinguishable chatter we heard Paul ask: "How many did you get, Jimmy?"

"I got three. How many did you get, Paul?" came the reply.

"Only two, darn it," Ramsey replied in a voice dripping with disappointment.

In this battle, fought in the rain from 5,000 feet right down to water level (Ramsey told me later he once found himself only 30 feet off the ocean), the boys in their Grummans had shot down seven out of the enemy nine. Lieut. Baker who had shot down two Zeros and a seaplane in the morning, failed to return. His wingman, Ensign Edward Sellstrom, said that Baker shot down one Zero and then appeared to collide with another which burst into flame. Both the ships then crashed.

By a strange coincidence another fighter pilot, also named Baker, was lost in this same engagement. This pilot came out of the fight safely but because our carriers were by now in heavy rain and almost complete darkness he was having difficulty locating us. He was from the fighter command of Carrier II but we were listening on the fighter frequency and could clearly hear him asking directions and the assistance which both Carrier II and our own Fighter Control were attempting to give, in order to get him back safely.

For more than an hour we stood around listening to this very real drama. Dinner was waiting in the wardroom mess but nobody cared to dine until this young flyer had been brought aboard. Finally after more than an hour with his fuel supply nearly exhausted he said he could see land below him—evidently one of the islands in the neighborhood. We judged that he had flown north again out of the thick weather and back perhaps toward the Louisiades. The last radio report was his announcement that he was going to alight on this land. I have still not learned the fate of this boy.

A group of us were standing on the flight deck following dinner when we saw the final, most amazing sight of this very full day. It came without warning when we heard a drone of aircraft engines in the murk overhead. Out of the rain squall on one quarter flew a formation of nine bombers that came right across the fleet only mast high. The leader picked out the *Lexington*, turned our way and flashed on his navigation lights. Every other ship followed suit and they strung out "like a flight of tired birds coming home to roost," one officer remarked.

The leader flew into the landing circle and began flashing his identification signal. It happened that there was some similarity between the identification he used and our own. Knowing we had only one plane then in the air we were momentarily taken aback.

At that moment, our missing scout returned, seeing the "strangers'" navigation lights, started shooting. We could see the sparks of his tracer as he fired at the last of the line. This was sufficient signal for the escort destroyers to open fire.

The Japs who had mistaken the *Lex* for their own carrier doused their lights and made off, disappearing almost as quickly as they had come into the blackness of the night.

I have often wondered since what would have happened had we allowed them to make a landing. As one of the boys said: "Heck, this ocean must be crowded with aircraft carriers." He was speaking with more perspicacity than he realized for our scout followed the direction taken by the enemy ships and a short time later saw them being taken aboard a carrier only 30 miles away.

This scout, directed home to the *Lexington* by radio, told us there was a large enemy force "with ships everywhere" just over the horizon from us. He said he thought there were two carriers but there might be more.

With this information we knew the Japs unquestionably were warned and perhaps hunting us through the darkness. For a time we were wondering if Admiral Fletcher would use his "tight" force of excellent cruisers and destroyers for a night attack. There was some speculation on this but it never developed. There was always a chance, of course, that the two fleets would run into each other before morning so the gunners on the ship were kept on the alert all night.

There we were, two powerful air-striking forces within 30 miles of one another wrapped in the invisibility lent by a rainy night. All of us felt that morning would bring a momentous day. In our enemy we recognized a tough, fanatical foe whose courage and cunning could not be discounted. Our forces appeared about equal. It seemed to be a question of who would get the first blow home. We had seen on the previous day what aircraft could do to a carrier and so we knew the consequences that day might bring.

All of us felt that with daylight, would come the world's first battle between two strong aircraft-carrier forces, each being aware of the other's presence so the surprise element was out. And all of us felt that history was in the making as our vessels groped through the inky night.

11

THE CORAL SEA VICTORY: TAGULA

Commander Mort Seligman, the *Lex*'s executive officer, brought with him to sea practically all his worldly goods except his house. With his civilian clothing, his golf clubs, fishing tackle, etc., he also had on board a superb combination recording and play-back machine. We often discussed the value of interviews with pilots, air commanders and air crewmen recorded on discs as a permanent record. Taken immediately after the men return from action while their impressions are still vivid and clear, such recordings would be of great value to supplement their written reports which often are laconic, stereotyped, and brief.

We had been so enthused over the idea that the commander arranged for me to assist as questioner in his cabin on the night of the 7th. He invited, for the experiment, all the commanders of the air squadrons that took part in the day's attack on the Jap carrier, later identified as the *Ryukaku*. Those who were present that evening after the air conferences were over and plans for the 8th had been laid, were: Group Commander Bill Ault, Lieut. Commanders Ramsey, Brett, Hamilton and Dixon.

My part was to see they were properly introduced for the recording (with Commander Seligman acting as the recording engineer) and to ask a question now and then to get them talking. We wanted everything they could remember about what each man saw and did in the fight. All of them were skilled observers, reporting about jobs in which each was an expert. What they had to say was precise and to the point. It was without frills of any sort and just about the most dramatic thing I ever heard. From their flying grandstands above these five men were eyewitnesses to everything that took place and was interwoven into the battle itself.

As each man finished his own statement he made a summary accounting for his squadron and then added his conclusions concerning tactics. They also gave their evaluation of enemy movements and defensive action, described and summed up the strength and weaknesses of enemy pilots, planes, anti-aircraft guns, and vessels.

I believe that had these recordings been preserved and sent on to Washington as Commander Seligman hoped and intended, they would have been of the greatest value to the Navy's staff, personnel and procurement sections. They would, in my opinion at least, have been of truly material benefit as supplemental to the paper reports that already go in on every phase of any action.

We played the four discs, each one of about 20 minutes' playing time, back for ourselves that night. So good were they that Seligman and I decided to attempt to make a recording the next day of any fighting that might take place around us. We were anticipating an air assault on the *Lex* and Carrier II almost as soon as it was light, so there was real point to the preparations we then made.

Earlier experiments along the same line had been unsatisfactory because the recording microphone had picked up too much noise from the ship itself. The rattle and slam of gunfire on the *Lexington*'s flight deck alone had been enough to jam the mike and create a noise level over which it was impossible to talk. So we taped the microphone so, that by cupping my hands over it and holding it close to my lips we could exclude almost any other sound and yet get a clear recording of the voice itself. We extended the microphone lines from the Commander's cabin up to the signal bridge—my battle station—and had about 40 feet of loose line there to enable me to move freely around the bridge and see everything that might happen. One of the orderlies was shown how to operate the recording machine. We rigged an intercommunications telephone between the bridge and his cabin so that he could be given directions when to start and stop the turntable.

By the time all this was arranged it was after midnight. The other officers had long since turned in. I wandered around the *Lexington*'s quarters for a time, being too uncomfortably hot to sleep.

The only light I found was in the cabin of Commander Brett who was busy tapping away on a typewriter. He looked up, smiled, and invited me in to show me the manuscript of a book on color photography he had almost completed after two years of work. He explained he already had published one book on the subject and his second volume was covering particularly wartime applications for color film. He hoped it would be of some value to the services, and believed that when this cruise was over he would be ready to send it to the publishers.

I finally left him and got to typing myself—getting my notes in order and doing rough dispatches to cover the action to date. I finally fell asleep at 4 A.M. So exhausted was I that when the pre-dawn "battle stations" call came at 5:30 I just rolled over and dug into the pillow again. But the "clang, clang, clang" of the scouts going off finally roused me. And suddenly I was wide awake. I had just remembered there was a very good reason for getting up this morning—there were Japs round and about us and a battle in the offing.

One becomes so weather conscious on a carrier that I had gotten into the habit of climbing up to the flight deck for a look around before going down to breakfast. A peek out the Island's exit showed me a beautiful, clear morning with the sun sparkling just over the horizon. It was a marvelous day—exactly the kind everyone in the fleet would have gladly done without, for an aircraft carrier, like a plane in enemy territory, is safest when it is running through fog and heavy rain squalls.

It turned out that the *Lexington* remained in clear weather throughout the hours of daylight. It was the Japanese who had the position of advantage, for their fleet was in ideal carrier weather—it was running from one patch of low scud and rain to another all day long. It had these natural curtains to hide in and its ships split up most skillfully to take all the benefits the weather afforded.

There had been every likelihood that the two fleets would be close together at dawn. It could have been possible that they might be almost within sight of us, and we of them. We of the *Lex* stood to general quarters in all departments ready to bounce into action the minute our scouts took the air just before daylight. Maybe they would find the enemy in their first 15 minutes of flying. If that was the case the battle would go to the force that struck the earliest blow. We intended to be that force.

Fifteen minutes, thirty minutes, then an hour went by and none of the scouts reported a thing. They had flown out from the ship in all directions like spokes of a wheel radiating from the hub. After that first hour we relaxed somewhat on the ship and got a good breakfast under our collective belts.

It was not until 8:10 that Ensign Smith, one of the scouts who had gone out due northeast, radioed a contact report. He had completed the full limit of his 225-mile outbound course, had flown his 90-degree cross leg and 25 miles of his return course, when he sighted the enemy.

"Two carriers, four heavy cruisers, many destroyers, steering 120 degrees, 20 knots. Their position 175 miles, roughly northeast," he reported.

It was the information we had been seeking. Pilots went to their readyroom and the deck crews began warming up the motors. The whole ship was alert and a few minutes later orders came down from the bridge to put the ship "into condition Zed." This is the order given just before the commander really anticipates battle. It means that every watertight door and hatch is bolted down. In the *Lexington* this divided the ship off into some 600 separate air compartments which made her virtually unsinkable.

All over the ship I could hear crews slamming shut watertight doors and dogging them down with clamps which held them in place and would resist the enormous pressures of outside seawater, should the hull be holed near them. Steel hatches separating the decks were battened down by tightening more than 40 steel nuts and bolts that held the edges. Cut into each hatch is a round hole (the Navy calls this a scuttle) large enough to allow a man to slip through. Each hole has a top with a large wheel that operates a threaded screw. This enables the scuttle to be opened to allow a man through and closed again behind him. In "condition Zed" there is a guard for every door and scuttle.

There was no more word from Smith but Commander Dixon who had been flying a scouting segment adjoining Smith's heard the pilot's radio and flew over to see for himself, in the hope of giving assistance. Within a very few minutes he was at the position where Smith reported the Japs.

Dixon couldn't find them. He began quartering the area which was full of unusually woolly clouds, hanging low. Under some of them was a veil of heavy rain. These vapor pillars filled the sky to overflowing, without however making a solid layer. Dixon found that some of the mist and rain made visibility zero right on the sea and extended up as high as 6,000 feet. Looking for a fleet in there was like looking for a deer in a forest.

Suddenly he saw them slipping across a clear spot, and he began amplifying Smith's reports at once. Also he corrected the position as given, announcing that they were 200 miles away from us. He saw two carriers, five cruisers and at least seven destroyers. And most important of all he stayed within sight of the enemy, circling overhead, slipping into and out of the clouds and continued sending radio direction signals to guide our air squadrons, which he assumed were already on their way to attack.

But Dixon was wrong on that point. Our attack squadrons, although ready to go, were still aboard. Admiral Fletcher evidently was awaiting word from the rest of the scouts before committing himself fully in any one direction. He was waiting to be sure there were no other Japanese fleets within the scouting circle around us. This is a logical precaution, almost a military necessity, but the pilots were chafing under the delay. They wanted to get off and trap the Japanese still on their carriers, before the Japs could make a pass in our direction.

This, of course, left Dixon in a spot. Alone, without support of any kind, he soon was discovered by enemy air patrols. Dozens of Zeros were in the air and one after another they began making feints at him. He avoided as many as possible by diving into clouds, but couldn't of course avoid them all. He had many brushes and did some firing, but naturally was evading combat.

His job was to stay alive and hold on to the Jap fleet. He did it superbly, for he remained hovering over and around them for two hours and 50 minutes. This was an hour longer than the time he expected our attack force would require to reach there. He finally had to start back because his fuel was getting dangerously low and he had still 200 miles to fly. In its own quiet way—typical of Bob Dixon—this lone vigil was one of the most heroic bits of work done by any man in the war.

Imagine it! A lone scout, holding its own over two, we now believe possibly three Japanese carriers, big carriers full of the best fighting planes and pilots the Japanese possessed. The airplane Dixon flew was a Douglas SBD—this is a good craft but definitely not a fighter. A standard Navy reference book says that this two-place plane weighs 7,400 pounds, has a 41.5-foot wing span, a top speed of 260 miles an hour, and cruises at 210.

Against it the Japs were using their vaunted Zeros. This is a single-seater plane with a top speed of better than 350 miles an hour, and is armed with two 20mm cannon and two .25-caliber machine guns. Furthermore, it is one of the most maneuverable fighting planes in the air, and with all this, plus numerical advantages, should have been able to knock down Dixon's aircraft without any trouble at all. Nevertheless, Dixon not only managed to stay in the air—he got home safely.

"How in the world, Bob, did you manage to survive?" I asked him. "When you started home and maintained radio silence for an hour and a half we became very concerned."

"We ducked in and out of the clouds," he answered grinning a little. "When they came after us (he had a rear gunner in the scout with him) they didn't press their attacks home. They seemed to prefer to make feinting runs, evidently hoping to get my rear gunner to use up his belts of ammunition so they could close in while he was reloading.

"My gunner refused to play this game, and held his fire until they were within killing range.

"If they came in too close I would make a steep turn and head toward them with one wing low. This allowed me to be in shooting position with my front guns and also permitted my gunner to fire forward over the wing with his twin flexible mounted guns."

Bob's long stay had helped us immeasurably. The weather was so rotten over the Jap fleet that it might have been easy for all our squadrons to have missed them. As it was he stayed—not knowing whether our groups were coming or not—until only 15 minutes before the first units arrived. His signals, given out until he started home, guided them practically to the goal, and made the search at the end very easy.

It was not until after 9 o'clock that Admiral Fletcher was satisfied he should launch all his planes at the fleet Dixon had been covering. The word to go came through; the pilots hurriedly copied their navigation information off the ready-room blackboards, and ran to their planes. The first ones to depart lifted into the air about 9:30 A.M. Ahead of them was a flight of approximately an hour and 20 minutes—they were enemy bound.

The *Lexington* sent an "attack force" of 12 torpedo planes, nine dive bombers, nine fighters, and four scout-bombers who were Group Commander Ault's command force. Carrier II sent off nine torpedo planes, 24 dive bombers, and six fighters. This time there were no bombers carrying less than 1,000 pounders. In all they totaled 73 aircraft—21 torpedo planes, 37 dive bombers, 15 fighters.

On the *Lexington* we learned just after the last of our planes got away that one hour earlier a Japanese scout had sighted us and escaped. This meant, of course, that the Japs knew where we were, our strength, and our course and speed. We did not doubt, after this word came through, that we would be the targets for a similar air attack group to the one we had sent away ourselves.

Our planes did not form one huge air fleet. The *Lexington*'s dive bombers climbed high—above 14,000 feet—accompanied by four Grumman fighters. The command force of four scout-bombers had two fighters as escorts, and three fighters went with the *Lexington*'s dive bombers. Four fighters had been scheduled to go but the fourth plane's tail was damaged by a propeller on deck as it was taxiing out to take off.

Carrier II's six fighters were distributed among the torpedo-plane squadrons and bombers from that vessel. With all these planes flying in separate formations, the 73 aircraft were split into five subdivisions. This became important later on, because the nine dive bombers from the *Lex* missed the Japs entirely in the fog and rain and took no part in the attack. These divisions also meant that the units were separated in time by intervals of from five to ten minutes.

When halfway to the target the three fighters escorting the *Lexington*'s dive bombers lost contact with their charges and returned to the carrier. This probably was just as well because these fighters then took part in the desperate defense of the ship, which began about the time they showed up. These details, however, will be explained later.

To describe this involved action in which time, height and space separations are so important let us choose, at random, Commander Brett's torpedo group from the *Lex*. They climbed to 6,000 feet and droned along unhurriedly which was the only way their heavily laden TBD's would fly anyhow. Part way along the route one plane turned back. Its engine was giving trouble, oil pressure was dropping and the cylinder head temperatures soaring so the commander ordered the pilot home to the *Lex*.

They went on, the other eleven. Escorting them were Lieut. Noel Gayler and a wingman whose name I do not know; and Ensign H. F. Clark with another wingman whose name I do not have. All four were flying fighters.

Cloud conditions developed as they approached the area where the enemy fleet was steaming and very soon after they began to clip along through the tops of these piled clouds they were intercepted by some wide-ranging Japanese fighters. These were Zeros, forming the outer defensive screen for the enemy.

While the torpedo planes ducked into the clouds the fighters engaged the enemy. Gayler said afterward the intention was merely to distract the Zeros for a moment but the quartet quickly found itself in a life and death duel because Zeros seemed to materialize from all directions and clung to the Grummans tenaciously. In a few seconds they were turning, firing, and turning again to keep the Japanese from shooting them down.

It was an unequal combat but Gayler—the sole American survivor—afterward said he believed that the other three men in his group got at least one Jap each. In the maneuvering and in the clouds they lost sight of each other. The boys whose names I have not been able to get were never heard from again. Clark some time later radioed that his plane was badly shot up and he was being forced to alight at sea. We all hope that the landing was successfully made and that he was able to get his little yellow rubber dingey inflated. If he was able to get into the dingey he had a good chance of being blown to one of the near-by islands by the prevailing southeasterly wind.

Gayler in telling of this action later said: "This swarm of Zeros kept me in defense maneuvers constantly. There was always one of them making a run at me. Early in the scrap I evaded the attack of one and then jumped his tail. He immediately resorted to the old Zero trick of zooming for altitude. Remember those babies will climb 4,000 feet a minute. They just love to have you on their tail trying to follow them up. If you do, they climb out of your range, flop over backward at the top of their zoom and you suddenly find them diving back at you when you are almost stalled and easy meat.

"I anticipated the pull up and gave him a snap burst

as he commenced his climb. My bullets hit him and he began to burn.

"I ducked into a cloud at once to evade the swarm again. They kept me in there for a couple of minutes. I'd duck out one side and they'd be there waiting. I'd climb to the top and find them up there. I'd go out the bottom and run into some more. That cloud was home to me. Finally I came out one side, saw a Jappie below me. The Jap saw me and made that instinctive pull up right in front of my guns. I gave it to him and he too burned."

That ended the fight and Gayler started after the torpedo group. He said he came out over the enemy fleet and through a hole in the cloud saw a carrier blazing furiously from end to end. He decided the attack was over and so turned back on his course looking down close to the water for the torpedo outfit.

While his escorts were in desperate combat with the Zeros, Brett and his torpedo pilots went. They approached the target area in time to meet Commander Ault's four-plane command unit. They joined up and started quartering the ocean because rain and clouds were hiding the Japanese ships. After 15 minutes of systematic search they sighted a carrier.

During the search Commander Brett had been trying to make radio contact with the *Lexington*'s nine heavy dive bombers. Failing to raise them Brett and Ault decided to carry on with the attack at once. Ault and his staff would do the dive bombing, coordinating their dives with Brett's more vulnerable slow, low approach that he had to make in order to launch his torpedoes.

This too was a gallant action. Every man flying in the two units knew that they were a very small force for the job in hand. The immunity the *Lex*'s squadrons had enjoyed in other actions arose in a large measure from the fact that there had been 70 to 80 planes attacking at once from all directions. This coordinated assault had the effect of confusing the enemy defenses, spreading the anti-aircraft fire thin and disorganizing the fighter patrols.

But this time the attack was to be made with 15 planes. Carrier II's planes were somewhere around but hidden from Brett and Ault in poor weather. They had made no contact with the *Lex* group and furthermore might be off somewhere attacking an entirely different division of the Jap fleet. This latter assumption proved correct, Brett learned later. And so they did not wait for more assistance.

"We caught this carrier and her escort of cruisers and destroyers in the clear," Brett told later discussing the attack. "We went over first at 3,500 feet, and there was no anti-aircraft fire. I judged that the Japs mistook us for their own planes, which is an easy mistake to make, because theirs and ours are almost alike. They've copied us freely. At that moment they were steaming hard toward the cover of a rain squall."

Ensign N. A. Sterrie in Brett's squadron explained the action in even more detail. "The clouds ranged from 2,000 to 6,000 feet and after the preparatory examination of the enemy disposition the squadron leader dived for the attack position.

"We fanned out and headed in at high speed. This time we were recognized and met by heavy anti-aircraft fire. And a lot of Jap fighters showed up but did not push their attacks home.

"Group Commander Bill Ault's four planes dived simultaneously with our torpedo run. All concentrated on the carrier.

"The Jap went into a tight constant turn when attacked. By the time it was my turn to drop she already was smoking, showing evidence of having been hit. I dropped my 'fish' on her starboard quarter 75 feet above the water, 500 yards out. At the time I was being subjected to heavy anti-aircraft fire and attack from a fighter.

"As I was joining up with the main group, one of the boys who had not let go of his fish said he was going to attack a cruiser. So I accompanied him making a dummy run to assist in absorbing the ship's anti-aircraft fire."

At least five of Brett's 11 torpedoes socked home into this carrier. This total is the Navy's official record garnered from many pilots who saw it. While Brett's squadron was attacking Bill Ault's dive bombers were making their dives and fortunately escaped most of the anti-aircraft fire because the carrier's batteries were busy with the torpedo planes. They were not molested in their swift straight descents. The result was that three of their heavy bombs plunged through the carrier's decks. Towering masses of smoke and debris rose after each blast.

"The bombs seemed to act in a dual manner," one of the torpedo pilots who saw the dive bombers come down said afterward. "Not only did they tear the carrier apart, but they also had an incendiary effect. Of course that's not so strange. Carriers have huge tanks full of fuel oil and high-test gasoline. Once this starts to burn it is good-bye."

With their job done the dive bombers and the torpedo bombers started home. The torpedo planes stayed right down on the sea and closed up in a tight defensive formation. A dozen Zeros hopped on them and as Brett told me later:

"They approached first from our starboard quarter. My formation was so arranged that we could bring all of our rear guns to bear on these Japs.

"As soon as the leader came within range we shot him down. The rest pulled away, swung around astern of us and made their approach from the port quarter. We repeated the performance, all 22 guns (they are in pairs) pumping shots into the leader. He fell burning. The rest, evidently impressed by our shooting pulled away and we were not molested again.

"But then we had other troubles. The long flight out, the search, the action and the long flight home was extending us further than we should have been able to fly. We leaned our mixtures, slowed down and trimmed for the most efficient angle of attack, to stretch our range to the utmost.

"During that whole last hour I was virtually holding up my own and every other plane in that formation, with my hands."

Commander Ault and his three comrades climbed up and rejoined their two-plane fighter escort as they started home. Before they had cleared the fleet area they were attacked by more than 20 Zeros. The fighter

Double .30 Cal. MGs

pilots, Lieut. Richard S. Bull, and his wingman Ensign Bain, were both lost fighting hard to protect their charges. Then one by one the scouts were dropped, three of the four going down.

The last we heard from Commander Ault he reported by radio he was making a forced landing on the sea. He said his rear gunner was severely wounded, his plane badly shot up, and he himself had been struck by a bullet. When men go down like this hopes are held that they can get ashore on some of the myriad islands in these seas. Many have done so.

Although separated from the *Lexington*'s groups, the torpedo and dive-bomber planes from Carrier II were also busy. When they arrived where the Japanese were cruising, they too found a carrier. This one was part of a big fleet, and undamaged—therefore obviously a different carrier than the one hit by the *Lexington*.

What this division of our planes saw and did was told well by Lieut. E. S. McCusky, one of four fighters that escorted Carrier II's unit of nine torpedo planes. The other fighter pilots with McCusky were Lieuts. Leonard and Woolen and Ensign Adams. They took off at 9:30 A.M., joined their formation, and had an uneventful flight to the bad-weather area.

"We sighted the enemy at 11:30. They were steering a course of 180 degrees, speed 25 knots. As we approached they were racing to get into the rain. We came round their port quarter at an altitude of 2,000 feet, our torpedo planes meanwhile flying down low.

"When the Japanese ships came into better view I saw three battleships and two carriers, with a numerous accompanying screen of vessels. The Japanese opened anti-aircraft fire and as the torpedo planes deployed for attack close to the sea I could see big pillars of water being kicked up by salvos fired from the cruisers' main batteries." (These must have been 6- and 8-inch guns, weapons ordinarily never used against aircraft. They were fired at the ocean surface so that a skip or burst would raise a column of water in front of a swift-flying torpedo plane. Should a plane hit such a water column it would be wrecked.)

"Thirty seconds later I saw three Zeros above, preparing to attack. I closed up and overshot, flying on past Leonard whom I was attempting to warn. The first Jap dived on me from above and behind. I applied full throttle and made a steep climbing turn toward him. As he fired, his tracer zipped behind my plane. A few seconds later I saw him pull up in front of me, smoke, hesitate, then fall away in flames. Evidently he had been hit by one of our fighters, I believe by Lieut. Leonard.

"At the same time I scissored another fighter who attacked, and his fire fell behind. As he climbed for another dive I kicked my plane around, pulled up and shot 400 rounds into him. He did not attack but turned and staggered into a cloud with smoke trailing. About this time another Zero attacked me from above. As I

was almost at stalling speed I took avoiding action by
diving into a cloud. Entering it I saw three other Zeros
beneath me and astern."

In the dive-bomber group of Carrier II was Ensign
J. H. Jorgenson who took up where McCusky dropped
his story.

"As we circled over the enemy we saw two carriers, two battleships, three heavy cruisers, three light
cruisers and a number of destroyers that seemed to be
opening out. They were doing 25 knots and spread over
an area of sea, five miles long and three to four miles
wide.

"At 11:34 our group dived on the starboard carrier.
The squadron skipper, Lieut. Commander William O.
Burch, led and I followed. We dived and released below 2,000 feet. I saw the skipper's bomb hit flush on
the carrier's deck amidships near the Island. While clos-
ing my diving flaps as I pulled out, the plane was hit
by anti-aircraft fire.

"It lurched and started into a left spin. After recovery I saw a shell hole through my left aileron and wing.
Fabric quickly ripped off and the wiring and tubing
protruded. As I gained a climbing attitude three fighters
jumped my tail. Their bullets peppered the plane, especially the wings and front end of the fuselage.

"Some passed in over my right shoulder and tore the
rear of my telescopic sight away. Others hit the back of
the seat and more came into the cockpit wrecking most
of my instruments. One bullet passed through the oxy-
gen tube lying on my forearm causing the tube to
smoke. Three bullets hit or grazed my right leg and I
got some shrapnel or powder burn in feet and toes.

"The plane flew very hard, the left wing being heavy.
I flew through clouds and saw my radioman shoot down
one fighter. Three more attacked from ahead and above.
One came in head-on and I fired into him until he
veered off smoking.

"After this attack my engine began to lose power,
missing on one or two cylinders. So I joined a group of
SBDs (more dive bombers) and followed them home.
Arriving I tried to lower my wheels with my flaps
down. But when I did this the plane dropped off quick-

Douglas SBD

ly. I then notified the carrier I was going to land in the water. I went into the sea near a destroyer, hit the water at 12:48 and was picked up at 12:52. The doctor aboard treated my leg.

"I desire to recommend Brunnetti, my radioman, for shooting down an enemy fighter and for good work at all times."

These are just samples of what happened to individual airmen with Carrier II's groups; collectively they did a good job on the Jap carrier on which they concentrated. It seemed that they ignored the port carrier of the two in sight, when first they arrived and bent all their efforts on the starboard ship. The battleships were completely ignored as being not worth wasting bombs on until air opposition was destroyed.

Seven of their 1,000-pound bombs and four torpedoes were rammed into the carrier which was left burning. The least assumption from the damage done would be that this carrier was gutted by fire. There can be little doubt, however, that it was sunk.

One of the most determined and gallant acts of the entire five-day battle came during this engagement. Lieut. John J. Powers, one of the pilots in our Carrier II's dive-bombing group, had told his comrades he was going to put his big bomb into a Japanese carrier "come hell or high water." Powers' dive was watched by a number of other pilots who remembered what he had said.

They related that he held his plane straight for the Japanese deck until he was down to 500 feet—point-blank range even for a dive bomber. There he released his bomb and commenced his recovery to normal flight.

The big bomb with its 700 pounds of high explosive sped true to its mark. The resulting explosion shattered not only the Japanese ship but also Powers' plane which had not cleared the blast area.

"There is no question that John knew what he was doing," one of his fellow pilots told me. "He knew that if you go below about 700 feet in your recovery, the blast from a 1,000 pounder will get you every time.

"To stay above 700 feet means you must release your bomb not lower than 1,000 feet. He held his to 500 and was probably below 300 when the explosion came. He just decided not to miss, God bless him."

The pilots told many more stories. Every one was replete with more action, more thrills and more destruction of planes than the wildest pulp-magazine thriller ever dreamed up. But in this case every one was true. And invariably they were told in the most self-effacing manner possible, by men who were proud of their flying mates but mentioned their own deeds as impersonally as though they themselves had had nothing to do with them.

12

UNDER SKY ATTACK

After we fired our air "shot" at the Japs at 9:30 that morning I wandered up on the signal bridge and stood around. Our flotilla was in tight formation, charging northeast at 20 knots on the trail of our planes. There were several reasons for this, the principal one being that of reducing the length of their flight back to the carrier. In going out more than 200 miles to hit the Japanese, they were operating at the extreme limit of their range and needed any help we could give to shorten that return trip.

Capt. Sherman who was living on the bridge in his emergency cabin in these days told me we had steam raised so that our speed could be stepped up to 30 knots at short order, should this be deemed necessary. We sat in his quarters speculating on what the morning might hold for us.

"There's a possibility," he said, "that the striking forces from both sides (ours and the Japanese) are right now in the air flying to the attack, and that both will get through.

"I feel that at the present time an air attack group cannot be stopped. It's likely that the position will be similar to that of two boxers, both swinging a knockout punch at the same time, and both connecting."

Later in the day I was to think of these words and the accuracy with which they summed up the situation. The Captain knew his stuff, and very evidently had weighed all the chances. He was fully aware of the facets in this sea-air war that is so new to the rest of the world but not to these two opponents.

The bridge of an aircraft carrier is the place from

which to see the action, because everything of importance occurs either in the air around the ship or on the
long, narrow flight deck that stretches away toward the
bow and the stern. The signal bridge on the *Lex* was a
six-foot-wide "open verandah" around the Island on the
starboard side. It was 25 feet above the flight deck
which itself rose 50 feet above the sea. Ten or twelve
feet above the signal bridge was a smaller open verandah affording the Admiral and his staff a post of observation. Finally, above that was a tiny little "crow's
nest" known as the "sky forward" lookout.

The Island was a light, unarmored structure. From
the deck, about 30 feet behind the Island, arose the vast
smoke funnel, which consolidated within its steel false-
structure the tubes carrying smoke and fumes from
the ship's 16 huge boilers, from her ventilating system,
and from her galleys. The funnel was carried to 60 feet
above the flight deck and around its upper rim was an
iron catwalk with a platform at either end. The after
platform was a lookout position known as "sky aft."
Round the catwalk were searchlights, signal lights, cam-
era mounts for the ship's photographers, and other
posts.

The signal bridge is the Captain's Country. Connected
to it from every compartment in the ship are telephone
lines and voice tubes. It is the heart and brain of the
ship. Everything that happens on the vessel is reported
directly to the captain. From inside the ship the reports
come by telephone. From outside, where lookouts and
signalmen always are on duty, they come in the form of
notes written on signal pads. The bridge itself extends
clear around the Island. The enclosed portion to the
bow is the wheelhouse where the helmsmen and officer of the watch are forever on duty. With them are
messengers.

The captain's emergency cabin is just behind the
wheelhouse. And behind that again is the chartroom—
the office of the ship's Navigating Officer.

This morning the bridge was "stripped" for action.
It meant that the heavy plate-glass windows around
the wheelhouse had been unlatched and slid down into
the sills leaving it open all around.

Today the ship's navigating officer, Commander James R. Dudley, was on duty in the wheelhouse, where he was noting every change of course. With him were Commander Seligman, the ship's executive officer and the communications officer Commander Winthrop Terry. Outside on the bridge was the ship's air officer, Commander Herbert ("Ducky") Duckworth and Lieut. Commander Edward H. Eldredge, ship's air staff. Marines, orderlies and signalmen made the bridge a crowded place.

In the chartroom an ensign, and the Chief Quartermaster logged in the permanent "big book," the speed and direction of the ship with every change, plus the time these changes were made.

A stranger looking on could not have identified the officers from the enlisted men. Everyone habitually there was deeply tanned. And everyone, from the Admiral down to the newest orderly, that morning wore working clothes. For Admiral Fitch and Capt. Sherman this consisted of khaki, Navy issue canvas windbreakers with a zipper front over a khaki shirt, cotton drill trousers of khaki, and battle bonnets, the new round-head type steel helmets.

So was everyone else on the bridge wearing helmets and either blue denim coveralls or khaki shirt and pants. The helmets are particularly good in the tropics because they have a papier-mâché liner which can be worn as a sun helmet when there is no danger of flying fragments. But today, by order, everyone on the flight deck or above wore a helmet. And everyone had to keep near by his post the Navy issue life jacket. Most of these are kapok vests. The fliers, and anyone with wings which included the Captain, Seligman and, of course, everyone connected with flying operations, had the new rubberized "Mae Wests" which can be inflated either with little compressed gas bottles—the kind you use in a soda siphon—or blown up by lung power. These are worn deflated until needed.

Early in the morning I met the Chaplain hunting through the cabins for a battle bonnet. He had obtained permission of Commander Seligman to watch from the bridge whatever action came our way. The permission, however, was contingent upon his being able to find a helmet. It turned out that he wasn't able to procure one and so missed a grandstand view of the last and greatest battle that the *Lexington* fought.

Capt. Sherman had a little solid black cocker spaniel, named Admiral Wags, aboard ship with him. Normally Wags was always at the Captain's heels. But as the little pup was terrified by the sound of the ship's guns whenever these were fired, he was put on an extended leash anchored in the skipper's emergency bedroom. The line was just long enough to allow him to poke his nose into the chartroom or see onto the bridge. This arrangement was his battle station. He was put there about 10 o'clock and for some time afterward he showed a mournful nose and ear at the door. It was here that I found him after the Jap attack subsided, and where after a fresh bowl of water and a pet, I was able to quiet him down.

In addition to zigzagging the *Lexington* was frequently moving out of the center of the fleet formation when she turned into the wind—which happened to be about north-northwest—to launch or take aboard aircraft of her defense screen. This meant a left turn for the big ship every time, and frequently carried her outside of the cruiser and destroyer screen on our port side. These ships were holding their fleet position and disregarding the *Lexington*'s maneuvers.

Capt. Sherman had at his command, for the defense of his vessel, eight fighters and eight scouts. A similar force had been retained by Carrier II. And in addition to the primary job of guarding the carriers (inevitably the most important targets) these planes also were guarding to some extent the escort vessels in the flotilla.

This day Capt. Sherman cut his fighter and scout groups in half. Four fighters and four scouts were aloft constantly while their counterparts were refueling on deck, rotating at brief intervals so all could fight at any time with maximum loads of fuel and ammunition. The fighters with their supercharged engines were given the high-level watches whence enemy dive bombers probably would appear, and the scouts were ordered to watch for low-level torpedo planes.

The first alarm on the *Lex* came at 10 o'clock when 12 "ghosts"—unidentified planes—were reported approaching from ahead. These never did come into sight and we never knew who or what they might have been. During the next half hour after we were certain they we not coming our way I dropped below for a cup of coffee. I found the ship absolutely emptied of her crew. Battle stations take every man, right down to the mess boys who pass ammunition, to some fighting post. And I had a quiet few minutes in the senior wardroom.

I returned to the bridge in time to hear the second alarm which came in at 10:50 A.M. One of the scouts called:

"Katie to carrier. Big force of enemy aircraft coming in from right ahead. They are 60 miles away."

The message went out over the ship's loud speaker system and every man aboard instantly realized we were in for a knock-down drag-out battle with the Japanese air squadrons. I remembered that Capt. Sherman, while we were talking in his cabin, had told me he believed the Japs would arrive, if at all, about 11 o'clock. Just one more point on which the skipper was dead right.

The *Lex*, following the Captain's orders, began a port turn into the wind so that all the airplanes then in reserve on the decks could get off. While we were launching the last of our scouts and fighters I looked over at Carrier II, two miles away on our starboard beam, where the same scene was being enacted. Both ships were getting every plane and gun into the air for both captains realized that the only real defense against an airplane is another airplane.

I could feel the change in vibration as the *Lex*'s big propellers speeded up to give us the last knot. This greater speed is needed for swift maneuvering, which is really a ship's best defense. And as I looked down from the bridge into the nests of light automatic cannon on the flight deck, I saw the gun teams standing by their pieces holding extra shell clips and eagerly looking ahead and upward in the direction from which the enemy was expected.

About this time a great deal began to happen.

Thinking back later I realize a thousand and one impressions were registering that I wasn't even conscious of at the time. Chiefly I was busy for the next few minutes getting my microphone and telephone circuits straightened out. With lightning suddenness the fleet was in the direst danger. One minute we had been shouldering our way through the Coral Sea billows in what might have been a pleasure cruise, the next we were prepared to fight for our lives. Such is the speed of sea-air war in this year of our Lord.

Perhaps the only way to give an approximately true picture of the speed of events in the next crowded minutes is to take the timetable of the action as I jotted it into my little pocket notebook as the battle thundered all around. From these jottings, some hours later, I reconstructed everything I had seen and heard, and it is some of this expanded material that the reader will get here.

While we were commencing our starboard turn back into the fleet formation, after having launched our last airplane, we heard the voice of Paul Ramsey coming in over the loudspeakers:

"Agnes to carrier. Enemy planes, 17,000 feet, four groups of nine each. Two groups dive bombers, each with mixed group of Messerschmitt 109s and Zero fighters in escort.

"I'm at 14,000, 12 miles northeast of you climbing hard. They are going awfully fast. Doubt if I can intercept."

Almost simultaneously we had a call from a scout, off in the same direction.

"Nora to carrier. Enemy torpedo planes, Nakajima 97s, spilling out of a cloud eight miles out. They are at 6,000 feet in a steep glide. We're intercepting now."

Red Gill in the fighter control room was calling all our dispersed defense planes, and directed them to concentrate against these oncoming enemies. The loudspeaker was full of orders, calls and notations as the Japs were sighted by our planes and coming closer by the minute.

I can fix the action of the next few minutes accurately from my own and the *Lexington*'s official notes:

Nakajima 97 ("Kate")

11:06 A.M. A huge column of smoke is seen falling into the sea far out on our port beam. Almost instantly we are told a scout has shot down another of those ubiquitous Kawanishi four-motor snoopers. The crew of this big plane evidently has been directing the Jap dive and torpedo bombers toward us. This is the third Kawanishi we downed in four days, every one of them within sight of the fleet. Each one made a beautiful bonfire in the sky and left a heavy smoke trail.

11:15 A.M. The *Lex* still increasing her speed gradually, is not quite back within the fleet formation. There is only one cruiser on our port side, slightly off our quarter. The destroyers and other cruisers that should be covering that side are astern, ahead, or to starboard of us. Might be better if they were keeping station on us rather than on each other.

11:16 A.M. I am watching that cruiser and suddenly see flames and belching smoke as they fire at something I can't see.

Not until seconds later does the thunder clap of the first shots, and then the steady roll of firing, as the cruiser's smaller weapons join in and keep pumping shells reach me. I see winks of flame all over that cruiser from those guns.

11:16½ A.M. "Here they come," sing the lookouts. "Enemy torpedo planes off the port beam." The skipper with a calm glance in that direction speaks quietly to the helmsman: "Hard astarboard." The maneuver is intended to swing the *Lex* so that she will present only her comparatively narrow stern and beam to the torpedo craft. But in comparison to the speed of those diving silver midges I can now discern low behind the cruiser, the gallant old *Lex* seems to be standing still. Even as the captain speaks they are getting larger, and fanning out to cover a wide front as they approach. They are coming in at a sorching pace—I judge that with their dive and wide open throttles they probably are doing almost 300 miles an hour.

As yet the *Lexington*'s guns are silent. Now the gunners are beginning to distinguish the nine planes of this first wave. Two of them are following a course that will bring them right across that blessed cruiser out there, 2,000 yards off our port quarter. These two planes are so low that they have to zoom slightly to pass over her. As they do one disintegrates in the air, simply disappears as if snatched away by some giant magician. Evidently it has been struck by one of the cruiser's heavier shells which also exploded the torpedo. The flash of this Jap blowing up is a beautiful sight: "Pretty shooting, boys. That's one that won't make it."

About this time the *Lexington*'s own batteries of more than 100 guns break into flame. There is the sharp, "Wham, wham, wham, wham, wham" of the 5 inchers, the staccato bark of the 1.1 inchers (37mm) and the rushing yammer of the 20mm batteries. A hellish chorus, uneven, jerky, but so forceful that it leaves us, there on the bridge, gasping in the partial vacuums created by the blasts. Out on the open bridge we are above the gun muzzles and with the first firing our nostrils are stung by the reeking cordite of the driving charges. Up from the port side of the ship goes a curtain of tracer, winking red and white in the brilliant sunlight. Our light automatics are firing.

11:17 A.M. The *Lexington* is still swinging. As her slender stern comes round more and more toward them, the Japs change course slightly, parallel us and when abreast turn once more toward our port beam. They are riding right in on a hail of the smaller weapons' tracer but they don't seem to falter once. Not even the destruction of their leading plane by our cruiser appears to faze them.

By now they are in close to us. The first couple is not more than 800 yards off and the last within about 1,000 yards. We can see the black blobs of the torpedoes fall away from the planes, their splash as they hit the water, and their trailing foam as their own internal machinery begins to drive their twin propellers and sends them shooting on toward us at 50 knots, just under the surface of the sea.

There are still eight of them coming on in spite of our fire. Each one drops its torpedo. But instead of turning away they continue straight on in toward us, with the leading pair right down on the water, so low they have to pull up slightly to get over us, following a track that will pass over the fore part of our flight deck.

Right here I see the results of all our battery training. The forward 1.1 battery has the range on that first Jap. I see their shells, bright crimson tracers, tearing through the wings and fuselage. This plane wavers, begins a slow roll to its left and veers off just enough to pass in an inverted position just under our bow. As it glides by I see flames coming from the tail, and the machine smashes itself into the water 50 feet off our starboard bow.

The port forward 5-inch battery manned by Marines concentrates its fire on the second Jap. As this plane zooms to cross almost directly over these guns, they hit it squarely with a shell. The explosion blows it to bits, its engine plunging into the water almost at the foot of the battery. Shreds of its wings and tail surfaces slither along the carrier's deck like sheets of paper swept in front of a gale. I can't see what happens to the crew —and I'm not interested.

The remaining six silver planes are trying to pass astern. Similar fusillades of fire from our after guns are concentrating on them but they seem to be weathering it and in a second they have zipped past and rapidly are diminishing, snaking in sharp banks to throw off the gunners' aim and staying low as they scuttle away.

This first wave has hardly passed when a second appears. They too come from our port quarter. But instead of being low they are at 1,000 feet or better. I can just make them out, coming down in a 45-degree-angle glide.

11:18½ A.M. The *Lexington* shudders under our feet and a heavy blast spouts mingled flame and water on our port side forward. A torpedo explosion, and we can see the wakes of others streaking toward us. These missiles dropped by those first eight Japs are only just now reaching us. I notice that some of them are porpoising (nosing up out of the water and then diving deeply as if their leveling-control mechanism had been damaged). Their wicked noses look to me like death incarnate. I have the illusion they are alive, and breaking water to peek at us, only to dive again after having made sure of their courses.

11:20 A.M.—"Wham"—again the whole ship is shaken. Another torpedo. And at the same place, on our port bow. Another spout of flame enclosed in sea-water. While we are still staggering under the lurch as the great old ship heaves and shakes itself, a lookout in "sky-forward" (just above the bridge) calls out "dive bombers."

Looking upward into the sun I see the first dive bomber flattening out, having just released its bomb. The plane is very low, no more than about 800 feet and I look up in time to see the long black bomb separate from the plane. There is a terrific "boom" and a blinding flash on the port forward gun gallery. A 1,000-pound bomb has hit among the three 5-inch guns there—wrecking them all, starting a fire, and killing most of the Marines in the gun teams.

The second wave of torpedo planes still untouched by all the fire directed at them are now dropping their fish. They have come on down to about 200 feet off the water and are still 1,000 yards away. I notice that they are not straightening out, nor flying parallel to the water surface when dropping their missiles. Instead they are still in their dive, and going very fast.

This group also comes straight on in toward us, and opens up with their machine guns. Their fire, incidentally, is pretty accurate: it killed and wounded some of the men on our after port gun platforms. Can't see whether any of these planes are finally knocked down by us, I don't know, for the action by now is at white heat, and all around us are geysers of water several hundred feet high from the dive bombers' near misses. The planes themselves are coming over us at not much more than funnel height, all of them bouncing their machine-gun bullets off the decks, the sides of the ships, and the lookout positions. At times the whole deck is sprayed with their bright tracers, but most of this fire seems a little too high to hit the exposed gun crews.

11:21 A.M.—"Baloom!!"—Another torpedo hit. Also on the port side, almost amidships. More torpedoes are coursing toward us, their white wakes ghastly warnings of the disaster in the water. The seas seem full of them on our port side.

This new batch of torpedoes is porpoising even more than the first lot. Two of them appear to be certain to hit us right amidships. The trail behind them shows they have been aimed as bull's-eyes. I glimpse their nasty black noses about 100 yards out. They looked like sure hits. I brace myself for the explosions—but they do not come.

I look out to starboard and see two torpedoes break the surface running away from us, still porpoising. They must have passed right under the ship—which means they dived more than 40 feet because the old *Lex*, loaded down as she is for war, is drawing at least this much.

About this time a light bomb hits the *Lex*'s funnel. It explodes and kills or wounds several men on the catwalk. A moment later some of the dive bombers' machine-gun fire wounds some more men stationed there. All in all this turns out to be a pretty dangerous post in the battle.

In the midst of all this, I'm attempting to dictate into the mike in my left hand and with the other hand make a few scribbles in my notebook while trying to see everything that happens, when a quite illogical thought passes through my mind: "There's so damned much noise here I can't hear any single explosion—it's almost like a complete silence."

Hardly has this thought intruded when there is a new sound—the moaning eerie wail of the *Lexington*'s steam siren. It seems a heavy bomb has passed through the 30-foot gap between the Island and the funnel, missed the ship and fallen into the sea on the starboard side. In its passage it struck and kinked the metal tube in which the lanyard, operating the whistle from the bridge, is housed. This glancing blow bent the tube and pulled the lanyard tight causing the whistle to continue to hoot and moan—the cry of something stricken—which continues until the last of the Japs have passed over us—only then someone turned off the steam.

"Wham!" "Boom!" "Tat-tat-tat-tat!!" "bang, bang, bang, bang" go our anti-aircraft guns. Then a prolonged "Whaaaaaaaaaaa" of the Japanese dive bombers coming down across our deck, all guns blasting. We can see their tracers lacing past, many of them too high to get the deck crews and too low to bother us on the bridge.

Another thought flashes through my mind: "These fellows don't dive bomb like our boys. They aren't coming down as steeply. They're only diving at about a 50-degree angle." As this crosses my brain I see a black blur whip across in front of the Island about bridge high. The object clears the starboard rail by inches, hits the water and explodes. It is one of those big Jap bombs (a thousand pounder) that would have removed all of us from the Island—the main control center of the entire ship, had the ship's 8-inch

Barbettes not been removed at war's beginning, for it passed exactly through space where the Number 2 Barbette used to be.

Instinctively I duck behind the bridge rail as it flashes by. And so does everyone else who see it come. Still squatting down behind the weather shield around the bridge, soaked by the geyser of water thrown up by the bomb blast, I reach out and measure between my thumb and forefinger, the thinness—one-eighth of an inch—of the metal plate. Ensign G. J. Hansen, the signal officer, sees this and reads my mind.

"It's not even waterproof, Mr. Johnston. Won't even keep out the spray," he grins.

11:22 A.M. "Whooom!" once more the *Lexington* lurches—the fourth torpedo hit.

11:22½ A.M. "Baloom! ! !" the fifth torpedo, all on the port side—amidships and forward.

Capt. Sherman is watching the torpedoes and dive bombers and swinging the ship, now to starboard, now to port in a snake dance, in an effort to evade the missiles. His orders to the navigating officer and helmsman continue to be in a tone of voice that might have been used in any drawing room.

About this time I am passing in front of the wheelhouse. The skipper is standing in front of the wheel looking out and listening intently to the reports being made to him from all round. As I pass I catch his eye and brashly enough put my hand out. The Captain takes it and as we shake hands I remark: "I think it's going to be all right, Captain." He smiles back and squeezes my hand: "I hope so, I hope so," he says in his quick quiet way.

Looking out to starboard to see how the rest of the ships are faring I count five planes burning on the water. Japanese planes escaping after having dropped their torpedoes or bombs, are being followed by our starboard guns pouring tracers into and after them. A huge waterspout leaps up near Carrier II, my immediate reaction is "She's hit." (Later I discover it was a near miss by a huge bomb.)

Suddenly I see a Grumman following a Jap as he dives down toward Carrier II. They disappear into the smoke of the umbrella of bursting, heavy anti-aircraft shells and emerge into a literal hail of the machine-gun fire thrown up from her decks. The Jap releases his bomb and begins to flatten out—he bursts into flame as the bullets from our fighter rip into his gas tanks. The Jap flames into the sea and the Grumman zooms back into the fight.

Dive bombers are still coming down, only a second or so apart. Most of the missiles are falling toward the after end of the ship, close, but not quite hitting. Above we see the Jap machines diving in a chain. Watching closely I see the bombs leave each plane. The aircraft follow, gradually flattening out. Their machine guns and wing cannon wink momentarily. Each plane sweeps over the *Lexington*'s deck and then becomes a tiny shape, swiftly diminishing in size as it speeds away.

11:25 A.M. "Seven more torpedo planes from the port side." The lookouts call our anti-aircraft fire is so hot now that the pilots in these planes are anxious to drop their fish and get away. They fail to press home their attack like the first groups. All of them are dropping their torpedoes while still in a 45-degree glide, and more than 200 feet above the water. They then turn away instead of boring in. They never come closer than within 1,500 yards of the *Lex*.

Again we swing to avoid the torpedoes. This time it is back to starboard. All the torpedoes seem to be porpoising badly.

"Hold her steady, Captain, hold her steady," Commander Duckworth suddenly shouts. He is out on the navigation bridge dancing up and down in his excitement, his arms spread out to each beam as if pressing the torpedoes away with his hands. "We've got three alongside—two to port and one to starboard—they are exactly paralleling us.

"If we veer," Ducky yells, "we'll collect one sure." The skipper "holds her" straight, and the torpedoes churn slowly on past us. We are doing 25 knots and they are doing 50 so they seem slow anyway.

11:26 A.M. A signalman reports to Capt. Sherman that one of our airmen (having been forced to bail out during the fighting) is floating on his little yellow inflated raft through the center of the speeding fleet. He is just off our starboard bow and only 100 yards from our track. As we sweep past him I can see him on his knees wildly cheering and waving us on. He is paying absolutely no attention to the Jap aircraft all around us and to the flying anti-aircraft stuff zipping past him from our own guns and other guns in the fleet.

Capt. Sherman glances his way, instantly understanding and over his shoulder directs a signalman to have our plane-guard destroyer—the last one in the fleet— "pick that boy up." This is done. The destroyer draws alongside him, spins quickly and as it slides past, engines in reverse, makes a sharp turn, drops him a line, and jerks him aboard.

11:27 A.M. Five more Jap torpedo planes suddenly appear. In the confusion we have not seen them until they are right in the midst of the fleet. But now our anti-aircraft have opened up on them too. These new enemies are almost at water level. They single us out, spread fanwise and bore into our starboard side—the first attack of the day on our right.

With the entire fleet firing on them they drop their fish a long way out. The old *Lexington*, still charging ahead despite her wounds, turns once again and all these torpedoes miss her, their feathery wakes lacing the water wide off our bow.

Two more Jap planes slide in through the fleet's fire, but these turn aside from the *Lex*, pass astern of us under the barrage of our AA guns, and drop their fish at the cruiser on our port quarter. Accepting the challenge this smartly handled ship swings quickly, avoiding both torpedoes. The cruiser's gun crew, meanwhile, is pouring its stuff at both the planes and someone gets a direct hit on one of them. The plane disappears in a clap of thunder and fire.

Commander Seligman is intently watching the diving Jap planes when a Marine approaches, gives a smart salute, and hands him a paper. The Commander reluctantly takes his eyes off the attackers and hastily reads the message. Crumpling the paper in his hand he disgustedly exclaims: "This is a swell time to worry me with this—as if I didn't have enough disturbance already."

I ask, "What's the bother now?"

Without taking his eyes from the bombers, he replies, "Someone wants me to worry because we have a case of *measles* aboard."

11:32 A.M. The last of the dive bombers roars by, raking us with his machine guns as he passes. His bomb falls close but definitely not aboard. The guns trail him out of sight. Suddenly there is silence. The attack is over and despite the hits suffered the *Lexington* is afloat, steering normally, and her engines are giving Capt. Sherman the speed he asks for.

By now, we have a six-degree list to port, and the lookouts report we are spilling oil in our wake astern. Smoke rising from the gun ports indicates fire inside the hull.

The whole assault has lasted only 16 minutes. More than 103 Japanese aircraft have passed over us. Our gunners have made an all-time record by shooting down 19 of the Jap planes—19 that we could see— from the *Lexington*'s decks. How many more were so badly damaged that they crashed after passing over the horizon, we will never know.

*   *   *

Ten minutes after the attack ended and while our gunners still had itchy trigger fingers, one of our scouts came back. He was flying somewhat erratically and went immediately into the landing circle with wheels and hook down—the landing signal. As the plane flew the downward leg of the landing circle some of our after-port machine gunners fired a few shots in its direction. They were stopped by others who recognized the type and the insignia.

The plane came up astern, too high and too fast, and though waved off by the landing officer the flier cut his motor, dropped down on the wet, sloping deck, bounced once, touched the left wing tip and then flipped over the port side. This plane was flown by Ensign R. F. McDonald with C. H. O. Hamilton as rear gunner. The two had formed part of our anti-torpedo-plane screen and had been in some hot air fighting over the horizon. While duelling, McDonald had been badly wounded in the shoulder and was now trying to land before he lost consciousness.

The wound was in his right shoulder (his stick shoulder) and in the ensuing crash he broke his right arm as well. Both men were picked out of the sea by our plane-guard destroyer coming along behind us. McDonald was sent to a naval hospital to recover from his hurts. And Hamilton was not injured.

Now the fighters and scouts began coming back. They were being rearmed and refueled and sent off once more—because we had no assurance there would not be another Jap wave.

Shortly after noon Commander Brett's torpedo squadron returned. As they flew forward on our starboard to get into the landing circle, one of our destroyers let fly a few rounds at them. Fortunately, all these shots missed and the over-anxious gunner was quieted.

Brett's 11-plane squadron had only 10 planes when it landed. All his boys had come through the attack safely except the missing plane which was forced down into the sea, with dry fuel tanks 30 miles out. A destroyer was sent to get the crew and all three were picked up.

The stories of the airfighting which took place in defense of the *Lex* began to filter in as reports from our patrols were brought to the bridge. They indicated that our air screens were probably more important to the defense of the ship than the anti-aircraft fire.

Ramsey and his fighters had told us earlier that they tried, unsuccessfully, to intercept the first two units of Jap dive bombers. They never caught these planes because the Japs were above and ahead of Ramsey before they were seen. The fighter escort of the following wave of Jap dive bombers mixed it with Ramsey's units.

One of our fighter pilots told how Ramsey had found himself momentarily in an advantageous firing position near one of the Japanese Messerschmitts in the ensuing melee. He dived on it and fired almost all his ammunition before it started to fall in a spin. In Ramsey's own words:

Kawasaki Ki 61 Hien ("Tony")

"That fellow was all painted up with yellow and red stripes. He looked like a Christmas tree, almost too pretty to shoot at, but I thought I'd better try him. He never did burn and he took an awful lot of shooting. If they're all going to be like that it's going to be tough to collect these things."

Because the fighters missed the dive bombers the real air defense was done by the scouts. Our losses among these defenders were heavy and we never will know the full stories of the sanguinary dueling in which they were downed. But from the survivors came reports of deeds of great valor.

Lieut. Hall, one of the scouts who made the initial interception of the torpedo planes, shot down two of the first nine he encountered. While he was battling these planes, five Zeros, probably the escort of the Jap torpedo craft—Kogekiki 97s—jumped him. Hall turned so effectively on the Zeros that he got two of them. His report of the fight regretfully ended: "The other three escaped into a cloud." In the latter part of this fight Hall was wounded in both feet by the Zeros but never let the wounds interfere with his fighting.

Our friends Lieut. Leppla and Gunner Liska were in the thick of this action too. These boys who on the 7th had bombed an enemy carrier and knocked down four Jap planes, were out in the torpedo-defense screen. They intercepted a group of the Kogekikis and knocked one down. Immediately they were surrounded by a flight of Zeros and in the fight shot down one Zero and drove several others off, after getting damaging bursts home on the targets. They wrote in their reports that they "broke off action when the right forward gun was shot up and the magazine of the left forward gun was empty." (There are only two forward firing guns on the scouts.)

Limping back to the *Lex* they were again attacked by two enemy fighters. Using only the rear guns, this team managed to drive them off, one with its engine smoking badly and obviously damaged.

In another fight Ensign W. E. Wolke intercepted one of the Kogekikis and shot it down. Ensign R. F. Neely got into another torpedo formation and downed two planes.

Four scouts from Carrier II were shot down by a large Zero formation while they were attacking incoming Jap torpedo bombers. Just then a four plane fighter group of our Grummans came into the area and in turn jumped the Zeros. Five of these Zeros were knocked down in two passes made by the avenging American pilot.

Lieut. Gayler, whom we left in the last chapter returning from the attack on the Japanese fleet after a prolonged duel in which he won victories over two Zeros, collected two more Japanese planes before he got home to the *Lex*. These were Japanese Kogekikis flying back toward their own base. Gayler saw them pass, turned and gave chase. He managed to shoot them both down with the last of his ammunition.

These four victories in one single flight raised this pilot's war score to eight clean kills, most of them against enemy fighter craft. In addition he received credit for bombing an enemy anti-aircraft installation at Salamaua. When he alighted on the *Lexington* the afternoon of May 8th he was the Navy's leading air ace with three more confirmed victories than "Butch" O'Hare, his squadron mate.

Lieut. Morgan and two wingmen, also flying fighters on escort duty with the *Lexington*'s dive bombers, had lost contact with their charges, as you may remember from the last chapter. They returned to the *Lex* in time to jump into the battle. Morgan intercepted the dive bombers but was himself attacked by their Zero escorts. He set one on fire and saw it crash into the sea. The Japanese craft, he reported, had a belly tank in addition to its regular fuel to give it greater range.

A summary of all the day's air fighting—including battles over the Jap fleet, along the 200-mile sea and air route that was flown by all the forces, and finally the fighting around the *Lexington*—showed that the American flyers had downed 63 Japanese planes. Nineteen of these were downed by the *Lexington*'s guns and 44 by our aircraft. We lost 16 planes, eight from the *Lexington* and eight from Carrier II. The Japanese lost one third of their planes according to the best estimates we were able to make.

13

THE LEXINGTON GOES
TO GLORY

While the flight deck crews were busy servicing the *Lexington*'s air-defense planes, Capt. Sherman on the bridge began getting the first reports from below decks by approximately 11:45. They came from men who had spent the battle period in engine rooms, battery rooms, the hospital, the various hull compartments and all the departments necessary for the efficient functioning of a ship.

These men, officers, and crew, had been busy long before the battle was ended, trying to offset the damage the Japanese inflicted on the *Lexington*. Their work began with the fall of the first close bombs and the first torpedo hits. It involved foremost a checkup on all compartments, to isolate those flooded from the rest. It meant they had to struggle, often far below the waterline, cutting and jamming timbers to strengthen bulkheads against the rush and pressure of the invading sea.

The first torpedoes exploded against the "torpedo bulges" up toward the port bow. A torpedo bulge is a false hull constructed along the sides of the ship below the waterline. It is like a blister and is outside the main hull within which the ship's real buoyancy is contained. These blisters are sometimes full of water, often full of some light, noninflammable filling. They are intended solely to provide a wall around the ship against which torpedoes or mines may hit, and explode well away from the real hull.

Naturally such blisters cannot offset hits entirely. The blast tears an enormous hole in the blister, usually punches a smaller hole in the main hull, springs plates and pops rivets or tears near-by welding. But this secondary damage usually impairs a big vessel only to a minor extent; if there were no blisters a hole 10 to 20 feet in diameter might be torn in the main skin.

The *Lexington* had another protection against torpedo blasts consisting of the vessel's enormous oil, gasoline, and water tanks. These were deep vertical tanks running parallel to the side of the ship just inside the hull. Forces applied to the outer skin were often dissipated against the fluids in these tanks. And there was the compartmentation of the hull, a last defense.

The *Lexington* had 600 compartments which could be closed off with watertight doors and hatches. As soon as a leak developed in one of the hull compartments, attempts would be made to plug it. If it was too large or impossible to reach, the doors to this compartment would be closed and the surrounding bulkheads shored up. In effect these bulkheads and doors then became the ship's side because they were keeping out the sea.

In speaking of torpedoes it should be remembered that these deadly weapons do not penetrate a blister-protected warship's main hull before exploding, as does an armor-piercing bomb or shell. A torpedo hits at only 50 knots' velocity and its supersensitive detonator in its nose bursts the warhead-load of explosive at the instant of contact against a ship's side. Consequently the blast does not reach into the ship's vitals but is expended against the protected outside hull.

In the case of the *Lexington*, five torpedoes struck her within a four-minute period, all of them on the port side forward of amidships. In one section two of these hits were so close together that the second torpedo seriously damaged the main hull. The net total of loss of buoyancy, plus the weight of water that entered many of the damaged port-side compartments caused the list (about 6 degrees) mentioned earlier.

Commander ("Pop") Healy with several hundred men in his department had the specific task of tending to all hull damage. While the *Lex* was still in combat they were working on repairs and those first accounts of the situation below deck were now (about noon) coming to the Captain. Commander Healy reported that explosions among our own 5-inch ammunition, ignited by the heavy bomb on the port 5-inch forward guns, started fires in the Admiral's country; these were being controlled and soon would be out. Their structural damage was immaterial to the ship as a whole.

Healy was also optimistic as to the harm done the hull by the torpedo attack and by the "mining" effect of the heavy bombs that hit close alongside our hull. He was able to state that the compartments were holding and bulkheads strengthened. His men were then busy trying to get things "shipshape" in the compartments adjoining those damaged.

He promised Capt. Sherman that the slight list which meant little as far as navigating the *Lexington* was concerned but was an annoyance and possible source of danger for flying operations, would soon be leveled. He had crews already pumping fuel oil from some of our port tanks into empty ones in the starboard side. This shifting of weight which can be controlled almost to an ounce, would bring us level in about an hour. He had just one plea:

"I would suggest, Captain," he closed his summary, "that if you must take any more torpedoes, take them on the starboard side."

So well functioned the damage crews that when the first planes of our air-striking force returned at about 12:40 from their mission against the Jap force, some 200 miles distant, the pilots couldn't tell from the air that we had been through an attack. Many were surprised after alighting to hear that we had been bombed, torpedoed and hit repeatedly by what seemed to be the entire Japanese naval air force.

The flight deck of the *Lexington* had not suffered in the attack except for a small ragged hole in its edge beside the port 5-inch gun gallery where the heavy bomb had struck. By the time our flyers came back the planes on deck had been wheeled up to the bow, their wings hiding this minor damage. (All landings onto a carrier are made over the stern.) The slight damage to the deck near the guns in no way interfered with the launching of planes, as it was confined to the outer six feet of the deck's edge. (The entire deck at that point was more than 100 feet wide.)

There was no decrease in the *Lexington*'s cruising speed either. She was holding her position with the fleet, doing 25 knots, and could have gone faster, according to Commander Heine Junkers, the Chief Engineer. He reported that one of the bombs that fell close to the ship near the tail (at the time he had thought it was a torpedo hit because the blast shook the vessel so viciously) put three of his fire rooms temporarily out of action. An hour's repair had brought them back into use and now all 16 boilers were again available.

On the bridge the satisfactory reports from below and the fact that everything aboard was operating in a normal manner, roused considerable optimism. An officer told me that the designers of the *Lex* had claimed she could take 10 torpedoes and still float. It seemed they were right. Nothing appeared to be seriously the matter with the old girl even now. Those near misses—the bombs which exploded close alongside and shook us so violently—having exactly the same effect as mines (and we had more than 10 of those) had not affected her at all, he claimed.

The *Lex*'s medical organization attended to our battle casualties all over the ship. The explosion at the 5-inch forward battery killed many men, and burned, shocked and wounded others. The doctors treated these wounded as they were brought away from the gallery where fire still raged, and gave them first aid in the passageways. Then they were sent forward (400 feet and two decks below) to the ship's hospital right up in the bow.

There were numerous other casualties, some amongst the Marines on the port aft 5-inch guns, from machine-gun fire and bomb fragments. Steel singing aboard from near misses had cost us men all along the gun decks. Several were killed and injured on the "sky aft" funnel position—again from machine-gun slugs and splinters —and a number had been overcome by fumes and shock in the ship's decoding room, and the Supply Executive Department.

The medical crews were having great difficulty in

getting the injured down from the funnel catwalk. Lines were rigged, the steel "cage" stretchers were hauled up and men who had already been given first aid, lashed into them and lowered 60 feet to the flight deck. These stretchers were also useful for helping to get the men around twisting and tortuous spiral steel stairways into the lower decks.

From among those I knew well aboard the first one hurt was jovial Commander Walter Gilmore (you may remember him as the Grand Inquisitor in the wardroom as we crossed the Line). The Executive Officer, who went below as soon as the first torpedoes hit, found him on the floor in the cabin next to the decoding room. This room was situated only 50 feet away from the point where that 1,000 pounder hit us. The blast had swept right across this deck tearing down the steel bulkheads that divided the deck into cabins.

In the room where Gilmore lay the steel-cabin separations had been pushed over and it was the hot breath of this blast that felled him. Chaplain Markle, one of Gilmore's closest friends, immediately gave him artificial respiration in the hope that the blast had merely stunned him. The Chaplain worked over him until Dr. White came along from the hospital and told him Gilmore was beyond all help. In the same cabin orderlies had found a few minutes earlier the body of Commander Wadsworth C. Trojakowski, the ship's dental surgeon. Both men had been together when the explosion occurred.

Much of this wreckage included the Admiral's Quarters where my cabin was. Immediately after the attack I came down to get my typewriter and found all of this section devastated, still burning and soaked with chemical fire-extinguishing fluid. Before the battle hundreds of 5-inch shells had been stacked all around to be near that (since bombed) gun position; these were now scattered throughout the whole section.

Relatively few of them were exploded but the continuing fire and heat caused their charges to swell. This pushed the projectile out of the brass powder cases of scores of them. Shortly after the projectile would fall away the fire would get to the powder charges and

burn with a great rushing "*Sssssssssssss*" throwing out a
searing tail of flame. They reminded me of the giant
firecrackers we used to break in half and then light to
see the powder hiss and burn.

When I saw this wreckage I enquired if anyone had
seen Duke, the Admiral's pantry boy with whom I
had become friendly during the time he took care of my
cabin. I knew Duke had no other battle duty except to
be in attendance upon the Admiral. During alerts he
used to sit in the tiny little pantry and play his accordion. When we searched, we found him there, killed
by the first blast.

Some of the happenings below as seen through the
eyes of Chaplain Markle follow:

"I arrived on the main deck (two below the flight
deck) to find dust and smoke drifting through the passageways coming from further aft. In the passageway
amidships I found four men who were nearly naked
looking for help. They were horribly burned. A Fili-
pino cook who was there assisted me to get the men on
the cots in the passageway and take off the remainder of
their clothes, give them a drink of water and a morphine injection. A hospital corpsman came along and
treated their burns with tannic acid jelly and took
over their care.

"Men kept coming in from the 5-inch gun galleries,
sometimes alone, others with the help of a comrade.
We had about 12 men on the cots and during a brief lull
I went to the gun galleries to see what had happened.
There I saw several bodies; they seemed to have been
frozen or charred into grotesque statues. Capt. Hauser
(Capt. Ralph L. Hauser, United States Marine Corps)
was there with a few surviving Marines manning Number 2 gun which was still able to fire."

At this time we felt we had the ship squared away
once more and we were pounding on northward intending to close in for another attack during the afternoon.
We had destroyed the enemy's carriers—eliminating his
air defense—and now the rest of the fleet would be
"cold meat" for the fliers. I was sitting in the navigating
cabin, writing up the events of the morning from my
notes when there came a jolt heavier than any of the

explosions during the battle. Then from deep down inside the ship resounded the dull rumble of an explosion. It was just 12:45 P.M.

The only other occupant of the room at the time was Chief Quartermaster Solomons. He was tending the ship's "big book" and he carefully noted the fact of the jolt and the time, along with his other information.

I looked at him. He looked at me. Each could see mirrored in the eyes of the other the unspoken question: "What *was* that?" I hurried below to see whether it was a mine, torpedo, or some of our own ammunition.

There was no one in the wardroom, so I turned toward the junior officers' mess, three decks below the flight deck. There was a glow of fire. A gang of men were moving about with portable chemical extinguishers, and leading hose lines down. I had no smoke mask and the air was getting pretty thick with fumes and dense smoke clouds. It forced me to return to the wardroom where I met some officers who had been on an inspection trip.

"We think it was a sleeper bomb," they told me. "Probably one that hit us during the attack, penetrated to the lower decks and only just now exploded."

But this we soon learned was wrong. The first explosion was followed in 20 minutes by a second. Each one left fires behind it. The blazes began to spread throughout the lower region and within a short time the full extent of that first internal blast's damage became visible.

The explosion had occurred in the vicinity of "Central Station." Central station is the room from which all damage control is directed. It was Pop Healy's office and he was in it at the time. The blast killed Pop, and a number of his men who were on duty in that section. It marked the end of the combat phase of the battle with the Japanese, but was only the beginning of an even grimmer, more bloody trial of the *Lexington*'s officers and men.

During the next five hours we suffered more casualties than we had in all the fighting against the Japanese. The bravery and gallantry of the crew was above and beyond the sort of valor that actuates men in the heat of killing.

These men already had been smashed and blitzed by 103 Japanese planes that did their darndest. But now, attacked from within by subtle enemies that fed upon the fuels and stores within the great valiant old ship, they rose to a second desperate fight. With dogged determination and unshakable courage all members of the ship's company, from the humblest to the highest, strove together in a long, torturing, and deadly hazardous effort.

If they had but known that the first shattering internal blast sounded the *Lexington*'s death knell! They didn't or refused to recognize it. For hours their efforts, in which flesh was seared from bone, in which men repeatedly were smashed to death against steel decks and bulkheads, as more and more explosions followed with ever increasing frequency, warded off the heartbreaking finish.

Many of them who fought on with such downright guts, and completely without heroics, and without the compensation (the satisfaction of shooting back) that battle brings, had been in the Navy for only a few months. They were choking and burning as they strove, unseen, deep inside the smoke-filled galleries of the lower decks. They were aware every second that the *Lexington*'s own ammunition stores might shatter her at any moment sending them to the bottom with her. Yet they never faltered; they battled on unselfishly.

At least 600 aboard were on their first sea cruise. When the fight was over the oldest tried sea dogs in the crew, from the CPOs (Chief Petty Officers) to the captain, declared that these as yet unsalted tars had behaved like "man-o'-warsmen"—the fighting Navy's highest tribute.

No one person could have seen all there was to see aboard the *Lexington* during these final hours. I saw what I could and made straggling notes that later served merely to jog the memory. I talked to many Lexmen and among them to Lieut. H. E. Williamson who was standing just outside the doorway to Central Control when the main blast shook us.

"There was a terrific explosion that seemed to be either in the Internal Communications (telephone switchboard) or Central Station," he reported. "The concussion hurled me against the guard rail which broke and against the switchboard. Immediately following the explosion a gale of wind with the force of a hurricane blew through the door from Central and pinned me to the board. The wind seemed to be made up of streams of flame and myriads of sparks, very similar to the flames of an explosion in a gasoline engine cylinder.

"The flames were between a cherry red and white, and the sparks were crimson. The gale lasted for only a few seconds and left nothing but heavy choking fumes. I was already partially blinded by the flash and could not breathe because of the fumes. There were cries from the surrounding rooms, so I shouted at the top of my voice: 'Take it easy and hold your breath, and we'll all get out.' "

Williamson said the lights remained on but the corridors were so filled with the smoke and fumes that it was impossible to see far. He and the other men with him climbed out of the scuttle into the hangar deck and called for help. Crews came and began dragging out the injured and those overcome at Central Control, when, as Williamson tells it, the second blast occurred:

"After about five minutes I again went down the scuttle and was standing over it when a minor explosion occurred seemingly in the machine shop, and smoke and flames came out onto the deck. I reported to the chief engineer that it must be gas fumes that were igniting. Eleven men were brought out of that room through the efforts of Lieut. Frederick W. Hawes and Ensign Rockwell. Lieut. Hawes was overcome by smoke twice but went back each time to direct his men."

Williamson said the crews used plane-handling dollies to remove the burned and injured to the after end of the hangar deck. While engaged in this two more concussions occurred below.

His conclusion that the blasts were gas fumes, was borne out by the later analysis of our engineers. Their investigation showed the first explosion had been caused by the ignition of the highly volatile vapors escaping from our damaged 100 octane gasoline tanks which seeped through fractured bulkheads.

This first heavy blast tore strong steel watertight doors from their hinges and twisted massive steel hatches from bolts, thus opening up the decks below the water line. Particularly it smashed down every steel door in the compartments extending forward from Central Control right through the Junior Officers' Mess, the Chief Petty Officers' Mess, and to the main hospital 300 feet away right in the bow.

As soon as the blast punched open these airtight compartments the gaps allowed air to circulate freely. The air assisted combustion and fires on all the lower decks increased in intensity. Smashed doors and hatches prevented the burning quarters from being isolated until they burned out.

The fires could not be shut off any longer, nor could they be extinguished with water, because the explosion had shattered the water mains that fed the fire hoses on these decks. Pumps—small electrically operated auxiliary pumps that were scattered all over the ship to provide pressure in any area—were useless without water.

Then, before extra lengths of hose could be led in from undamaged sections of the ship, the fires consumed the electric mains, cutting off light and power where they were needed most. Hoses from remote auxiliary pumps still operating did not supply nearly enough water. All the available chemical extinguishers were rushed into use but it was a losing and discouraging battle, for no sooner would the Damage Control make progress in one place than another explosion would occur and extend the burning area.

By this time the engineers were aware that the main fire was being fed from huge storage tanks in a section which could not be flooded. And the increase in frequency and violence of the explosions indicated all these blasts were further damaging the storage-tank bulkheads, allowing a faster seepage of fuel oil and gasoline. This was evaporating in the heated air and either feeding the fire direct or forming vapor pockets that soon exploded and multiplied the damage still further.

The first concussion that swept through the hospital threw Dr. White through a door to the deck fracturing an ankle and severely injuring his shoulder. The doctor dragged himself back on his feet, however, and for the next three hours, while refusing to have his own hurts tended, he directed the hospital's work.

Dense smoke rolled into the infirmary through the smashed compartments within a few minutes after that first blast. All patients were moved amidships to the Captain's quarters two decks above, where an emergency ward was set up. Two hours later they were driven out once more as the fire continued to spread through the *Lexington*'s interior. This time they were moved to the forward flight deck from where they ultimately were taken aboard a destroyer that came alongside.

The first interference with the ship's navigation developed when the blast destroyed the telephone switchboard, disrupting communications throughout the ship. Speaking tubes were still in operation from the bridge to the engine room and to one or two other departments, but for the rest of the ship, messengers had to be used.

The second interference came when the fire consumed the main electric cables—perhaps an hour later (about 1:50), putting the electric steering controls, centralized at the bridge, out of action.

Normally the *Lexington* was steered without a wheel and chains. A small hand lever—not unlike the power control of a street-car motorman's—was electrically connected to a pair of motors right in the lowest reach of the ship in the aft compartment. Its movement on the bridge started one or the other and they in turn operated a huge hydraulic ram that moved the ship's vast rudder.

With the burning away of the main cables there was no method of controlling the ship's movements except by manning the auxiliary steering apparatus or "trick" wheel located in a blind position near the great rams.

As long as the auxiliary speaking tube from the bridge to the trick wheel was functioning Capt. Sherman found the *Lex* could be handled satisfactorily. Soon, however, the speaking tube also was destroyed by flames and the bridge cut off from the wheel completely.

The Captain's temporary answer was the establishment of a live line of men extending from the trick wheel to the bridge, and spreading over 450 feet of deck four decks deep. Officers directed the steering orders to be passed by word of mouth as quickly as possible, but delay between the giving of an order and its execution was naturally unavoidable. Initially the *Lex* managed to hold her place in the formation of ships which had slackened speed as Admiral Frank Fletcher in Carrier II was informed of our troubles. Soon, however, her bow was yawing back and forth in unintentional zigzags. The yawing increased until eventually we became a menace to the other ships around us.

"Open out formation around the *Lexington* and disregard her movements," came Admiral Fletcher's order to the flotilla. It was his instruction to them to stay out of our way because we were gradually losing control of her.

Efforts to repair the electric lines to the rudder were being made and one of the brave acts of the day was that of an electrician volunteer. These vital cables are strung down inside one of the legs of the tripod mast, a hollow steel tube about two feet in diameter. The electrician asked to be lowered on a rope down the mast leg to the point where the wires were ruptured so he could attempt to repair them.

A sling was quickly rigged and a telephone connected to him. Then he disappeared down inside this black tube. The men payed out the line swiftly as he descended. I'd like to report that he was successful in getting those cables spliced, but when he reached a point where the fires were raging all round the outside of the tube, the heat was too much for human endurance. He gasped a word or two into the telephone and was drawn up quickly just before he collapsed.

The loss of the main electric cables, which robbed Capt. Sherman of steering control, also cut off the current to the thousands of electric bulbs that illuminated the interior of the ship. Pitch darkness that never afterward was lifted fell throughout her length.

The men knew the corridors and passageways by heart, of course, but these were now clogged with debris, smoke and fumes. Battle lanterns were lighted —electric bull's-eye lanterns with high-powered lenses —but they couldn't penetrate more than a foot or so into the smoke. Every man below was wearing a smoke mask, and still some were overcome.

At 2:30 P.M. there was another particularly violent explosion. It seemed to shake the ship all over. Into my notebook where I was logging significant events, I found later I had written: "The end."

This explosion wrecked the ventilation system of the fire and engine rooms. Ordinarily they are swept by fan-driven blasts of air which keep the temperatures down to liveable levels—about 100 to 105 degrees. Now with the fans wrecked and the draft ceasing, the temperatures amid the great boilers with their hot oil fires and pounding machinery jumped quickly to 145 to 160 degrees Fahrenheit.

"We felt the explosions a lot more strongly toward the stern than you did amidships," one of the fire-tenders told me afterward. "The heat after the fans stopped turning affected us to a point where it was difficult to keep our minds clear. We became dizzy and had violent headaches."

Captain Sherman asked of the Navigating Officer the "distance to the nearest land," and "distance to the nearest point of Australia." A few minutes later came the command to plot a course to a designated point on the Australian coast and Chief Quartermaster Solomons was working out this course when it became apparent that it was impossible to keep the men in the fire rooms any longer.

At 4:00 P.M., the final orders to draw the fires and abandon the engine rooms were given.

The orders were passed to Lieut. Commander Mike Coffin, then in charge of the watch below. Coffin personally visited every nook and cranny in the boiler and engine rooms to see the men there got the word. He had them douse their fires—in the case of the *Lex* this was merely turning off the oil feed lines—and open the safety cocks to allow the steam from the boilers to escape. The noise topside was terrific as the steam from these 16 boilers roared up through the funnel.

This sound was properly interpreted by all on the flight deck and above. The four great bronze propellers at our stern ceased turning and slowly the great vessel coasted to a stop.

All the normal exits from the engine room to the deck were cut off by fires which by this time had spread aft to the hangar deck and actually were burning right above the engine compartments. In order to see that every single member of their gangs got out, Commander Junkers and Coffin stayed to the last directing their men through the intricate maze of narrow passages and emergency steel ladders that finally led to the open deck aft.

The fire fighting gangs under the leadership of Commander Seligman, who took over when Pop Healy was killed, were still struggling against all odds. I came across Commander Seligman several times in different sections of the ship with his fire and rescue squads. Every explosion killed or burned some of his men; others were getting their lungs full of the smoke, or blinded by fumes. As the injured or blinded men were brought up to the flight deck for treatment other men stepped forward, donned the smoke helmets taken from the casualties and went below in their places.

There never was a call for volunteers; there was no need. Men were waiting constantly on topside for a smoke mask to get down into the fight.

By now more than 25 percent of the below decks area was a blazing inferno. Bulkheads adjoining burning sections turned red with heat and thick layers of paint (repeated painting over 17 years had built these layers as deep as an eighth of an inch) curled off, their burning flakes acting as agents which transferred their fire straight through even closed bulkheads into ever new areas.

The conflagration engulfed the machine shop where 20 armed bombs—all 1,000 pounders—were stowed. They had been made ready for loading onto our dive bombers in preparation of possible afternoon attacks. Further aft there were stored 48 torpedo war-heads filled with tons of the finest explosive the Navy knows how to make. This locker was on the hangar deck, and now in close proximity to the fire.

One violent explosion occurred at the moment Seligman was starting through a manhole. It tossed him back like a feather caught in a draft. As one of the men who saw this and other narrow escapes Seligman had during the afternoon put it:

"The Exec was continually being blown through doors and out of scuttles like a cork out of a champagne bottle."

It was impossible to estimate the number of casualties caused by these fires but our medical records show that at least half of our injured were burned in fires or explosions. Most of them suffered burns or combinations of burns when slammed against the bulkheads by blast.

At 4:30 P.M. Capt. Sherman sent a messenger to Seligman to get the men up from below.

Then commenced a hunt through smoke-filled smoldering passages to make sure that every man on duty in the various compartments received the order. The loud-speaker system which made it so easy to transmit orders while the ship was functioning normally was gone when the electricity failed, so the job was one that had to be done methodically by men who groped from door to door and deck to deck.

Some of these messengers went down to decks around and below the fires to pass on the word, for there were men in these lower regions on pumping stations and watching the water levels in the bilges who had to be told.

There were many scenes of courageous action as when Commander Seligman asked if there was anyone who knew his way to a certain station, then almost isolated by fire. A colored mess boy stepped forward and said he would go.

"Are you sure you know the way?" Seligman asked. "And do you fully realize the chances are that you might never get back?"

"Yes suh," answered the boy.

"All right then," said the commander, "thank you very much for offering to go. On your way, and good luck. I'll be here and you report to me when you get back." He made his way, found his men, and returned safely.

It was just at this point I suffered a great personal disappointment. I found my way through the smoke to Commander Seligman's cabin to recover the recordings. In all we had made a dozen or more records. The first of these from the squadron commanders on that wonderful attack on the *Ryukaku*. Then there were several that I had made during the attack on the *Lexington*. In addition to getting the stuff as it was happening, and getting onto the wax the sound of the Jap bombs, plane engines, the torpedo explosions and the sounds of our own guns, I had gone down when the attack was over and amplified everything with 15 minutes more of my own explanation.

I had played these disks back and found them superb. I knew that this was a set of records of value to the Navy, and had hoped to secure one set for myself. Several times I had started down to get them but always was sidetracked. When the order was given to get everybody up from below I remembered them again and this time went in through the smoke to the cabin. I was too late. Fire and explosions had gutted the Executive's office. His recording machine was smashed and everything else in the place was destroyed.

I hurried to the chartroom to gather some last-minute particulars to complete my notes. A small leather-cased chronometer lay on the desk and thinking this was possibly the property of Commander Dudley I offered it to him, but he said, "It hasn't worked for years."

The figures showing the distance steamed since we entered the war I noted from the distance recorder—a gadget not unlike a car's speedometer—which also showed the ship's speed when moving. The *Lexington*'s coffee pot was lying on the table and I have regretted ever since not taking it to present to the Captain later as a souvenir.

After having gotten the latitude and longitude, about the only detail not available was the depth of that part of the Coral Sea into which we were about to plunge. The radio depth-finder, which was also in the chart room, had caught my eye, but when I asked the quartermaster if we could use it to add this last detail, he mournfully shook his head, "It won't work, the power is off."

In the radio room one of the operators, having had nothing to do during the hours since his radio had gone out, was busy dusting the shelves and switchboards with a fox tail.

* * *

A destroyer now came alongside to take off our wounded and give assistance to our fire fighters. When it was found after the hoses had been rigged up that the flow of water was inadequate, the order came to have all men brought up to the flight deck.

About 5 o'clock I was standing on the bridge when I saw Admiral Fitch lean over his upper balcony and call down to Capt. Sherman:

"Well Ted, let's get the men off."

That was the "abandon ship" order. Nothing dramatic about it. Just the word of one good seaman to another. The Admiral could see as well as the Captain that further efforts to save the *Lex* were useless. They had both been told a few minutes earlier by Commander Seligman that a devastating explosion was imminent. The heat of our explosives was already far above the theoretical detonation point and might go off at any instant, as one of our flying officers discovered to his sorrow. He became curious about how the torpedo war heads were cooking, and slipped into the hangar deck. Avoiding the fires as best he could he reached the stacked torpedoes and laid his hand on the sleek nose of one, only to immediately jerk it away with an exclamation of pain—the metal casing had turned so hot it blistered his palm.

Execution of the abandon ship order was Seligman's duty. He at once got a score of different details of men busy. Some produced heavy lines that were secured to the flight deck net railing and streamed down into the water. Others got out huge doughnut rafts. These had a fat balsam-wood perimeter, oval in shape about 8 feet wide and 10 long. Inside was a wooden lattice floor attached by lines. When filled with men the flooring sank several feet beneath the surface leaving the men standing in water up to their waists.

Still others checked off the men belonging to certain departments of the ship who were to go first, dealt out spare kapok life jackets, and carried on the preliminary business which made the abandonment an orderly affair.

Meanwhile Admiral Fletcher on Carrier II, his flagship, had been notified of the decision to abandon the *Lex*. He answered by asking what assistance Capt. Sherman would require, and after the Captain signalled his reply, three cruisers and four destroyers were directed to stand in close and prepare to aid in taking the *Lexington*'s crew off.

The rest of the fleet continued on out toward the horizon. Carrier II had to keep moving to keep her patrols in the air; these were now doubly important, because they formed the only air screen for the rest of us. Some of our own pilots were flying these patrols for with his usual foresight Capt. Sherman hours earlier had ordered that as many of his aircraft as could be accommodated aboard Carrier II be flown to its deck. In this way about 25 percent of all the *Lexington*'s squadrons were saved for later battle. Only aircraft that had escaped battle damage were chosen. They represented a material reinforcement to Carrier II—and more than replaced her losses.

Almost as soon as the ropes had been rigged over the 50 foot high sides, men began dropping into the sea from where they climbed onto the rafts. It was about 5:15 o'clock. One of the destroyers came alongside to starboard, and took between 400 and 500 men aboard who climbed down the ropes to her deck. Ensign Martin, who had gone into the Captain's smoke-filled cabin and had rescued the still cowering Wags from under the bed, now wrapped him (though undoubtedly the best swimmer on the carrier) into a life jacket and had Swift, the Captain's Marine orderly lower him aboard the destroyer.

As this destroyer, loaded with the *Lexington*'s wounded and hundreds of her men, pulled away from us, there came spontaneously from her a roar which developed into three lusty cheers for Capt. Sherman. It was an amazing and uplifting thing there in those grim moments. The men who cheered were the men the skipper had led into battle. They knew he was the stuff and they cheered him to the end.

Most of the men lowered themselves to water level on the port side aft. The ship drifted away from them as she floated down wind and left a stream of swimmers and loaded rafts strung out for nearly 1,000 yards. All the vessels except one cruiser and the destroyer standing to our starboard, formed up along this line of men and pulled them aboard as quickly as possible.

But even working rapidly at this, it took a long time to bring the men aboard because each destroyer and cruiser had only one power whaleboat. In war time Navy craft are stripped of small boats when they go to sea, hence the types of rafts used by the *Lex.* In all, the abandonment of the ship was spread out over more than two hours. It allowed those of us who stayed behind to see most of the men off, and gave us plenty of time to have a last look around, and to note everything that took place.

There was calmness and order. Men would go to the edge of the flight deck, look over and then shrug their shoulders and come back. Someone would ask: "Not going over yet?" They would reply: "Oh no. It's too crowded still. I'll wait till they thin out a bit."

I had another walk around the gun deck. The forward port gun platform, where the big bomb had dropped, was a shambles and it amazed me that any of the crew had remained alive to handle the single gun left after that catastrophe. Amidships on the port side had been a small steel sponson, hinged at the bottom so that it opened outward to form the floor of a four 20mm gun battery. I found it slammed and jammed shut although all the others were open.

Later I learned that a bomb had almost grazed this platform while its crew of 12 were working their guns. The bomb went into the sea directly beneath and the blast had whanged the heavy steel sponson shut. The men were thrown sprawling to the deck inside the ship. They jumped to their feet, took their detachable gun barrels and ammunition to the next position (after finding the sponson so buckled it could not be reopened) and rejoined the fight.

Back, on the aft 5-inch gun position, where the gun crews were still standing-by on the chance of a late afternoon Jap attack, I heard of the casualties they had suffered from machine guns and bomb splinters. They told me one of their men was busy feeding 5-inch shells from the ammunition hoist into the automatic fuse-setter when a wave of torpedo planes sprayed them with machine-gun fire and passed on. This man went right on working, lifting two more of these heavy shells from the hoist to the setter, before suddenly dropping dead. He must have been hit minutes before and yet kept right at his job.

On the starboard a second destroyer had come alongside to pick up more wounded. I found the gunners busily handing down whole sling-loads of 20mm gun barrels—these are replaceable when they get hot with much firing—and clips of ammunition. The gunners knew that the destroyer used the same type of light quick-firing gun and instead of letting them go down with the ship they dismounted them so as not to be wasted.

The heavier 5-inch ammunition was being tossed into the sea to prevent it from exploding, because the fires were now beginning to reach their store.

When I got back to the flight deck I ran into Commander Hamilton who had gathered around him the fliers, mechanics, gunners and aircraftsmen of his squadron. He was giving them a general talk on the fortunes of war, a sort of classroom lecture out there on a deck that already was burning their feet from the blazes below. One of his mechanics had just come up to report he had completed fitting a new wobble pump to the Commander's plane. In jest Ham said: "Took you a long time."

The man replied: "Yes, sir. I had to draw a new one from the store, and had an awful job to get to it. There's a terrible big fire down there."

Ham grinned and continued his discussion. He told the assembled group who stood or sat around him in postures of ease: "The squadron has been in many battles and to date hasn't lost a man. And yet we've wreaked heavy toll on the enemy. We've got to hand it to our maintenance crews and chiefs because we had no mechanical trouble in all our flights over the enemy. We got through because we all stuck together and when attacked we defended each other."

We were scattered all about under the wings of planes, most of which bore bullet scars from this day's action. Someone called over to us: "There's plenty of ice cream over here if any of you care for it." It developed that some bright lads, remembering the ice cream from the ship's service canteen would soon go to Davey Jones' locker, had gone below and brought up several armloads of gallon cans. They even remembered to bring a supply of paper cups and wooden spoons.

It was most welcome because the scuttle-butts (water-drinking fountains) had been dry since 1 A.M. Now standing on the hot decks with the sun still beating down, the ice cream was delicious and refreshing. Particularly so as we had been unable to get any real meal after breakfast. We were at battle stations during lunchtime and while the cooks had made up sandwiches and coffee to be passed around with apples during the afternoon, most of us were hungry.

I stayed with Ham for quite a while, eating my ice cream and heard him exchange jokes with his pilots about the plane he customarily flew. This machine had developed a peculiar quirk—the electric synchronizing gear governing the firing of one of the forward guns had gotten out of tune and Ham repeatedly shot holes in his propeller.

All sorts of efforts to correct this were made, because each time it cost the ship a new propeller. And propellers don't grow like mushrooms. They changed the synchronizing gear, checked the electrical system, and on the night of May 7th, even changed the engines.

On the morning of the 8th this aircraft was flown by Lieut. Robert B. Buchan. Before he took the air the new chief warned him that the ship's last propeller (of the proper type) was on the plane. When he returned to the *Lex* some hours later the crew was disgusted to see—as the engine stopped—the usual holes in the propeller. But Buchan told his story: he intercepted a Japanese torpedo plane and lined it up before he remembered the difficulty with the guns. He hesitated only a moment, however, before squeezing his trigger. There was the usual jar and vibration as the guns fired. This time he didn't mind. The Jap went down afire. He figured that he'd shot the Jap down with part of the prop as well as with the slugs.

Some of the fliers were getting out their little yellow rubber boats and giving them to the mechanics who now were sliding down the lines. These craft carry one man most buoyantly and a number of boys who used them didn't even get their feet wet. One crew chief in Ramsey's squadron got into his little rubber boat and commenced to paddle away, his cap at a jaunty angle and his flare pistol at his side. Ramsey whistled to him and the man sculled his way back to ask: "What do you want, Skipper?"

"Nothing," said Ramsey. "Just wanted to say you look fine and that it's only 400 miles to Australia."

Commander Duckworth came along and remarked: "My word, you've got a real story to tell your paper now, haven't you?"

"Yes," I replied, "and you haven't given me a contribution yet."

"Here's one. We handled the *Lex* during the last hour she was under steam just like Columbus handled the *Santa Maria*," he grinned. "We'd lost our steering, communication and gyro compass, and our gyro pilot.

We were back on the old magnetic compass and were steering by hand with directions passed by word of mouth."

Commander Junkers told us how a rookie had reported on one of the early torpedo hits. The boy telephoned in to Damage Control to say a torpedo had holed his compartment right on the waterline, with the greater part of the hole above water.

"Why don't you plug it up?" the hard boiled CPO (Chief Petty Officer) demanded.

"I can't," the boy replied. "It's that big I can see a cruiser through it."

"Then shut the door and forget it," the CPO admonished.

There were only a few men left on deck. Just leaving was Lieut. Gayler. He dived off the 50-foot-high deck into the water and swam out about 100 yards. Then I saw him turn round, swim back, and in a few minutes he had climbed one of the ropes and reappeared.

"What did you come back for?" one of the fliers asked.

"Oh, I got a bit lonely out there. I didn't know any of those guys. When are you fellows goin' to come?" he replied.

At no time was there any hurry or scramble to get off the ship. A roll call taken later revealed that 92 per cent of the *Lexington*'s personnel had been saved. Capt. Sherman discovered when his records were completed that only 8 per cent of the original complement were missing. It is believed that all of these were the victims of air fighting, bombing and torpedoing, and finally of fire fighting and internal explosions. The Captain believes that every man who was alive when the abandon ship order was given, was rescued.

I did a last turn round the deck with Lieut. Commander Edward Eldredge, air officer for the ship. While we walked we met Lieut. Commander Brett who looked somewhat worried.

Earlier in the day, as he alighted from his attack on the Japs, I had chided him because he had not shaved.

Now his beard was longer still and I reprimanded him:

"What, not shaved yet?"

"Heck," he answered, "I've nothing to shave with. That bomb completely destroyed my cabin. Worse still it burnt that manuscript I showed you last night. There went two years' work."

Jimmy said that as far as he could learn the last of his men had gone off and he was going off too. We thought it a good idea so Eldredge and I took up a position on the starboard quarter and waited until an empty boat from a cruiser lying off that side approached us.

My preparations for going over consisted of transferring all notes to the breast pocket of my shirt where I hoped they would stay dry. Then, selecting a rope with a big knot at its end—I cautiously lowered myself down hand over hand. Eldredge was a bit careless in securing his grip and he did a trip to the water in one scorching flash that left him with blistered palms and a friction burn on one leg.

I climbed into a raft and then across into a whale-boat with others. This boat towed several filled life rafts to the cruiser where all disembarked. I stayed aboard the cutter with the coxswain and we started off again to pick up another load.

This time we headed out on the port side where there were a number in the water who had been swimming for a long time. Those on rafts would be safe till we could get round to them, but some of these others were near exhaustion and soon would be in trouble if not gathered up.

We chugged across the stern of the *Lex* ignoring all rafts, and while the coxswain handled the engine and rudder I began heaving swimmers into the boat. The first one we picked up was Lieut. George Raring, ship's meteorological officer who was swimming strongly, wearing only his skivvies. He and his wife were good friends of mine, and to my greeting "Home was never like this, eh, George?" he came back with:

"This is a fine time to remind a man of home."

We were hauling them in thick and fast and had

almost gotten 60 aboard when we ran up alongside Ensign H. B. Shonk of Scouting 2. He was swimming on his side with one hand raised high holding a water bottle (empty as we discovered later) and a tin of 50 cigarettes out of the sea. He held them up saying:

"Take these quick, Mr. Johnston."

I took them and tossed them into the boat over my shoulder among the already rescued, many of whom lay on the bottom trying to cough the seawater out of their lungs. A second or so later, after he was pulled aboard, Shonk was pounding me on the back, he had found the cigarettes and was holding one in his lips.

"Have you got a match," he questioned. I didn't—then, "has anybody got a match?"

As we again passed the *Lexington*'s stern on our way back to the cruiser there was a heavy explosion aboard her that sent the amidships portion of the flight deck hurtling into the air. Flames burst through. Almost immediately there came another blinding flash, a tremendous shock and a billowing cloud of black smoke soaring skyward as the 1,000-pound bombs exploded. Bits of the steel deck and side plates showered the sea for hundreds of yards around, endangering all in the water and boats.

I later learned that Commander Seligman and Capt. Sherman were still on ropes, just making their way off the *Lexington* when this blast shook them loose and threw them into the sea.

Only a few minutes later the after tip of the flight deck was blasted away. Planes were tossed into the water when the torpedo war-heads let go. Captain Sherman and Commander Seligman were swimming to a cutter when this happened, from where they were transferred to a cruiser already crowded with more than 800 *Lex* survivors. They were the last men off and had just made one more final inspection to see that everyone else was clear.

Seligman told me of this later:

"We were walking back to the stern and I was urging the skipper to hurry because I knew those bombs were overdue. He seemed to be thinking and suddenly stopped, asked me to wait a minute and trotted over

to the island. I saw him go into his emergency cabin
for a minute and as he came out a minute later he
was firmly adjusting his No. 1 cap to his head—the
one with the newest and heaviest gold braid.

"He grinned as we walked over to the side and
said: 'I hear there's not to be any more gold braid till
after the war, and I wouldn't like to have to use that
yellow cotton substitute. Thought I'd better save my
best one."

Seligman tells that when they reached the stern the
skipper ordered him to "lower away." He selected a
rope and started down, but Capt. Sherman stood above
him, musing as he looked back over the smoking ship.

"Come on, skipper, don't wait any longer," Seligman urged him. Capt. Sherman looked down at him
and slowly replied: "I was just thinking . . . wouldn't I
look silly if I left this ship and the fires went out?"

14

AFTERMATH

The water of the Coral Sea is hot, one might say. The *Lexington*'s automatic seawater thermometers registered it as about 90 degrees Fahrenheit—only a few degrees lower than blood heat. These waters also rightfully merit the description of "shark-infested," for enormous ferocious sharks of all sizes and varieties range the reefs and follow vessels that cross the Coral Sea.

From the *Lex* our lookouts who suspected each curling whitecap as the periscope wake of a submarine and whose vigilant gaze ranged the surface of the waters day and night, had seen thousands of sharks in the few days just preceding our final battles. So every man on the ship rather expected that if the time ever came when he would have to abandon ship those sharks would be a menace.

"If we ever had to swim in this ocean the sharks would get us," the deck crews used to assure one another in their leisure-moment huddles—the Navy calls this "shooting the breeze."

But when the time really came, and we were abandoning the *Lex* by the thousands, not a shark was to be seen. Neither we watching from the flight deck nor the sharp eyes of lookouts on the rescue vessels ever saw a fin or the betraying flicker of a tail.

Several explanations were offered. One group held that it was pure luck—the luck of a Lady, as the *Lexington* was often referred to.

The more analytical however, attributed the total absence of sharks to the fact that they were frightened off by the repeated heavy explosions in the great hull.

These blasts, which shook the whole 46,000 tons of her several times a minute toward the end, traveled for great distances through the water. Any heavy underwater explosion kills fish for hundreds of feet around because fluid transmits shock over long distances. Air is compressible so explosions soon lose their force, but water is incompressible and spreads explosive shocks further. To this fact we probably have to attribute the disappearance of "the denizens of the deeps."

It was into this clear warm water that Capt. Sherman and his Executive Officer plunged when the bomb blast amidships shook them off their hemp ropes. Both men spluttered a bit and then began swimming toward a whaleboat searching for the last few men still in the water. Both were unceremoniously hauled aboard, the Skipper still wearing his gold-braid-loaded No. 1 cap.

Reminiscing about this a few weeks later, after he had been made a Rear Admiral and was called to Washington from San Diego, he told me:

"The boys picked me up by one arm and the seat of my britches and hauled me over the gunnel to drop me flat on my face."

"That's about the only way you can pull a man out of the water."

"Yes, that's true," he drawled, smiling. "But I thought they might have a more elegant way of bringing a captain aboard."

It was 6:30 P.M. now and almost dark, as night descends quickly in the tropics. The sun had dropped into the sea and the rescue work was nearly over. Our whaleboat was filled with weary swimmers, some of whom were very ill after having swallowed seawater on top of ice cream, and was disembarking its cargo. All the men except Ensign George Markham and myself had climbed the boarding netting dropped from the cruiser's deck when there was another terrific explosion, one of the heaviest of all, aboard the *Lex*. The 16,000 to 20,000 pounds of torpedo war-head guncotton finally had detonated.

"Everybody take cover," came the shout from the deck officers.

George and I stole one look at the poor old *Lexington* and saw bits and particles, airplanes, plates, planks, pieces large and small all going up into the air in the midst of a blinding white flame and smoke. We pressed lovingly against the heaving steel sides of that cruiser, hugging her for seconds while the debris splashed into the sea for hundreds of feet around.

But even then the apparently indestructible old *Lex* didn't sink. Instead she began to burn harder than ever. The flight deck was now ripped wide open from stem to stern. Apparently this last blast had ruptured great holes in the oil and fuel tanks, for the flames now were shooting hundreds of feet high up into the air where they were crowned by thick black smoke.

In the deepening twilight it was a sight of awful majesty, one that wrung the hearts of all who watched.

After clambering aboard I finally went down to the cruiser's laundry to get myself thoroughly dried. There I met a friendly Marine who was in charge and who loaned me—at his own suggestion—shirt and pants while my own scorched and torn uniform was being washed and dried. My shoes, a favorite pair I had bought in London while covering the Battle of Britain, were put into a hot air drier. I got them back within an hour none the worse for the soaking.

While I was waiting for a dry change of clothing I fished from my pockets sheaves of loose leaf notes and my little black notebook. By drying them in the laundry's steam presser I saved every one and was grateful to find that my hen tracks were still legible though blurred. These were the only items I had salvaged. My watch, money, clothing, typewriter, my valuable tooth paste tube (six weeks later in Washington, D.C., when I tried to buy a tube I was refused because I couldn't produce the old one) and my favorite straight razor had gone down.

I then went back on deck. Night had fallen. It might have been a starry night—but none of us could tell. The leaping, towering flames from the *Lexington* hid all feebler light from the skies. Every bit of flotsam and every outline of the great ship showed up in a blinding glare. Around her the velvety tropic night was the deeper for the contrast. Two destroyers were easing slowly around her burning bulk, nosing in here and there to be sure no one was left in the water.

At 7:15 P.M. Admiral Fletcher aboard Carrier II gave a signal for the fleet to re-form and move away. We had been lying there immobile for at least three hours—the best way of asking for trouble in submarine-infested waters. It was time for us to go but the ships moved off slowly as though reluctant to leave their gallant comrade.

We didn't leave her entirely alone. One destroyer stayed behind, circling around her now cherry-red hull and the maelstrom of fire within her bosom. It was evident that she might burn for hours before sinking. What a signal beacon in the darkness she made! Japanese subs or snooper planes could see her for 100 miles or more and pinprick our position on their charts without any difficulty.

So the Admiral gave orders to sink her.

That lone, remaining destroyer did the job. Standing off 1,500 yards her crew sent four torpedoes coursing—this time into the starboard side. Their explosions were almost lost in the terrific updrafts created by her fires. But their effect was not.

She had been settling slowly through the hours, almost on an even keel. Now she shook herself as the torpedoes pierced her last internal ramparts.

Clouds of steam began to hiss upward with the flames. Her white-hot plates groaned and screamed as the water caused them to shrink and buckle. Inside her there were new blasts, rumblings, concussions—as pressures caved in bulkheads, as gasoline vapors exploded. And now the settling was more rapid.

Still she remained upright, dipping neither bow nor stern. Gradually the waves folded over her. One of her officers standing beside me, watching this final act, murmured, "There she goes. She didn't turn over. She is going down with her head up. Dear old *Lex*. A lady to the last!"

*   *   *

And so we went down to eat. A man has to eat. As I walked into the wardroom there rose mingled cheers and friendly boos. It stopped me for a moment until I looked around and there, for heaven's sake, were all the familiar faces with whom I'd been dining all those weeks on the *Lex.* It looked as if we were back on her except for the fact that the room was a different shape. Right there I realized that the *Lexington* still lived—lived in the spirit of the crew who had manned her. They would carry on.

The whole wardroom was cheery. All those friendly, sunburned, unshaven ugly mugs. They had fed, they had seen every man led to laden mess tables, and now were relaxing as guests of the cruiser's officers and men.

For the sake of her so hospitable company it's too bad the name of this smart cruiser cannot be mentioned. Nothing was too much. They shared everything they had with us.

Everyone, right through the ship, opened clothing lockers and duffle bags to us. They handed out uniforms, skivvies, singlets, dungarees, shoes and, best of all, their beds. Cigarettes and cigars, by the carton and the box, went our rounds. Cola, ice cream, all those little delicacies that mean so much to a crew cut off from land by long periods of sea duty, were forced upon us. And our money was no good on that ship.

After dinner I fell into conversation with the Supply Officer, who among other things asked if I had a place to sleep. He was way ahead of me for I hadn't even looked around yet. He offered me his bunk with: "Well, you can use my cabin. I won't be turning in for a couple of nights because I have to get this ship squared away."

He showed me to it and then got out his Navy Regulations to see what were our "rights" under the circumstances. He found one paragraph under "Shipwrecked Mariners," which allowed him to supply each one of the 800 of us with clothing, bedding, towel, toothbrush, toothpaste, soap and razor. And he immediately ordered his staff to get busy stretching the ship's available stores as far as they would go.

Straight through the list arrangements were made for

the cruiser's crew man for man—to house and bed
their opposite number from the *Lex*. For instance, the
Captain of the cruiser took into his cabin Capt. Sherman. The cruiser's executive officer took in with him
Commander Seligman. The chief engineer of the
cruiser threw open his quarters to Commander Heine
Junkers. And so on down, all were bedded in exactly
the same manner. The *Lexington*'s gunners doubled
up with the cruiser's gunners. Her engine room bunked
with the cruiser's engineers. the black gang with the
cruiser's black gang. Our Marines went in with the
cruiser's Marine unit, our signalmen with theirs. The
cruiser could even accommodate Admiral Fitch and
his Staff for though there were quarters for an admiral on the cruiser, no admiral had been aboard.
Now our Admiral and his staff moved in.

The situation with our pilots was a little different.
The cruiser's complement was eight pilots whereas
we brought on board dozens from our squadrons.
The cruiser's airmen nevertheless absorbed as many
as they could into their own cabins and arranged accommodations for the others wherever these could be
found. It meant, however, putting down cots in galleries and passageways and, in some cases, mattresses
on deck.

One arrangement, made among the men, impressed
me. On the cruiser there had been a bed for every
man in her crew. Now the crew voluntarily doubled
up. Two men with opposite watches would turn over
one bed to a Lexman. The other bed between them
would be used, watch and watch, since when one was
off duty the other always was on.

I went down to the crew's mess decks to see if I
could find any of my friends among the enlisted men.
Scores of them were sitting around contentedly puffing
on cigarettes and talking. I asked the lot: "How are
you getting on in this ship? Are you all fixed for beds
and feeling all right?"

"How could we help but feel all right," they replied, "with all this wonderful hospitality. They've
practically given us the ship."

That evening the cruiser's band got together and

gave off some hot music for our jitterbugs, boogie-woogie hounds and hot licks experts.

The lieutenant who edited this cruiser's newspaper offered to get out a special *Lexington* issue if some of the rest of us would help him with the material. We held a meeting and assigned several *Lexington* men to write stories about the carrier, and finally put out an eight-page issue.

The front page held a drawing of a Minuteman from Concord Common—the *Lexington*'s crest—for she was known as "The Minuteman's Ship." This symbolic figure stood on a silhouette of the *Lex* herself. Beneath her was the old quotation, *"Sit Tibi Mare Levis,"* (Light Lie the Sea Upon Thee).

Page two held a short poem by Lieut. Commander Weldon Hamilton:

> "We saw her live
>   Gloriously; her memory will give
>   To all who saw her noble end
>   Strength this nation to defend."

With it were messages from Admiral Fitch and Capt. Sherman. I think they bear repeating here:

"To the officers and men of the *Lexington*," wrote the Admiral. "I want to express my highest admiration for your performance in action, and conduct during the day when every effort was made to save the ship. You have upheld the highest traditions of the Navy. We were opposed by at least three carriers of the enemy against our two; they lost two for our one.

"It is my hope the crew of the *Lexington* will be kept together to commission another *Lexington* which will return to avenge the loss of our ship. I am honored to have served with you in action and hope to be with you again."

Captain Sherman penned the following words:

"I have never experienced such hospitality and warmhearted treatment as we have received on the U.S.S. ———. I speak for all of us from the *Lexington* in saying we are deeply grateful.

"Our sorrow at the loss of our ship is softened by the reception we have received.

"The *Lexington* was a grand ship that we all loved. We hope we can be kept together as a unit and man a new *Lexington*. Before we lost our ship the enemy paid dearly many times over.

"We are proud of our record and to have been associated in these operations with such fine comrades in arms as the officers and men of the U.S.S. ———."

Page three of the paper was a short history of the *Lexington* by Chief Boatswain's Mate John B. Brandt, who had been aboard her since before her commissioning; and a cartoon of a gob drinking a toast: "She lived as proudly as she fell; may all the damned Japs go to hell."

The acey-ducey tournaments aboard the *Lexington* —"temporarily postponed" as the writer said—were described on page four. Page five contained sidelights of the last hours of the *Lex*. And the last three pages were given up to the *Lexington*'s war history which I sat up all night to compile and pound out on a borrowed typewriter so that the paper could be printed by morning. What a life we morning newspapermen have.

At the foot of that last page was a sea scene with a wreath floating on the waters and the inscription: "Adieu."

About midnight Commander Seligman appeared in pajamas. He had been put to bed by the doctor as soon as he staggered aboard the cruiser. The pounding he had gotten in the explosions as he led the *Lexington*'s damage control gangs in their five-hour fight, the strain and exertion and the fumes and smoke he had breathed, had worn him to exhaustion.

Taking over one corner of the wardroom he requisitioned a few of his officers and commenced to gather a list of our survivors. He also asked that a *Lexington* officer aboard each of the other rescue ships compile a complete list of all the Lexmen aboard their ships the first thing in the morning. Then he asked the doctors for similar lists of the wounded. Finally he asked all officers to turn in reports of men they knew had been killed in air fighting or aboard.

Thus began the long task of preparing the mountainous paperwork required by the Navy after a ship's demise.

In the hospital the doctors were going top speed, working over 60 of our wounded. They were setting bones, preparing splints and casts, using tannic-acid jelly on burns, and treating bullet and bomb-splinter wounds. The operating room was filled right through the night. The same scene was being repeated on other ships with us. Probably twice the number again of those hospitalized, who suffered from minor injuries and lesser burns were treated and then returned to their own bunks.

It truly amazed me to see men severely burned, apparently sleeping peacefully. The doctors explained that as soon as these men were brought in the effected areas were lavishly covered with tannic-acid jelly. Besides having a soothing effect it formed a skin which protected the burned tissue. At the same time morphine injections were given against the suffering of pain from the burn. Those very badly burned were given plasma transfusions primarily to replace lost fluids, and to offset the shock of their injuries.

This combination of treatments tremendously reduced the percentage of lives formerly lost from deep, large area burns. And when properly and immediately applied the jelly enables the skin to heal almost without the formation of scar tissue.

"But don't you have to struggle hard for the lives of some of these patients, doctor?" I asked, remembering my own battle experience and the scenes in British hospitals less than a year before.

"No," he replied. "Once we get the boys all fixed up, the new sulpha drugs and the use of plaster casts, which eliminate the continuous dressing of wounds, turns doctoring largely into a matter of watching cases, feeding them, and giving them time to heal. A sailor, you must remember, lives and dresses cleanly, on his ship at sea and is subjected to a minimum of polluted air. It's not like trying to treat soldiers who must live in dust or in the ground. There's little likelihood of complicating infection with sailors."

Returns on the *Lexington*'s survivors that began to come in at this time showed some of the ships were badly overloaded. One destroyer, for instance, housed more than 400 of our men in quarters that were already crowded by the ship's wartime crew. The presence of all these men, scattered widely throughout the fleet, interfered with the fighting ability of the flotilla at large. Admiral Fletcher was anxious to free as many of his ships as possible to have them ready for instant combat, and so ordered a reshuffling and re-concentration of the men.

This was carried out at sea while the fleet continued to hold its cruising speed, and although somewhat spectacular it was neither difficult nor dangerous. The procedure was about as follows.

Two ships from or to which men are to be transferred are brought close together—about 50 yards apart. Each shoots a line to the other by rocket gun. These are rigged well above the deck, and generally attached to the upper structures so that the lines are clear of the water in their sag. A mail bag then is attached to the lines and pulled back and forth from one ship to the other.

In our case the men were transferred two to a bag. A single bag can transfer an average of 80 men an hour or better than one a minute. A number of these transfers were carried out simultaneously on a number of the vessels until the dispositions desired by the Admiral had been made.

On the fourth day—May 12th—we pulled into the French harbor of Noumea, New Caledonia. The government of this port recently had declared itself for Free France, and several thousand American troops had landed there only a day or so before. Here we were shifted to a new group of U. S. warships that carried us to a more westerly island port. Behind us we left our friends of Carrier II and their escorts.

All this time no one had been allowed ashore. We

did not know for certain whether the enemy knew we had lost the *Lex* and we were not going to simplify matters by helping them find out.

When we reached the second island port we all were changed again to transports that had brought a United States Army garrison to defend a Pacific island group against Jap encroachment. We remained for four days, before starting our final trek back home, during which time men and officers got leave in rotation so that everyone could have four hours ashore to get dust on his boots.

The port town was a tiny, hot and dry little place under British administration. The few little native stores were almost devoid of goods because their usual supply ships had not called on them for months. While strolling I met a fine upstanding native who told me he was a member of the island Queen's bodyguard.

The Queen had moved out of her palace, taking all her native subjects far inside the island, and there set them to work growing food and vegetable crops for themselves and the American soldiers. She had given over her palace—a big white-painted stone house—and all the houses of the town to the troops.

Her bodyguard said he was glad to see the Americans arrive, because before when they had no army, they had been much afraid that Japanese planes would come and bomb them. Now they felt much safer with soldiers and airplanes protecting their island. He said that in the past many nationalities had come to his island, Germans, French, English and New Zealanders, but he liked the Americans best because they were always laughing and joking.

The only items procurable ashore were grass mats, grass bags and tapa cloth. Only small quantities of these were left because our advance guard—the army—had bought most of the stocks. Ordinarily these native products sold at prices ranging from 25 to 50 cents a piece. Now, with sales booming, the native craftsmen had an entirely new price range. Their quotations were: "One dollah; two dollah; t'ree dollah."

The Lexmen for the first time really relaxing found to their complete disgust that the liquor store had long since sold its counters and shelves dry. They went around hopefully, however, sampling cocoanut juice and oranges by way of compensation. Some of them spent their shore leave scampering around on hired horses.

After "doing the town" I spotted a fine new vessel —a large merchantman—flying the Dutch flag in the harbor. This brought back fond memories of quaint places I had visited in Holland, memories of The Hague and Amsterdam, where I had lived for a spell and where Netherlanders had become my friends. On the basis of this friendship I went out to visit the captain, and if possible to beg, buy, borrow or steal a bottle of his Scotch.

I was taken aboard, and greeted by Capt. Van Dulken, a stout, beaming sea veteran, who like so many of his countrymen spoke excellent English. We got on famously at once. He was entertaining another Dutch captain, W. H. Berger, whose ship also was in the port.

Both of us paid proper reverence to Capt. Van Dulken's excellent Bols (Holland gin) and were invited to stay to dinner. The captain had several young Americans with him who manned the ship's guns. These boys always dined at the captain's table and that evening we were a merry little crowd.

The dinner too was a memory of Holland—fine Dutch cooking well served in the luxurious and serious manner with which good food and drink is, or was, appreciated in that country. Every course was accompanied by the right wine and when we reached dessert and champagne there was only one toast left: "To the United Nations."

For the Captain this was a particularly happy evening for that day he had received a letter that had followed him around the world for 15 months. It announced the marriage in Holland of his son and was written by his new daughter-in-law who commenced it to his vast delight: "Dear daddy."

"Fancy," he laughed, "this little girl I used to know running around in pigtails has married my son and now is my daughter. They wanted to wait until I could come home, but with the war being what it is, who knows when I'll get back to Holland. I'm glad they went ahead with it."

When we slipped out of this port every man from the *Lexington* except eight wounded whose cases were judged too seriously to be moved were in our convoy. Commander Seligman had insisted that only those whose lives would be endangered should be left behind. His word to the doctors again and again was, "I want to take every man home that's fit to travel. The best medicine you can give them is the knowledge that they're going home."

Some of us had made book on the bet that we would be kept in this little port for months, to hide the loss of the *Lex*. We were paying off now and delighted to do it.

The days were lazy and long. We were homeward bound, with nothing to do but eat and sleep until we arrived. Naturally, conversations turned to the war, to new and future developments, and to appraisals of Japanese equipment, methods, personnel, and the Japanese mind. This time we had our own ideas to draw on; our men had fought the Japs themselves, had met them in their Zeros and bombers and had seen the enemy's fleet. With anything like even odds they knew they could handle them. This and similar topics were expounded and milked dry until finally we arrived back at a west coast port. I suppose one could go on forever, were one to relate every incident, every conversation, every action. But even a book has only limited space. For every name mentioned there were countless others who could have served equally well as examples to illustrate the valor of our airmen and ships' crews. One group was no more brave, daring, or self-sacrificing than another. It was impossible to see and record everything that merited recounting. But if this serves to convey to the reader the knowledge that Americans have not forgotten how to fight, and shows that the boys of today are as good and as valiant as earlier heroes in our national history, the book has served its purpose.

SPECIAL MONEY SAVING OFFER

Now you can have an up-to-date listing of Bantam's hundreds of titles plus take advantage of our unique and exciting bonus book offer. A special offer which gives you the opportunity to purchase a Bantam book for only 50¢. Here's how!

By ordering any five books at the regular price per order, you can also choose any other single book listed (up to a $4.95 value) for just 50¢. Some restrictions do apply, but for further details why not send for Bantam's listing of titles today!

Just send us your name and address plus 50¢ to defray the postage and handling costs.